Lazarus, Home from the War

E. H. Lupton

Winnowing Fan Press, Madison, WI

Library of Congress Control Number: 2025908495

Print ISBN: 979-8-9883944-3-3

Cover design/art by E. H. Lupton.

Winnowing Fan Press logo design by Bryan Metrish.

Author photo by Bryan Metrish.

For all the doctors I number among my friends and loved
ones, but especially for my mom,
Dr. Laura Simon.

Chapter 1

L AZARUS LENKOV WOKE UP at 0820 on Monday, the second of November. It was something of a personal victory to oversleep; since coming home from Nam, he'd been stuck on the schedule the Air Force had picked out for him, which included getting up at 0445. This kind of lie-in was a goddamn triumph, right until he looked at the clock on his bedside table and realized how late he was running. His brother Ulysses was going to be on the porch at 0840 to walk him to work, which was a silly gesture, but one he appreciated enough that he didn't want to fuck up and make Ulysses late.

He rushed through his shower and threw on some clothes. Carla, his boss, wanted him to look "hip," because "people want a whole *experience* when they buy art, Laz. It's not just about the art qua art anymore. They want to feel like they've walked into something just a little outré." Laz neither understood nor cared what that meant, and most of his civvies had been picked out specifically so he could work on engines in them. Eventually, he'd settled into a uniform of jeans and a sweater, and he didn't shave very frequently, and that seemed to satisfy her.

Ulysses was already in the kitchen, drinking coffee and doing a two-day-old *New York Times* crossword puzzle.

He raised an eyebrow when Laz emerged from the stairwell, and offered him a mug.

"Thanks," Laz said. He looked around. His grandmother, usually grumbling around the kitchen at this hour, was conspicuous in her absence. "Where's Babushka?"

"She went out just as I arrived." He held out Laz's coat. "Think she was going over to see Celeste and the baby. You good? Can we go?"

As an explanation it was fine. Lila, the family's first great grandchild, was nearly six weeks old, and Babushka doted on her. But he wasn't sure he believed that was the only reason she'd made herself scarce around the time of Ulysses's arrival. "Are you guys—"

Ulysses shook his head. "Don't worry about it."

Laz shrugged. "I wasn't going to *worry* about it." He followed Ulysses through the house, juggling his coffee cup from hand to hand as he pulled the coat on and buttoned it. "I just want to know what weird bullshit I'm going to have to listen to both of you bitching about for the next couple months."

Ulysses finished his coffee and left the empty mug on the corner of the porch. "Things are fine between us."

"Is that why you and Sam didn't come to the Samhain party?"

Silence.

"Are you two coming to dinner Sunday?"

They started down Gilman toward State Street. The sun was just touching the tops of the trees without spilling over into the street, making it feel like twilight despite the hour. It was late autumn, and most of the leaves were gone; the ones remaining were brown and curled, shaking against the breeze. Ulysses walked quietly for a while. Then, unconvincingly, he asked, "Is there dinner on Sunday?" Like he was playing some sort of game.

Fine. "Do you need an invitation?" Laz asked. His coffee was cooling rapidly in the chilly air, but he put off taking another sip to dig a pack of cigarettes out of his pocket.

Ulysses waved them away when he offered. "Are you inviting me now?"

"Do you doubt that I am?" He lit a cigarette, then juggled the lighter and pack away without spilling any coffee. It was going to be a good day.

Ulysses's eyes narrowed. "Would you say that I'm typically the type who doubts things?"

"Would it surprise you if I said yes?" Laz said, struggling to keep his face straight.

"Should I be offended by that?"

Laz wanted to say, "What do you think?" but it sounded too much like a rhetorical question, which would have been a loss. Instead, he squinted and said, "Do you find yourself getting offended a lot when we talk?"

"Do you really want me to answer that?" Ulysses shot back.

"Do you think that I think you *should* be offended by me?"

Ulysses took a deep breath. "What if, instead of this dinner, you and I went out for a drink on Saturday?"

"Without Sam?"

Ulysses made a face. "Would it bother you if he were there?"

"Would it bother *you* if I said we should go by ourselves?"

"Do you think that I get bothered by that kind of request?"

"I think you wouldn't admit it," Laz said without thinking.

"Statement!" Ulysses said, and snapped his fingers. "I win."

"Damn you," Laz said, and laughed. "Saturday, then? Boys' night?"

"Sure." They'd reached State Street, where Ulysses would turn right and continue on to campus and Laz would turn left and meander up to the gallery. "Does it really bother you when I bring Sam along, Laz?" he asked. He raised a hand like he was going to put it on Laz's shoulder, then hesitated and dropped it back to his side.

Laz rolled his cigarette between his fingers. "It's not—no. Sometimes I, uh. You know, we can do things together. Like old times."

Ulysses gave him a long look, then nodded. "Like old times. Sure." And he turned away. "I'll see you tomorrow morning."

"See you."

Laz opened the gallery most mornings; Carla didn't find 0900 to be a fashionable time. "No one buys art before noon, Laz." But she paid him for the hours before she arrived and trusted him to take calls from other dealers, so he didn't care. The quiet was actually pretty nice, most of the time.

He put the coffee on in the back room and went through the mail. He swept the floors and dusted the frames. And then he waited.

Occasionally people wandered in, and he glared at them. The brave ones continued to look around. The really brave ones asked him questions. Everyone else fled.

At 1000, Oran walked in. They were a local painter, skinny in oversize clothes, a magic person who acted a little like they'd been in the war. Maybe they had; he'd never asked. Magic wasn't entirely unknown in the armed forces—there were enough poor bastards with shaky sigils scribbled on their helmets, making inadequate sacrifices before big pushes on the theory that it couldn't hurt. But true magicians were rare. Their powers were too scattershot and considered a liability, and were grounds for transfer or even discharge in some situations. Still, he was pretty sure he hadn't been the only bloodline magician in the barracks, and Oran had a certain exhausted twitchy look that he sympathized with.

Oran never spoke about it. They'd come by one afternoon a month ago with a portfolio of small surreal landscapes done in bright acrylics. Laz had taken seven of them on consignment and, after a ferocious argument with Carla, thrown them up on one of the walls under the label *Outsider Art*. It didn't mean much—the art was in a gallery—but he'd sold five pieces for twenty-five bucks each. That had made Carla thoughtful enough that when two more "outsider" artists presented themselves, she let him manage it.

"How's it going?" he asked brightly. Oran gave him a dark look.

"It's November," they said. Their tone wasn't exactly morose, but they sounded tired. "I'm not really a winter person."

It was a little jarring to be the person in the better mood in a conversation. Laz reached under the counter to pull out the notebook with the sales recorded in it. "Not excited about the holidays?"

"No."

Laz wasn't so much either. Thanksgiving was Babushka's least favorite American holiday, and Ulysses had already announced he was taking Sam out of town on a *honeymoon* from the winter solstice through to New Year's, so that was likely to be a long, boring stretch of nothing to do. But it was a beautiful fall morning, sunny again after a long, rainy October, and thinking about the future wasn't worth it.

"Looks like I owe you eighty dollars. Do you want a check?"

"Cash." They set a large brown portfolio on the counter. "I've got some new ones, if you're interested."

"Yeah." He got the money from the safe and counted it out while they pulled out a few canvases. Three still lifes, four landscapes, and two portraits that felt a little too Tretchikoff but would probably sell fast.

"What do you think?" they asked after a moment of silent study.

He considered them. The landscapes were bright, like the ones that had sold. One was clearly an abstract view of the Union Terrace with its bright sunburst chairs, but the others were intriguingly dreamlike. They left him with a sense of houses on dark streets lit from within, or lights seen from high above. The still lifes were very well executed and more subdued in color. The best one included a number of tropical fruits—a luxuriously textured pineapple, a yellow mango, and the black, white, and magenta of a cut dragon fruit—set among shiny grapes and gleaming peaches. The dragon fruit in profile looked almost like a human heart, sliced in half. They couldn't have seen half of those around Madison; the composition was as much a fantasy as the landscapes. "I like that a lot, but no one will buy it. The others are good." Laz gestured to the landscapes and the portraits. "Twenty bucks each?"

They nodded and started to put the rejected paintings back into their portfolio. Impulsively, Laz added, "Could *I* buy that one?" He tapped the tropical still life.

Oran stared wordlessly, and then shoved it across the desk at him. "Take it."

Laz blinked, feeling he'd not explained himself properly. "I can't sell it. Let me pay—"

They gave him a look. "Then keep it."

"Oh," he said, caught off guard. "I—thanks."

Oran rolled their eyes.

After they'd left, Laz cut some mats for the new paintings and hung them on his outsider wall. They looked good.

Carla came in at 1100, grunted at his acquisitions, and poured herself half a pot of coffee. "We have big, big people coming in this afternoon at two," she said, right before shutting herself in her office. "A dealer from Chicago. I need you back from lunch by one to strategize."

'Strategize' typically meant making Laz look up figures in a Christie's catalog while Carla paced. "Sure."

The next time he glanced at the clock, it was not quite 1145. But he'd missed breakfast and was starving, so he tapped on her door and then left.

There had been a regular grocery store on the isthmus until May, when anti-war radicals had set it on fire in the wake of the Kent State shootings. Ulysses and Sam, in recounting the story, acted like this was an understandable choice. Laz hadn't been back from the war yet, and also he didn't really care if hippies wanted to make things harder for themselves, but there weren't any other biggish grocery stores nearby, and the lack made *his* life somewhat more complicated. He stepped out into the bracing fall air and wandered down State Street toward campus. Triangle Superette was open and had a sandwich counter in addition to selling a somewhat random assortment of groceries. He ducked inside and browsed the shelves, looking for sweetened condensed milk and thinking about the lunch menu tacked up on the wall.

Three other patrons were also wandering through the small shop: a gray-haired, dark-skinned woman in a pillbox hat who was frowning at the apples on display, a younger, ghostly pale woman with shoulder-length blond hair who was probably a student, and a short, wild-haired man who raised an eyebrow at him impishly when they locked eyes. Laz smiled to himself, noting the way the man's eyes swept down Laz's body. The other guy wasn't bad looking—trim and well-dressed in a long black coat, slightly rumpled white shirt, and bow tie, he had a strong nose, strong jawline, wry mouth. There was something about his wiry cloud of black curls that made him look a little like a mad scientist. It wasn't a look Laz had realized he'd find attractive, but there they were. And he had nice eyes, gray like the ocean, and clever.

Laz turned away to pretend to study the canned goods for a moment. When he looked up, the man was perusing the sandwich menu. He had just enough time to register disappointment before the man glanced back at him. Their gazes met again, and Laz felt his smile widen into a grin. Maybe he wanted Laz to come over and say hi. That felt like something he was capable of today. He'd slept; he'd had a pretty good morning. He could—

Something exploded. He hit the deck, and everything was lost in the shouting and confusion and smoke.

He was in the jungle. He knew it before he even opened his eyes just by the humidity on his skin, the underlying scent of decay when he inhaled. But it was no jungle he'd ever been in before. For one, the plants were wrong. Or at least, they were not plants he'd seen in Southeast Asia. For another, it was cold. It was quiet, too. In Vietnam, the jungles Laz had encountered sounded like distant gunfire, helicopters, and rain. In Thailand, the jungles had sounded like insect calls and birdsong, occasionally the crunch of something bigger. Quiet only happened when something bad was going on.

He felt panicky, but there was a path in front of him, so he started down it. There was something desperately wrong, some emotion beyond fear that was keeping a tight hold on his chest, but he couldn't identify it, just as he couldn't tell whether the noise he was hearing was footsteps or something else . . .

When Laz came back to himself, he was lying down somewhere outside. The soft, fleecy collar of his bomber jacket was pressed against his face, and beneath that was something warm. That was okay. Not exactly comfortable, but comforting. It was—

He blinked a few times until his eyes focused. He could see the Orpheum's sign about a block away, sticking out above the other signs that lined the street. Interesting. Hadn't he been . . .

It all came back in a rush, and his breath caught in his throat.

He was lying on a bench on State Street with his head in someone's lap, looking up into the nearly bare branches of a tree. There were still a few yellow leaves, bright against the blue of the sky. And there was a voice in his ear, a nice tenor with a polished British accent, talking about—he frowned. Football?

"I'm afraid the article is not at all complimentary to the coach after losing at homecoming last week." There was a pause and a rustle of paper. "Homecoming apparently being some tedious American football ritual. The author does single out the quarterback for praise in the face of a tough defense." He made a clucking noise. "Still. I hardly think that public criticism is going to improve anyone's performance, do you?"

"I think they're hoping UW will dump the coaching staff," Laz said. His voice came out all crummy, but it worked. He cleared his throat.

There was a pause. "Glad you're feeling better," the voice said. Laz finally forced himself to sit up and look at the man he had been lying on.

It was the mad scientist. Of course it was.

He groaned.

The man said, "Do you have these episodes frequently?"

"Depends." Laz stretched. His back hurt from how he'd been slumped on the bench, and his face hurt from . . . from . . . He fumbled through his pockets for his cigarettes, but the pack had gotten crumpled when he fell. "I must have hit my face when I dove."

"I think that was me. You were struggling when I brought you out." The mad scientist grinned. He had a scrape on his cheek that hadn't been there before the episode.

Laz's eyes tracked from the mark down to the mala he'd wrapped around one wrist; the smooth wooden beads hung there innocently enough, but he shut his eyes and cursed in Russian. "I'm so sorry," he managed.

"I've had worse. Besides, you haven't seen *your* face yet."

"Still."

Silence for a moment. An employee of the Superette appeared and said, "Doctor Sobel?" and handed over a sandwich wrapped in brown paper. Sobel murmured his thanks, not looking away from Laz. "What set you off?" After a moment, he added, "My *old man* used to flinch when they tested the air raid sirens." The Americanism sounded odd in his mouth, although Laz was distantly amused by the obvious enjoyment he got from saying it.

Laz said, "Something loud happened."

"The older lady knocked over a glass jar," Sobel said. "It shattered on impact. Tomato sauce everywhere."

Laz groaned. "Yeah, that would do it."

"What were you seeing? Combat?"

"It's all jumbled together. You run away, in your head, and who knows where you end up." He took a deep breath. "I wasn't—well, I was, but. It wasn't as bad as some. Most." He took another deep breath, feeling like his lungs weren't quite processing the oxygen. "That wasn't what I was remembering." He looked at the ground. Let the man stitch together something coherent out of that, if he could. "What's your name?"

"Eli Sobel." He extended a hand. "What's yours?"

"Laz Lenkov." Sobel had smooth, uncalloused hands, cool to the touch. Laz saw his watch as they shook and realized the time was edging close to 1300. "I'd better get going. Sorry to have taken up your lunch break like this."

"No problem." Sobel got up, refolded the newspaper, and left it on the bench. "I'll walk with you. Where are you off to?"

"You must have better things to do."

He shrugged. "I don't have any patients until one thirty. I can see you to your destination and still get back to the office in time."

"Physician, dentist, or vet?" Laz asked, setting off up the street. Part of him wanted to walk fast enough that Eli Sobel would have a hard time keeping up so he could be rid of him. The rest wanted to drag things out, never let him get away. Instead, he found the doctor setting the pace at a good clip, and he had to take an extra step or two to catch up.

"I'm a neurologist." Sobel shoved his hands into his coat pockets. "You're ex-Army?"

"Air Force," Laz said. "I was a pilot." He winced inwardly; Ulysses had warned him to be careful about mentioning his history in Madison.

"When did you get out?"

Laz looked away, up the street toward where the Capitol stood, tall and unfriendly, just a little unreal at this distance. "August," he said finally.

Laz could feel Sobel staring at the side of his face. "That must have been a difficult transition."

"A bit." He'd forgotten the sweetened condensed milk, and now he could never go back to Triangle Superette. "It's really cold here." They came to a stop outside the gallery, and Laz gestured vaguely. "This is me."

"Ah," Sobel said, putting a lot of meaning into it that Laz couldn't parse. Laz wasn't sure what he'd experienced before, in the store—was the attraction real and mutual, or had it been ginned up by his overheated imagination? Eli Sobel seemed to be asking himself the same question as he stared into Laz's face. Or maybe he was just assessing Laz's neurological defects from a professional point of view. Eventually, Sobel said, "It seems wrong to say it's been delightful, since that was doubtless very stressful for you. So I'll just say please be careful." He shot Laz a benign little smile and headed off toward the Square.

Laz leaned back against the filthy freezing bricks of the gallery building and let the world spin on without him for a while.

Chapter 2

T HERE WAS A WORLD in which Eli never saw Laz Lenkov again. He certainly had no specific intention of looking the man up after he left him at the gallery. He'd been handsome, rakish in a way that immediately had all of Eli's attention, but clearly a mess. Eli had to fix enough people in his professional capacity; he wasn't interested in doing it in his spare time as well.

Then, on Thursday night, he was leaving the office and decided to walk back to that little market to pick up a few groceries before heading home. The route would take him past the gallery, but that was neither here nor there. It was an art gallery, probably long closed for the day.

He was surprised, checking his watch, to see that it was only eight o'clock in the evening. It felt later than it was, because in bloody Wisconsin the sun set at four in the afternoon in November. The wind was cold and sharp, with a hint of snow, although the other physicians he shared offices with had assured him that serious accumulation was unusual before mid-December.

Probably Eli had been in California for too long. It had made him weak where the weather was concerned.

When he came around the corner, it took him a moment to realize that there was a police car, lights still flashing, parked on the curb in front of the gallery.

His stomach twisted as he hurried forward. The young man had seemed stable when he'd left him on Monday. Not exactly happy, but calm. He wouldn't have hurt himself, surely.

But there was Lenkov, standing in the center of the sidewalk, an old rag held to his forehead. Judging by the blood on the cloth and his face, he'd been there a while, but despite the cold he was only wearing a sky blue sweater and jeans. Eli frowned. There were a couple of cops, one trying unsuccessfully to schmooze with Lenkov and two others talking to a man in a leather jacket and engineer boots.

Eli sidled up to Lenkov and the cop, carefully inserting himself into the space between them when the latter turned away. Lenkov's eyes widened just slightly in recognition, and the corner of his mouth twitched up.

"What happened?" Eli asked quietly.

Lenkov leaned toward him, voice pitched low. "Some motherf—some guy made an appointment for an after-hours viewing of our current collection. My boss was going to handle it, but she had a family emergency at the last minute and I offered to stay. And then the guy showed up with his friends and—anyway, their motives for coming were not what they'd claimed." He made a wry face. "If there had been fewer of them, I might have had a chance, but five against one . . ."

"Christ! Are you okay?"

He shrugged. "They hit me with a bottle or something. My brother found me on the ground when he came by to see if I wanted to grab dinner. He thinks they ran out the back."

Eli's eyes flickered to the other man, who seemed to be concluding his conversation with the officers. "That's your brother, I take it?"

"Ulysses," Laz Lenkov said. After a dry pause, he added, "I've been told we look similar."

Perhaps hearing his name, the brother turned toward Eli. They were indeed similar, dark hair and pale skin, the same wide lips and high cheekbones, except there was something refined and collected in Ulysses that in Laz looked wilder and more dangerous. Eli shrugged in answer. "A bit."

"Laz," Ulysses Lenkov said, putting a hand on his brother's arm, "they say you can leave now."

"Groovy," Lenkov said, and lowered the rag. "How's my head?"

He was looking at Ulysses when he asked, so Eli couldn't see for himself, but the expression on the brother's face told him everything. "I think we need to get you to the hospital, man," Ulysses said.

"Nope," Lenkov said cheerfully.

"It looks really messed up." Eli guessed Ulysses Lenkov was the older sibling, and used to getting a certain level of obedience, going by the tone his voice was taking on. "And it's still bleeding. Just let me call Sam, and then we can—"

Lenkov's tone went serious. "I'm not going to the hospital."

Eli, torn between slipping away and sticking his nose further in, made a snap decision. "Could I have a look?"

Laz Lenkov whirled, then waited without comment as Eli fished his penlight out of his pocket. The cut was jagged and wider than he would have liked, running from Lenkov's forehead, an inch or so above his left eyebrow, up into his hairline. "That's messy," he said, inadequately. "How long have you been standing out here?"

"Thirty, forty minutes," Ulysses Lenkov supplied.

"You definitely need stitches," Eli concluded. "Also a coat. What kind of lunatic are you to be standing out here for forty minutes without a coat? It's thirty degrees out!"

"Sorry," Ulysses Lenkov said, in the measured way that Midwesterners spoke when they weren't yet sure if they were going to have a row with you or not. "Who are you?"

"This is Eli Sobel," Lenkov said. "He's a doctor."

"Friend of yours?" Ulysses Lenkov's eyes were tracking between their faces, one eyebrow raised. "Maybe you should take his advice, then."

"No hospital," Lenkov said again, and then looked at Eli. "You're a neurosurgeon, right? Why don't you just sew me up?"

"I'm a neurologist," Eli said. "That's not—"

"You know how to suture, right? And your office is near here." Lenkov glanced at his brother. "Then everyone will be happy."

"I rather think it's just the opposite," Eli muttered. "If I sew you up, it won't look pretty. I can't guarantee you won't have a scar when I'm done. A good plastic surgeon could."

"I got plenty of scars," Lenkov said, clapping the rag to his head as blood began to trickle down his forehead again. "One more isn't going to ruin my beauty."

Eli sighed. He glanced at Ulysses Lenkov for help, but the other man only looked pleased to have the situation dealt with.

"Give me your keys," Ulysses said. "Cops are leaving. I'll go grab your coat."

Eli pulled his own coat closer around himself as they waited. Lenkov hummed tunelessly to himself. Finally, Eli said, "Five men, huh?"

"Sounds like I'm making it up, doesn't it," Lenkov said. His tone was still affable, but there was something closed off behind his eyes. "I'm pretty sure the cops thought so. Especially seeing as how there's nothing missing except some petty cash."

Eli peered through the front window of the gallery, but the view was unenlightening. "What did they want?"

"Hell if I know." Lenkov let out a bark of laughter. "I realize this doesn't sound especially promising."

"Something clearly happened. I certainly don't think you hit yourself in the head with a bottle." Eli swallowed his concern and tried to hide behind his normal mask of professionalism; he didn't feel entirely successful. "Hopefully it will become apparent in the morning."

Ulysses Lenkov returned, locking the door behind him, and held out Laz Lenkov's keys and the dark brown bomber jacket he'd been wearing when they met. "Do you want me to come along?" he asked.

Lenkov somehow managed to get into his coat without either dropping the rag or getting blood on anything else. "No, I'll be fine. We'll go around the corner, little iodine, three stitches, and I'm done by twenty-two hundred." He glanced at his watch. "Maybe twenty-three. Go home. Tell Sam I'm sorry I fucked up dinner. I'll call you tomorrow." He added something in Russian that made the corner of his brother's mouth curve upward.

Eli recognized deflective optimism, delivered reasonably steadily, and didn't try to intervene. Ulysses Lenkov probably recognized it too, but said nothing, just gave Laz a measured look and a nod and headed across the street to a parked motorcycle.

Eli turned and led Laz Lenkov back up the street toward the Capitol. His office was on the Square, on the third floor of a professional building. He shared space with a dermatologist and an ENT, as well as the other neurologist he practiced with. All of them had gone home by now, so there was no one to comment when he opened the first exam room and led Lenkov in.

The other man squirmed back out of his coat and hopped up on the table. He was looking a little peaky; Eli found a pillow in one of the drawers so he could lie down, then draped a thin blanket over him, wishing it was warmer in the room. Lenkov's eyes followed Eli restlessly as he dug up the appropriate tools from different drawers.

"I'm going to suggest one more time that you go to the hospital," Eli said. "The fact that I'm trained in suturing doesn't mean I'm the best person to do it."

"I don't think the last person who stitched me up even had a college diploma," Lenkov said.

"What?"

Lenkov tugged up the hem of his sweater, exposing a long, gnarled scar that began in front of his right hip, below the waistband of his jeans, and curled up and around toward his right kidney. "You've actually got a medical degree. It's fine."

Eli bent closer to examine Lenkov's flank. It was fairly neat work. It still had the uneven, raised look of a recently healed injury, but he thought that in time it would heal to a thin white line.

"What happened?" he asked.

Lenkov looked at him with hooded eyes. "Flak."

"Is this why you didn't want to go to the hospital?" Eli said, his fingers ghosting over the scar before he could stop himself. Lenkov's skin was cool, and he smelled of soap and smoke, and the faint iron tang of the blood on his sweater.

Lenkov closed his eyes at the touch. "One of the reasons."

Eli tore himself away, and Lenkov put his shirt back in place. Eli was wildly off-kilter, and it got worse when Lenkov caught his eye and winked at him. "Just do your best, Doc. It'll be fine."

"Stop flirting or I really will make a hash of it," Eli said. It felt better to put a name to the tension between them, even though saying it aloud made him doubt he had read the situation correctly.

Lenkov, on the other hand, just chuckled. "Sorry, I was trying to distract myself."

"Is it painful?" He carefully took the rag and tossed it in the bin.

Lenkov sighed. "It hurts, but that's not what I need distracting from."

Eli suddenly understood and hesitated, his fingers an inch above the man's hair. "Is there anything I can do to help?"

"Talk to me. Tell me what you're doing before you do it." Lenkov held up his hands in front of his face, turning them this way and that. They were mottled from having been out in the cold for so long. "I'll take an aspirin if you have any." He folded his hands across his stomach.

"Demanding little blighter, aren't you," Eli said, turning away to rummage through the drawers. Luckily, this was the dermatologist's exam room, and she kept all kinds of useful things on hand, including a small chemical warming pack that he crushed and tossed to the other man. "I can't give you aspirin. It's a blood thinner, and you're still oozing. I have acetaminophen, though, and I can give you a shot of lidocaine."

He held up the vial as he said the word, and Lenkov hesitated. "No morphine."

"Are you allergic?"

Lenkov shook his head. "No, I don't have any allergies. I just don't like it."

"Makes you queasy?" Eli guessed, and saw Lenkov make the barest nod of agreement. "I see. No, lidocaine is just a local numbing agent. It'll make this a little more comfortable for you."

"All right."

Eli swabbed the skin on Lenkov's forehead and injected the lidocaine, then set the syringe down and busied himself with cleaning the cut while he waited for it to work.

"Do you have to cut my hair?" Lenkov asked.

"No, I don't think so." It was dark and wavy, not quite two inches long. He carefully combed his fingers through it, looking for loose glass.

"It's fine if you do." Lenkov was watching Eli curiously as he stepped away to scrub his hands at the sink. "Cut it all off if you need to."

"I'm not a barber," Eli sniffed, and Lenkov laughed.

"There. You don't have to treat me like I'm going to fall apart."

"I'm just trying to be kind." He held up another syringe. "This is saline. I'm going to wash off as much blood as I can." Lenkov made a noise of agreement, and Eli stuck a towel under his head. He took his time swabbing everything off, then inspected the wound again. "I'm going to suture your face and scalp separately. Your face is going to heal a little faster, and this will let us remove the stitches when we want to, instead of having to wait."

He wasn't sure if the other man cared about the minutia, but Lenkov said, "All right."

"I'll begin now." Eli pulled on his gloves and poked Laz's forehead with the blunt end of the needle. When he didn't react, Eli made his first stitch. Lenkov didn't look pained, but he also didn't look comfortable, and he was breathing more rapidly than Eli liked. He grappled for a question to distract the patient. "How'd you get to be a pilot?" he asked, and then winced inwardly. It didn't seem like quite the thing to ask someone who was worried about having a flashback. "I just . . . heard you had to be pretty keen for that."

But Lenkov didn't seem to mind. "I went to the Air Force Academy. Got a degree in mechanical engineering, graduated top of my class, got commissioned, went to flight school, and then there was a war on, so off I went."

"Commissioned? You were an officer?"

"A captain by the end."

"Very gallant." Eli made another stitch. "So why are you working in an art gallery and stopping bottles with your head?"

"Someone has to do it." He looked like he wanted to shake said head, then thought better of it. "Carla knows my family. She needed someone who could be counted on to show up, and I needed something to do other than sitting around all day."

Eli tied off the suture and inspected his handiwork. "How long were you in Vietnam?"

"Five years. Well, I was stationed in Thailand for most of that. I just worked in Vietnam." Lenkov smiled weakly, in a way that seemed to indicate the whole story was more complicated than he was letting on.

"Still." Eli picked up the blue suture and pushed Laz's hair to the side. "Did you get shot down?"

Lenkov exhaled loudly. "No," he said a little sharply. He moved to the side, slightly out of range, and scowled up at Eli. "You're really good at putting your fingers directly on sore spots, aren't you, Doc."

Eli pulled his hand back. "I'm sorry, I thought the lidocaine—"

"I mean—find a different topic. I don't want to discuss that."

"Ah." He took a deep breath. "Sorry. I—yes."

Lenkov stared hard at him, but all he said was, "Tell me about yourself."

"Me?"

"Yeah. What are you doing in Wisconsin?"

He cleared his throat. "I came to the States to do a fellowship in San Francisco, and then a friend of mine was coming back here to take over a practice and invited me along." Belatedly, he recalled that he was still meant to be suturing and moved back toward Lenkov's scalp.

"Do you have any siblings?" Lenkov's eyes were half-closed now, the warming pack still clutched to his chest with both hands.

"A twin sister." He did the first stitch, then another. The light was not ideal, and he had to get his face really close to Lenkov's head in order to see what he was doing. "Can you move the lamp a bit toward me?"

Lenkov complied. "Where is she? Back in England?"

"Chicago, actually."

"Expand on that."

"Expand on her living in Chicago?"

"Stop being difficult." Lenkov opened one eye. "I find your voice soothing, okay?"

Eli wasn't sure what the correct response to that was, and instead of laughing it off or acting puzzled, he wound up making a weird, strangled noise.

"I find I can't move my eyebrows, owing to the lidocaine, but consider them raised."

Eli did snort at that. "Very well. Ahh . . . my sister's name is Ayala, and she is an orthopedic surgeon. She came to America the year before I did. She felt that the medical establishment in the UK, and especially London, was very hierarchical with a lot of senior physicians already at the top. Therefore, had she stayed, she would have been stuck doing rather menial tasks for years, whereas the States have more opportunities at the moment." He glanced down at Lenkov, who was finally looking calm again.

"Is that why you came?" he asked.

"It's why I stayed."

"Is she married, your sister?"

"Why?" Eli had to ask. "Are you looking, as they say?"

"Would that be weird?" Lenkov asked. "Don't answer that. I'm not, no."

"Your brother, perhaps?"

"No. God forbid." Lenkov opened his eyes again. "I'm literally just trying to remember what civilians talk about."

"What did you talk about in the military?"

"Cars, mostly."

"God, you're a prat." He tied off the suture.

"I don't know what that means, but given your intonation I'm sure you're right." He grinned up at Eli, who found himself grinning back.

"The worst part is done," he said, clipping the tail of the suture. "You'll be right as rain this time next week." He set the needle and the forceps down and busied himself dressing the wound. "Keep it covered for twelve hours," he said, stepping back. "If it starts to look puffy or you become feverish, let me know and we can get you some antibiotics. Otherwise, come back sometime next week and I'll take them out."

"If we're done, does this mean I can recommence flirting with you?" Lenkov asked.

The room was abruptly too small, Eli too warm. "That's right, I totally forgot about your concussion."

"One would have thought that would be your first concern, as a neurologist."

"Not letting the patient die of exsanguination is always the first task," Eli said, gathering up the detritus of his work. "It's unfortunate, but the brain does need blood to function, so that gets prioritized." Lenkov sat up, and Eli stepped in front of him, keeping a hand on his arm in case he got dizzy. His sweater was surprisingly soft. "Besides, you seem pretty oriented to where and who you are, so—"

"So the only sign I've had a head injury is my insistence on flirting with you?" Lenkov asked. "That feels very unflattering to at least one of us."

Eli shrugged. "You know," he started, gesturing to himself, and trailed off when Lenkov looked at him intently. He had very striking amber eyes; Eli had noticed them immediately when they'd met on Monday. He'd been trying not to think about them in the intervening time.

"I'm not sure I do," Lenkov said, sliding off the table and almost directly into Eli's body. Eli tried to steady him, but lost his own balance and wound up clinging to the other man's sweater in a way that was distinctly not what he'd been going for. Lenkov, meanwhile, grinned at him like a feral animal and snaked an arm around his waist to keep him upright. "You started it," he murmured, almost too low for Eli to catch.

Eli shifted slightly. He had just enough time to recognize what was about to happen before Lenkov—Laz—leaned down and kissed him, surprisingly gentle for how wolfish and wild he was.

The abrupt course change from competent professional to object of lust made Eli's head spin, and for a second or two all he could do was clutch at Laz's arms and not fall over. Then he got his feet under him, metaphorically speaking, and managed to kiss Laz back. Laz kept going, threading the fingers of one hand into Eli's hair, keeping him close. Beneath the metallic scent of the iodine, Laz smelled of distant cigarettes and faded cologne, and his jaw was stubbled under Eli's fingertips, prickling against his lips. It had been a while since anyone had kissed him like that, so intent, and he knew he probably needed to put his foot down before this got out of hand, but he didn't. He kept on not. He put a hand on the back of Laz's neck. He selfishly didn't want it to end.

Laz pulled back eventually, which was disappointing, but when he smiled as though at some shared, private joke, Eli found he was smiling too. Laz pressed their foreheads together and murmured, "Come home with me."

It was the brush of the gauze that reminded him, with a pang of guilt, where his responsibilities lay. "You've had a head injury."

"You keep saying," Laz said, drawing back slightly to meet Eli's gaze. "But I'm fine. You said so yourself."

Eli hadn't performed an exam, but he doubted pointing that out was going to convince either of them. "It's not really my thing," he said instead, bracing himself, because most people didn't like having that kind of invitation rebuffed.

But whatever reaction he'd been envisioning, it wasn't what he got. Rather, Laz said, "I'm sorry if I misjudged things, Sobel. I didn't mean to make you uncomfortable."

"Eli," Eli said. "If you're going to kiss me like that, you might as well call me by first name." That brought the smile back to Laz's face. Eli felt like he was fourteen again, on the verge of blushing. "I just like to get to know a fellow before I sleep with him."

Laz considered this for a long moment, and then said, "All right." He looked like he was going to say something else, but the office phone rang.

Eli squeezed his eyes shut for a moment. Patients were supposed to call the hospital or the answering service after hours, and someone there would triage whatever was going on to the appropriate party. But if someone had forgotten that, he couldn't just leave them to twist in the wind. "I should get that," he said reluctantly.

He was still standing pressed against Laz, who mumbled something apologetic and stepped back. Eli felt his absence and wondered about the nature of the mistake he was making. How big was it, how much was he going to kick himself for this a week from now when it had finally settled in? And the phone kept ringing.

He stepped out of the exam room and grabbed the receiver on the reception desk. It was a resident named Morrison down at the Wisconsin General ER. Sorry to be a bother. Concerned that one of Eli's patients had suffered a stroke, but symptoms had come on slowly, which was unusual. Appreciate a second opinion.

Bad headache with hemiparesis. That got his attention.

"I'll be there as soon as I can," he said, and hung up while she was still thanking him.

"Sorry," he said, stepping back into the exam room. "I'm afraid I'm needed elsewhere."

Laz had put his coat back on and was perched on the exam table, features carefully schooled. Maybe that was what one learned in the military. Hurry up and wait, wasn't that the phrase?

"My car's just outside," Eli went on. "Can I drop you anywhere?"

Laz nodded and got to his feet. "I live around the corner from here."

"At a place with other people who can keep an eye on you?"

Now Laz looked distinctly amused. "Sure."

"I mean it," Eli said, trying to sound stern.

"I live with my grandmother."

"All right," Eli said, mollified, and led him down the stairs to his car.

It was a little green two-door BMW of recent vintage, which got him an interested look from Laz, and then a pained one when he heard the engine. "What the hell?"

"I know," he said, reversing out of the parking space. They had to go all the way around the Square because of all the bloody one-way streets. "It's awful. But I was on call last weekend and I haven't had a chance to take it in yet. And, well, the wheels haven't actually fallen off yet, so . . ."

Laz made a face. "You going to have time this weekend?"

"Never say never." He changed lanes, tried to think of a different subject. "I didn't ask. The men that hit you . . . do you think they were going to steal something, but your brother interrupted them?"

Laz frowned. "It's possible. We just got a painting in that's pretty large. Worth a lot, too. If they were planning on taking it, that might explain why there were so many of them." He exhaled loudly. "Ulysses heard feet as he came in but he didn't see anyone."

"What kind of painting was it?"

"A landscape. Kind of surreal, I guess. A ziggurat standing in a jungle." He huffed to himself. "The kind of thing Rousseau would have liked. Or that Mexican bird, Remedios Varo. We handle a lot of landscapes."

Eli took another left at Laz's indication. "When you say large . . ."

"About sixty inches by sixty inches." He gave Eli a sly look. "Do you need that in metric?"

"I'm aware of Imperial units, thank you. It was our empire," Eli said.

Laz laughed again. Out of the corner of his eye, Eli saw an abortive motion, like he'd started to run his hands through his hair, then stopped himself. "The dealer was in on Monday afternoon, and the painting arrived yesterday. I wish I'd paid more attention to him, but I was still—"

He glanced sideways at Eli, who said, "In a bit of a state."

Laz nodded. "I'll look up the records when I go in tomorrow." He pointed at a big cream-colored Victorian manor house on one corner. "This is me."

"*That's* your gran's place?" Eli asked, forgetting to offer any warnings like, 'Please take it easy for a while, I am serious about you having a head injury.'

"If you met her, you'd understand." He glanced over at Eli, who suddenly wondered if Laz was going to kiss him again. But then Laz just tilted his head a little, mumbled something that might have been a thank you, and got out of the car.

"See you around sometime," Eli said, trying to sound jaunty and American and optimistic.

"You know where to find me," Laz told him, and went up the steps and into the house.

Chapter 3

L AZ WENT DOWN TO the gallery early after a restless night and swept up the glass with long, careful strokes of the broom. It was a moving meditation, something he could do with total focus and control for about five minutes, and it made him feel a little better. Maybe someday, when he could tolerate the idea of being in Thailand so close to the planes he wasn't flying, he could go and be a monk for the rainy season, lose himself in chanting and chores until his head stopped screaming at him.

Phra Nok would laugh at him, he was absolutely sure. Silly Americans and their obsession with monasticism, the lingering belief despite all evidence to the contrary that solitude and prayer would fix what was wrong with them. But then Phra Nok would welcome him in and offer to take him out for a Coke.

There were a few droplets of something red on the floor in front of the new painting. He stared at them for a moment, disconcerted. Then he retrieved the putty knife he used for patching holes in the walls and scraped them up.

In Carla's office, he copied out the contact information for the man who had made the appointment, knowing as he did that it was a pseudonym and the phone number he'd given was almost certainly fake as well. Why make an appointment to steal a painting under your own name?

As an afterthought, he checked the back door and found it locked. Had Ulysses done that?

Laz sat down behind the desk. He opened the copy of *IEEE Transactions on Mathemagical Research* he'd brought in to read. And then, for some reason, he found himself staring at the painting instead.

It was exactly the same as it had been the previous night, but something was wrong. He stared at it until he was dizzy, trying to compare it to his memory of the painting from before, without luck.

Carla arrived around 1030, took in his stitches and wild eyes, and sent him home for the day.

"Look, Laz, I'll deal with everything, don't worry." She frowned, eyes locked on his forehead. Eli's handiwork was neat, but the thread was dark, like insect legs against his skin. The rest of the stitches, farther up past his hairline, were blue and looked a little odd when the light hit them. Everything was a little gnarly, but Laz was actually pretty sure that despite Eli's protests, it was going to look fine once it healed. He tried to explain that.

Carla just clicked her tongue. "Go home and rest," she said. "I'll see you on Monday."

State Street was filled with hungover teenagers shuffling around like the living dead, although he could hear the distant chant of protesters and bang of drums somewhere down the street, echoing off the buildings. The weather was cool and cloudy but bright; the light hurt his eyes even with sunglasses on, but everything else felt reassuringly normal and solid.

He stopped at the Coffee Collective and got a cup of coffee that cost a hundred times more than anything he'd ever gotten overseas and tasted a tenth as good. Sitting in the shop, he watched college students—babies, really—come and go. He wanted to be cynical and glare at them; nothing really bad had ever happened to any of them. But then, nothing bad was happening to Laz at the moment either, except that he had a headache. There was something refreshing about that.

He drank his coffee and opened the journal again. But instead of the paper on advances in algebraic optimization in sacrificial algorithm construction, he found himself dwelling on the—what *was* it? Not a break-in. The door had been unlocked. It was, in the bloodless parlance of the police, an incident.

The painting was not just large. It was by a weird, secretive painter from Michigan who went by S. Rochester and sold through a particular dealer out of Chicago. It had been something of a coup for Carla to get one. The mystery, plus the air of exclusivity, combined to make the paintings pretty hot commodities in the current market. And maybe people thought they were good, too. Who could say with art buyers at that level?

And then there was Frankie Argent. Or that was the name the man who'd scheduled the appointment had given. Tracking him down wasn't going to be as easy as calling the number he'd left or looking him up in the phone book. But his method of—whatever the hell he was doing—was unique. Could he have been pulling this scheme at other galleries?

Laz got up and talked a phone book out of the café staff. There were a lot of art galleries listed in Madison, but most were small—one artist or a little collective. Carla had mentioned two or three of them in passing over the last few weeks, and he copied those names and phone numbers onto the back of the slip he'd written the other info on. If they were big enough that she saw them as competition, they were big enough for the possible attention of an art theft gang.

There were a few other places that might be worth calling, galleries they'd worked with in Minneapolis and Chicago. He jotted down the names he remembered.

He had a plan. That was very satisfying. It was like a mission, something he hadn't had since . . . well. A while, anyway. It was time to go make some calls.

Laz got up, left his cup in the bus tub, and stepped out onto the street. It was still bright, the November air crisp. He put his sunglasses on. A car drove past, making a terrible squealing noise when it turned the corner, and Laz winced. And thought, without meaning to, of another car.

On a whim, he didn't go home. Instead, he detoured to the garage at the corner of Johnson and Broom and picked up a new drive belt. Then he wandered back up State Street to the Square, keeping his eyes peeled for a certain 1968 BMW 2002 in British racing green.

He had a favor to return.

Saturday morning, Laz made his way to Ulysses's apartment. It was comfortably after 0900; he'd learned an important lesson about barging in too early back in September.

The Baskerville was an old, wedge-shaped building south of the Square on the outer loop where a lot of roads came together. Someone coming out held the front door open for him, so he didn't have to buzz. He went up to the fourth floor and knocked.

There was silence, both outside the apartment and from within. The hallway that bisected the floor was a mix of eras, with dark wainscoting below plaster painted golden yellow. The carpet was pale gray and industrial-thin. The window at the far end of the hall let in enough light that none of it felt oppressive. Ulysses claimed that it had good vibrations or something.

There were worse places to rent, anyway.

The door finally opened, revealing a tall, olive-skinned man with curly hair and light green eyes: Dionysus Samuel Sterling, who had once been a god, and who preferred to go by Sam. He gave Laz a confused look before stepping back to let him in.

"What's up?" Sam was bleary, still wearing a pair of pajama bottoms and a white T-shirt. He was looking at Laz's forehead, where the sutures had developed a bit of admittedly ugly bruising around the edges. "Your face!"

"Where's Ulysses?" Laz said instead of answering.

Sam shrugged. "I don't know."

"What do you mean, you don't know? Don't you have some kind of—" He waved his hands in a way he hoped indicated 'magic bond.'

Sam snorted. "Do you want a cardinal direction or something?" He folded his arms and yawned. Unusual to see him looking so tired. As though sensing Laz's curiosity, he said, "We were out all night at the behest of some guy who needed information on a cursed watch that had gone missing. But we couldn't trace it. So we come back and go to bed, and then ten minutes later Ulysses is out the door, shouting that he had some kind of brainwave and was going to the lake." He glanced at his naked wrist like he was looking for his own watch and made a face. "That was probably three hours ago. You're welcome to wait."

Laz bent to unlace his boots. When he stood up, the room swung unpleasantly around him. Sam didn't say anything, just looked at him from half-lidded eyes, then led him to the kitchen and pushed him into a chair.

"When did you last eat?" Sam asked, setting an empty mug on the table. "Solid food, not coffee."

Laz sat back. "Ah . . . lunch yesterday, probably." He'd eaten it at 1600, which was its own problem.

Sam nodded. "You have to remember to do that, Laz." He turned away and opened the fridge.

"I'm working on it," Laz said, looking down into the cup.

He watched Sam shuffle around the kitchen, filling the percolator and then digging through the fridge. Eventually, the other man pulled out a foil-wrapped dish. After a moment of banging through cupboards, he set a large slice of apple pie in front of Laz. "I'd make pancakes, but we're out of almost everything, including milk and eggs," he said with a wry smile, dropping into the chair opposite Laz.

"Can't you just psychically tell him to go to the store?" Laz asked, picking up his fork.

Sam pressed his fingers to his temples like a TV performer. "*Go to the co-op*," he intoned. "*Pick up bananas.*" He lowered his hands, laughing. "I wish it worked like that." The percolator boiled and he got up to pour them both coffee. When he returned to his seat, he was looking at Laz's forehead again. "He told me you got attacked."

" 'S true," Laz said. "But I'm fine. Really." Sam made good coffee. Laz would give him that.

"You didn't have an episode?"

Laz didn't respond. Sam didn't say anything either. It was a strategy he had apparently adopted from Ulysses specifically for dealing with Laz, and the most annoying part was that it worked. "Right before those bozos showed up, it was almost like I kept seeing people out of the corner of my eye," he admitted. It had reminded him of the strange electric feeling just before a thunderstorm—a potential in the air he barely understood.

Sam nodded slowly, his face schooled.

"What do you think it means?" Laz found himself asking.

"Ulysses has been through all the papers on precognition we could find," Sam said finally. "He didn't see any case studies that were similar to your"—he hesitated minutely—"condition. Something different is going on."

Laz knew that, but he still felt vaguely stung by all the euphemisms. "Different how?"

Sam shook his head. "I'm not a specialist. But it's not unreasonable to think whatever you went through over there changed the way your brain relates to your foresight."

"Caused it to deteriorate, you mean." Laz sighed.

"Hard to say. I think it's a way of protecting yourself. That doesn't seem entirely bad to me." Sam got up and cut himself a slice of pie as well. "Ulysses said you'd made friends with a neurologist. Did you ask him?"

Laz thought about asking Eli Sobel's opinion on the matter and died a little. "I saw a neurologist back before my separation," he muttered. "He said it was a psychological problem."

Sam said, "Mm," in a neutral tone.

They heard the front door open, and a few moments later Ulysses came in, carrying a paper bag of groceries in one arm. With his other hand, he reached into his pocket and withdrew a watch, which he set on the small kitchen table.

Sam bent to examine it more closely, not touching it. "Is that what he wanted?"

Ulysses shrugged. "I mean, it's cursed, right?"

Sam nodded, pressing a hand to a spot at the top of his sternum, where a little eye-shaped amulet made of blue and white glass hung on a thin chain.

"How many could there be?" Ulysses held up a hand. "Don't answer that. I'll take it over to him this afternoon. He said he'd be at the pawn shop over on East Dayton." He turned his attention to Laz. "What's up?"

"I've been looking into what happened," he said, eating the last bite of his pie and sitting back. "I called a couple of galleries and dealers yesterday, got a few more to call today."

Ulysses seemed to remember he was carrying a bag of groceries and went over to the fridge. "Isn't that the cops' job?" He bent, removing a carton of eggs from the bag.

"Do you really think they're going to do fuck all?" Laz asked. "You saw them. I was covered with blood and they were trying to figure out how to pin it on me." Laz caught Sam looking at him again. "Scalp wounds bleed a lot. Eli said I'm fine."

"It's Eli now?" Ulysses loaded a few more things into the fridge, then turned to set a bunch of bananas on the counter. Sam hid his grin behind the coffee mug; even Laz found himself smiling. Oblivious, Ulysses went on, "So what are you thinking? Did I interrupt an art heist?"

Laz hesitated. "Is it possible that they could have been enchanting the painting or something?"

"Enchanting it how?" Ulysses sat down in the third chair and put his feet up on Sam's lap. "Like *The Picture of Dorian Gray*?"

"It's a landscape."

Ulysses snorted. "Anything is possible. I just don't know what they'd be trying to accomplish."

Laz thought about the events of the evening in question, especially the less fun part before Eli had shown up. "Did you lock the back door when you went in to get my coat?"

Ulysses tapped his fingers on the table. "No, I didn't think—did they come back?"

He wasn't sure how he would have known. "If they did, they didn't steal anything, and they locked up when they left again."

"What did you say the dealer's name was?"

"David Bothwick," Laz said, pulling a scrap of paper from his pocket. "He lives in Chicago. Exclusive dealer of the works of S. Rochester."

Ulysses shook his head. "I don't know the name. Doesn't mean anything, though. What about this S.

Rochester?" He leaned forward and stole Sam's coffee cup. "How widely distributed are their works?"

"I mean, they're one contemporary painter. Their works are in demand among those who care, but they don't have a Factory or anything."

"Right." Ulysses sipped the coffee, expression thoughtful. "Do you posit that S. Rochester and Bothwick are in on this? Some vast art conspiracy?" He paused. "But then why wait until the painting got to Madison to enchant it? If the artist is in on it, the magic could be done in the studio, or at the dealer's place."

Laz sighed. "Now you're making me sound paranoid."

Sam took his coffee back from Ulysses. "How much was the painting worth?"

"About twenty-five thousand dollars, I think," Laz said.

Sam nodded like that was a rational amount of money to pay for a painting. Ulysses looked faintly taken aback. "That's double the median yearly household income," he said.

Laz shrugged. "Sorry, comrade. Welcome to capitalism."

"I know. I'm just—" He shook his head.

"Try not to think about it. It's just play money."

But Ulysses was clearly thinking about it. "How much does she pay you?"

"Not so much that I'm tempted to buy something like that." He took the mala from around his wrist. "There was wax on the floor."

Sam reluctantly surrendered the coffee cup again. "Candle wax?"

"Yes." Laz rolled the beads between his fingers, feeling polished wood, then a rough spot where the bead had a little chip on one side. "Red. I thought it was blood at first."

Ulysses drained the last of Sam's coffee and set the cup down gently. "It's not like candles are obligatory for casting spells, but fine. We'll come by sometime and check it out. Now get out of here, go call your other galleries."

"What are you going to do?" Laz asked, and his brother laughed and got to his feet.

"I'm going to bed. I've been up all night." He said it matter-of-factly, but he glanced over at Sam while he was speaking, and suddenly Laz felt very much like a third wheel. It made him squirm.

"We're still going out for drinks tonight?" he asked.

"Yeah. Nick's?"

A classic State Street dive. "Sounds good."

"We can talk about the guy who made the appointment. What was his name?"

"Frankie Argent."

Ulysses yawned jaw-crackingly wide. "That's a hell of a name."

Laz and Sam got up too. Laz collected his coffee cup and drifted back into the living room. "Thanks," he said, making a gesture that he hoped encompassed everything.

"No problem," Ulysses said. "Now get out of my hair."

Nick's on a Saturday night was hopping. The crowd was mostly townies rather than students, despite the restaurant's location halfway down State Street. The place had opened in the late fifties and maintained what felt like a bobby-soxer aesthetic—black and white tile floor, red bar with polished wood rail, vinyl booths that smelled like generations of cigarettes. It was the sort of place that college students came to have a quiet beer while they read, and townies came to have a burger and a game of pool. There was a jukebox in one corner that was playing The Monkees when Laz came in; he dropped in a nickel and pushed a random button to queue up something different.

Ulysses wasn't there yet, so he slid into a booth and inspected the menu. What was the probability that he'd be able to convince Eli to come out to a place like this sometime? It was not the kind of sophisticated night spot Laz instinctively felt that Eli deserved, but perhaps he could pitch it as an interesting experiment in American sociology. Not that Eli had seemed too interested in sociology.

The man was going to drive him crazy. If he'd come back with Laz the other night, if they'd fooled around, he would . . .

What?

It was a familiar dance: spot someone who thought you were attractive and give them the eye. Sneak off somewhere and have some fun. The size of Bangkok and the variety of cultures its inhabitants hailed from made it easier to find someone interested in a little fling. Udon Thani, the town adjacent to the base, was a little too small and overrun by airmen, although he'd met a few interesting people there as well.

The point was, though, that was where it ended. It was essentially a way of blowing off steam. Everything he'd done in the war—search and rescue, intel, unarmed recon—was difficult, stressful, and tense. Why not have some fun? It wasn't Eli's thing, and that was fine, but Laz was too messed up to be worth having some kind of relationship with. The whole situation was just a setup for heartache, a protracted getting-to-know-you period that was going to lead to Eli deciding that no, he wasn't actually interested in whatever little Laz had to offer, have a nice life.

So why was Laz still thinking about the tiny mad scientist?

"If the menu is that depressing, we can go somewhere else."

Laz jumped and met Ulysses's quietly amused eyes. "How long have you been there?"

"Not long." He leaned forward. "Are you okay?"

"I was just thinking." He put the menu down. "We can stay. I want the gyros."

"All right." Ulysses looked around and caught a waitress's eye. When they'd ordered, he said, "Do you want to talk about it?"

"About what?"

"Whatever you were brooding about just now."

"No. I—no," Laz managed, hoping he kept the horror out of his voice.

Ulysses nodded slowly. "How did calling the galleries go?"

Laz stared at him for a moment, his brain revving uselessly. "I called a bunch. Two have a painting each by S. Rochester, although one got it out of an estate sale rather than directly from Bothwick." He took a deep breath. "The other place has had the painting in for a while without any incidents. So I don't know. I started to wonder halfway through the afternoon if the appeal of robbing Carla was that she's—well, she's tiny, and a woman, and one might assume, therefore, helpless and easily overcome." Or sane enough not to try to fight five grown men for a painting.

Ulysses started to crack his knuckles. "Are there any wards on the gallery?"

"No," Laz said. "None that I know about, anyway. Most demons are not interested in stealing art. We have, instead, a burglar alarm. Which was disabled, because fucking Frankie Argent had an appointment."

"Mm."

Their drinks arrived, a beer for Ulysses and a whisky on the rocks for Laz, and he took a while staring into the glass, watching the greasy swirl of liquor and melting ice. "Where *is* Sam?" he asked abruptly after an uncomfortably long silence. "I hope I didn't—you, that is—I—"

Ulysses laughed. "No, don't worry about it. He's having dinner with some friends to talk about the spring show their theater company is putting on."

"Sam does theater?" It felt strange to have missed that. It seemed like a key piece of intel. He should have been paying better attention.

"He stage manages their productions." Ulysses took a sip of his beer. "Ellen and Harry write musical adaptations of Shakespeare. Harry does the words; Ellen does the music."

"Sure. That sounds fun." Or like the third circle of hell. He turned the glass of whisky in his hand. "What are they planning?"

"Scenes from the lives of various Caesars." Ulysses scratched the back of his head. "I think initially they planned to start with Julius and go all the way to Nero, using some material from *I, Claudius* and Shaw's *Caesar and Cleopatra* as well as Shakespeare's *Julius Caesar* and *Antony and Cleopatra*. But Harry is finishing his dissertation, so they're going forward with a slightly circumscribed version called *Cleopatra in Love*."

"Yond Cassius has a lean and hungry look?" Laz suggested.

Ulysses grinned and shook his head. "She's not in that one."

"Oh." He thumbed through his mental store of quotes. "Caesar's spirit, ranging for revenge, with Ate by his side come hot from hell, shall, ah"—he fumbled—"cry 'havoc,' and let slip the dogs of war?"

"That's still Julius Caesar. But it is one of Antony's lines, so you're closer."

Laz laughed. "How do you know all that? I thought you only went in for Russian lit."

"I read all kinds of stuff," Ulysses said. "But Sam is a Shakespeare buff, so . . ."

He trailed off, and Laz studied his face, the little half-guilty smile. It was as though he felt he shouldn't mention his lover too much in Laz's presence. "On some level, it baffles me that the two of you wound up together," he said abruptly. Ulysses raised an eyebrow, and Laz waved a hand. "Don't get me wrong; now that I know him, it makes sense. But when I first came back . . ."

Ulysses shrugged, and then had to sit back when the waitress arrived with his burger. He ate a french fry, looking curiously at Laz. "What was the surprising part? Him, or me?"

"I couldn't tell you exactly." Laz picked at the pita bread wrapped around his gyros. "It barely seemed plausible that you would've bumped into someone like him on campus. And then when I found out about the god thing, I didn't understand how you could have taken up with him . . ."

Ulysses shrugged and looked down at his own hands. The shiny silver ring on the left one still looked out of place to Laz. "Does anyone's relationship really make sense to outsiders?"

"No. I mean—" Laz started to rub his forehead in frustration, and had to pull his fingers back when they grazed a suture.

"One answer is that Dionysus decided that he wanted me, so I stayed," Ulysses said finally. "But I'm not sure that's what you're asking. Also, it makes me sound kind of powerless, which is not how I remember things happening."

Laz sighed. "Actually, mystical magical bullshit is about what I'd expect from you, coming and going."

"Touché." Ulysses took a bite of his burger, watching Laz thoughtfully as he chewed. "Is this about that doctor?"

"No." Laz took a bite of gyros so he didn't have to speak for a minute. For a while they stared at each other over the table.

Finally, Ulysses said, "I didn't get the sense that he was a magic user."

"No."

"And you haven't told him about the—"

Laz exhaled forcefully. "No. Christ, Ulysses, I met him on Monday right before I lost my mind and hit the deck at Triangle Superette. I didn't expect I'd ever see him again. I still don't."

"Sure you will," Ulysses said. "You've presented him with a mystery." He grinned. "I bet you'll have a hard time keeping him away now." Laz must have looked skeptical, because he added, "I know, I only met him for a minute. But he seemed nice."

"Normal," Laz said. "He's normal."

"You sure about that?"

Laz didn't answer.

"Anyway, he still has to take the stitches out, right?" Ulysses ate a french fry and grinned at him. "Look, don't worry about it. Things will work out the way they should."

"Very zen of you," Laz groused.

"It's easy to be zen about other people's problems," Ulysses said. "But if you ever want to talk . . ."

Laz wondered if that last, awkward, elliptical sentence was really the change that Sam had wrought in his brother. The Ulysses he remembered from his last leave didn't want to talk about feelings. Laz had taken him out for a drink and tried to draw him out about Livia, who had recently dumped him. It had been like talking to a brick wall. But now Ulysses was happy. What a bunch of bullshit.

"There is nothing to talk about." Laz scowled. "Thanks, though. Glad we've found one more topic on which you can play the all-knowing older brother."

Ulysses grinned and stole one of Laz's fries and changed the subject to methods of tracking down the mysterious Argent. And for a while, it was like nothing had changed at all.

Chapter 4

ON SUNDAY, ELI DROVE from his house, which was on the east side where the Yahara River crept across the isthmus to meet Lake Monona, down to the Capitol and then around to the weird old place on Pinckney Street where he had dropped Laz off on Friday night. It was only about two miles, but he was still transfixed by his car mysteriously no longer making noise when he drove it. He wanted to keep driving to see if it would break again, like an injured man poking a bruise over and over to see if it still hurt.

He parked up the street from the old house. There was a car in the house's driveway when he approached—a red convertible, bonnet open. As he came around the corner of it, he saw Laz, bent at the waist and leaning over the engine. Eli admired the line of his legs and arse, his gaze trailing up to the small of Laz's back where his shirt had ridden up and his trousers were creeping down—more scars there, no surprise. He was a looker, though. And then Eli scuffed his shoe on the asphalt and Laz glanced over at him.

"Hey," he said. "Is there a wrench over there?"

"Sorry?" Eli stared at the pile of tools.

Laz shifted, trying to get a better look over his own shoulder. "A spanner?"

Eli found one and passed it to him. "What are you up to?"

"Fine-tuning." There was some clanking, and a moment later he pushed back and stood up, tugging the hem of his shirt back down.

"I should've known you were a car guy," Eli said as Laz wiped the grease off his hands and looked over the engine again.

"I have a degree in engineering," Laz reminded him. "Get in."

"You're insufferable." Eli sniffed in mock disapproval. "Are you going to put up the top?"

"It's above freezing." Laz reached out and wiggled one of the hoses a little, then shut the bonnet. He'd been wearing only a white undershirt despite the chill, but now he grabbed a plaid shirt off the driver's side door and pulled it on, cuffs flapping. Eli idly watched him button it, then looked up and realized he'd been caught. Laz fished his coat out of the back, lips quirking up at one side. "Let's go for a ride."

Eli pulled himself together. "You sure you know what you're doing?"

"I'm a fighter pilot," Laz said, sounding somewhat offended. "Are you asking if I'm sure I can drive a midsize muscle car?"

"Yes."

"Why'd you come?" Laz asked suddenly.

"To bother you," Eli said, because he couldn't figure out how to say 'I was worried.' "And to check on your stitches."

Laz glared at him. "Mission accomplished. Now get in the car."

He got in the car. "Not very practical, is it."

Laz got into the driver's seat and turned the key, cheering when the engine caught in a way that was loud, muscular, definitely worrying. "I didn't buy it to be practical."

"Why did you buy it?"

Laz leaned toward Eli, and Eli's heart skipped. But Laz opened the glove box and pulled out a pair of sunglasses. Eli watched him slide them onto his face. "It goes fast," he said, like Eli had asked a ridiculous question, and reversed out of the driveway.

They took Highway 14 out of town and turned down a series of nearly identical rural roads, passing farmstead after farmstead, fields all fallow now, each road slightly too narrow for the speeds that Laz was taking the car up to. Eli tried not to grip the door handle. At least the car had safety belts.

Periodically, he caught Laz giving him little looks out of the corner of his eye and smiling to himself. At first Eli wondered if he was making some ridiculous face. Then he realized that maybe Laz was just checking to see that he was still there, having a good time.

They wound up at a park called Devil's Lake an hour or so later. Laz pulled into a gravel lot with a flourish and pulled the hand brake. "Fancy a hike?" he asked. At Eli's tentative nod he was out and bounding over to the trailhead. "The view from the top is worth it."

"The name seems a little inauspicious," Eli said some time later, following Laz along a trail that seemed to be mostly up.

"Hmm? Oh." Laz shrugged. "I don't know. You'd have to ask Sam; he's the one with the entire history of south central Wisconsin crammed into his head for some reason. Probably the Ho-Chunk had a name and the settlers misinterpreted it." Before Eli could ask who Sam was, Laz added, "Ulysses won't set foot anywhere near here, so maybe there's something to it."

"Is he very superstitious?"

Laz glanced at Eli curiously. "He talks to ghosts."

"Presumably this is some form of magic." At Laz's affirmative grunt, Eli pressed on. "Any ghosts in particular?"

"No." Laz stumbled over a tree root half embedded in the path and cursed under his breath but didn't fall. "He's not a spirit antenna. He has to be where the ghost is." He rubbed one knee. "He gets real twitchy about places that have a lot of bad things in their past, too. I don't know if he can sense it or something. It can make him kind of a pain in the ass to travel with, that's for sure."

"How fascinating." Eli mentally thumbed through everything he'd had cause to learn about magic in years past. "Is he the only one? I've heard it runs in families."

"Yeah, no," Laz said, somewhat incomprehensibly. "Everyone has their little thing. My gran reads cards, my dad predicts the stock market, my aunt does herbal stuff, my sister does protective warding and . . . all kinds of things, really. She's great. Ulysses is a professor of magic at UW. He thinks there's a gene that's responsible for all of our magic."

"Our magic?" He narrowly avoided a slender branch, which caught at his collar but didn't scratch him. "I take it this is more than the usual—" He waved a hand.

"It's not the three S stuff." Laz must have sensed Eli's confusion. "Sacrifice, sigil, spellcraft?"

"Americans and their marketing slogans," Eli grumbled, but he thought he saw Laz grin.

"You don't do magic, then?"

Laz had asked the question in a light tone. Eli couldn't decide what to make of that. "Jews doing magic has been associated with considerable antisemitism over the years, especially during the war. Whether my parents have any talents or not, they long ago opted not to get involved. They didn't—don't—have any particular antipathy, I suppose, but we were warned off." He pushed a low-hanging branch aside. "All right, if your whole family has magical talents, what do you do?"

"I see the future." Laz was looking determinedly up the trail, as though he'd admitted something vaguely embarrassing.

Eli turned this information over in his mind. "Why did you kiss me, then?" He was slightly horrified to hear the words leave his mouth. "If you knew I wasn't going to go to bed with you."

Laz laughed, head thrown back. It was an absurdly attractive sound, rich and rough, and Eli felt better about his slip. "First of all, that's not how it works. I don't see anything so complex. I get a few seconds of feelings, sometimes an image. It doesn't happen all the time, or even most of the time, and I can't control what I see. I didn't have any particular insight into what you'd do if I kissed you. I just did it because I thought I would enjoy it." He stopped and turned back, looking intently at Eli the way he had in the exam room. "And I was right."

"Ah," Eli said, in a distant voice that felt a little bit like his. "Good."

After a long, steep climb, the trail emptied out onto the top of the bluffs. Laz waved a hand at the view before plopping down on a rock near the edge to catch his breath.

It was an incredible view, Eli had to give him that. The lake was a large blue pool at the bottom of a rocky basin carved out by glaciers tens of thousands of years before. Standing five hundred feet above the water's surface, Eli felt as though the entirety of the park was spread out at his feet. On the far shore, the trees were a beautiful wash of oranges and reds punctuated by some green firs. He shuffled as close to the edge of the rocky bluff as he could stomach and looked down, then stepped back decisively, dizzy, and sat down next to Laz.

"Did you ever look at something like this and just . . . want to throw yourself over?" Laz said in what he clearly thought was a conversational tone a few minutes later.

Eli looked at him sidelong. "The French call that l'appel du vide," he said carefully. "I don't think it's all that uncommon."

"Mm." Laz drew his legs up and wrapped his arms loosely around them. "When I was a kid, I always used to fantasize that I would grow wings on the way down."

"Is that why you joined the Air Force?" Eli asked before he could stop himself.

"I mean, look at it." Laz waved a hand at the sky. Eli looked. The sky was vast and blue, almost too beautiful to look at. Here and there, big, fluffy clouds hung in the air and let the light dance around them. More clustered on the western horizon. Other than that, it was just them and the sun and a few turkey vultures wheeling in the distance. They sat for a while in silence. It was still November, and despite the sunlight and his coat Eli wished he had a hot drink, not that Laz would've permitted him to bring anything along in the car.

After a while, Laz seemed to notice that he was cold and shifted so that Eli was leaning against his side, Laz's body blocking the wind. Eli let himself forget the complicated calculus of touch for a bit and curled into the warmth.

"Could I ask you a question?" Eli said. They'd been sitting for a while, watching the clouds on the horizon slide closer.

"You just did," Laz said unhelpfully.

Eli decided to ignore him. "Did you break into my car, for lack of a better term, and fix it on Friday?"

After a long silence that was, in itself, telling, Laz said, "It was the timing belt."

Eli nodded. "Is this you trying to be charming?"

"I'm not charming," Laz said. "I'm useful."

"Mm." Eli looked at the side of his face; Laz was gazing out across the basin, amber eyes distant. Damn, he was handsome with a little stubble on his jaw. He smelled like motor oil and tobacco, which felt masculine in a way Eli hadn't entirely realized he was into. If only he weren't the oddest man Eli had met since moving to Wisconsin.

Although that thing with the car was actually kind of sweet. Peculiar, but sweet.

"Thank you," Eli said belatedly. "It was very kind of you."

Laz looked embarrassed. Eli decided he liked seeing the other man slightly off-kilter. It softened him, for lack of a better term, took away some of that military remoteness. "I wasn't. . . . That is, you . . . I . . ." He shifted, and Eli realized he was toying with that string of beads again, giving each a little twist as it slid through his fingers.

"Steady on."

Laz glared at him, then looked back out across the lake. "The timing belt controls makes sure the intake and exhaust valves open in time with the pistons. Important to take care of it before your engine gave up." He sighed. "And I owed you for the stitches."

Eli looked at his profile and laughed abruptly. "You like me," he muttered, digging his elbow into the other man's ribs. "You did it because you like me and you wanted to get my attention."

Laz snorted, but then glanced over at him. "Did it work?"

"I'm here, aren't I?"

There was a long silence, but Eli felt him relax slightly. "That's true."

Eli let time unspool between them, not making an effort to speak, just watching the birds swoop and the wind ruffle through the trees on the opposite shore. They'd been sitting there for what was likely the better part of an hour when Laz abruptly shifted.

"We should get back to the car," he said, standing up. "It's going to rain, and we left the top down."

Eli looked at the clouds again. They were larger, certainly, and one was looking—pointier? Darker gray, but that was about the sun's changing angle. "Is it?"

Laz extended a hand down for him and pulled him to his feet. Before he could second-guess himself, Eli let his momentum carry him closer, one arm sliding around Laz's waist until the taller man's body was pressed against his, not exactly warm given the weather but a firm, muscular presence. Laz was already looking at him, expression curious, and it was all too easy to tug him down into a kiss.

Laz's face was cold, and Eli was sure his was no better, but it didn't matter. Kissing was less overwhelming than last time but somehow more fun, because they were out in the sun and wind, standing on the top of a rock like they were on the outstretched palm of god.

Eventually, Eli had to disengage to take a breath. Laz held on to him for an extra moment before he stepped back.

"You should know I don't know what I'm doing here," Laz said. "I don't exactly date much."

Eli shrugged. He still had his fingertips on Laz's waist, curled through the belt loops like he was afraid Laz would abruptly turn and throw himself into the air. "You strike me as a fast learner," he said.

Laz laughed. "I'll remind you of this when I inevitably fuck up and hurt you."

"Nothing is inevitable," Eli said, feeling unexpectedly, brashly earnest. "I thought you must understand that better than most."

By the time they reached the foot of the trail, the first droplets were already beginning to spatter down, and Laz rushed to get the top up.

After the heater kicked on, the car felt like a tiny tropical island speeding through the cold gloom back to the city. Laz was probably going too fast, but Eli found himself relaxing, drowsy from the hike and the warmth.

"I forgot to ask," he said. "Did you hear anything from the police?"

Laz shook his head. "The cops aren't going to waste their time investigating an art heist where nothing got stolen."

Eli frowned. "I suppose not."

After a moment, Laz said, "I've called every art gallery in Madison and a few in Chicago and Minneapolis. There was one odd incident about six months ago." He paused. "They didn't want to talk about it at first, but then when I called back this morning, I got the woman who was actually working when it happened, and she was still so angry she told me everything."

"What did she say?"

Laz let the car slow a bit as they went up a hill, then downshifted as they crested it. There was a stoplight at the bottom. Eli watched it go amber, then red. Laz carefully brought them to a stop. "A man and woman came in together and looked around. They seemed to be bickering about one of the paintings, so she left them alone. Then they left. He came back that night after she'd turned off the sign but before she'd locked the door." The light turned green. Laz lowered a hand to the gear stick and put the car into first.

If Eli hadn't already been watching, he would have missed the moment where Laz hesitated, foot on the clutch. He shut his eyes, almost a wince. When he opened them, he looked in both directions, all without letting the car engage.

A dump truck trundled through the intersection from their right, running the red light. It didn't pause as it passed through where they would have been if Laz had already hit the accelerator.

Eli sucked in a breath, but Laz just put the car into gear as if nothing had happened and turned left.

"The man didn't hit her," Laz continued, and it took Eli a moment to remember they were discussing the art gallery. "He threatened to, I think. Locked her in the back room. By the time she got out, he'd gone, and nothing was missing. Not even the petty cash."

Eli cleared his throat. "That's unexpected."

"Yeah." Laz tapped one index finger on the steering wheel. "I asked if I could come see the work they were interested in, but it's been sold already."

"To whom?"

"A Mrs. Ryan Greenfield from Edina." He finally glanced over at Eli, then back at the road. "I haven't found her yet."

"That's proper weird." Eli pulled himself together. "Do you *want* to find her?"

They were approaching the edge of Middleton now, and Laz carefully guided them onto University Avenue. He downshifted as they started to hit more lights, and the engine revved louder. "I'm curious, but I'm not Ulysses," he said a bit cryptically. "I can't just go running after every mystery because *someone* should."

Eli looked at his face in profile for a moment. "I'm sure you'll figure it out."

The look Laz shot him was oddly grateful.

Laz pulled into the driveway carefully and set the hand brake. There was a motorcycle parked in front of the garage. It had a teal blue gas tank and chrome fittings. It was familiar, somehow, not that Eli made a habit of remembering motorcycles. Laz stared at it for a long moment; Eli thought he heard him mutter, "What's he doing here?" Then he shifted in his seat, leaning toward Eli. "You never said how my stitches look."

Perhaps the sun was still up, somewhere beyond the clouds, but the light was pale and rain-washed, growing dimmer by the minute. Eli fished a penlight out of his pocket and turned in his seat to examine Laz's forehead, leaning awkwardly over the armrest between them.

"No, don't move," he muttered, reaching out to adjust the other man's head. "They're fine. Everything is healing nicely. Drop by the clinic in a few days and I'll remove them for you."

When he let the penlight flicker out, Laz's face was very close to his. Eli swallowed, aware of the way their breath pooled together between them, knowing he should move but wanting to stay exactly where he was. Laz inhaled to say something, and then froze, looking past Eli's shoulder toward the porch. "Shit. Busted."

Eli twisted and saw Ulysses Lenkov standing on the porch, arms crossed in a way that emphasized how muscular he was. His face was impassive, one eyebrow quirked at the two of them; Eli genuinely could not tell if he was inclined to burst into laughter or hit him.

"Suppose I'd better go," Eli said, glancing at Laz, who was glaring out the window at his brother.

"Yeah." Laz looked back at him and smiled wryly. "Sorry, he's just—" He shook his head, and Eli snorted. "A day or two for the stitches, Doc?"

"Yes," Eli said, one hand on the door handle. "Tuesday would be fine."

Chapter 5

L AZ WOKE UP EARLY in a puddle of sweat, wrapped up in the lingering remains of a nightmare about blaring proximity alarms that wouldn't shut off, shouted orders and reports of anti-aircraft artillery on the radio, flak, the yawning feeling in his stomach as the plane responded to his evasive maneuvers, confusion and the smell of smoke.

It was 0400. Terrific.

Probably it was good that Eli had turned him down. Imagine having nightmares around someone else. Imagine trying to explain that. He couldn't.

The sheets were unpleasantly clammy, so he got up and dragged himself out for a run.

He stuck close to the lake. His hands went numb almost as soon as he stepped out of the house, and his nose and ears were painfully cold in the breeze. Then he started out too fast, and his chest felt tight, lungs burning from too many cigarettes. It was good, in a way; kept him from thinking about the lingering pain in his back, where there wasn't any shrapnel left but his nerves still thought something was wrong. He pictured himself as a projectile launched from Thailand across a vast frictionless plain, designed to splash down into Lake Mendota. How high could he rise and still reach the target? How fast would he be moving at impact? What if instead the world was made of friction, entirely of friction?

Equations swam through his head. Standard parabolic motion was $y = ax - bx^2$. Assuming 8,400 miles between Thailand and Madison. Assuming a maximum altitude of no higher than sixty-two miles. Assuming twenty-two hours of travel time. What was he trying to find? What did he need to prove?

He jogged down the path to Picnic Point, feet crunching on the gravel, and reached the end just as the sky east of the Capitol was starting to pink. He stared at it, breath fogging in the air before the sound of someone else's feet on the gravel made him turn.

It was Sam, in his running shorts and an old sweatshirt, watching him with a curious expression. "You are not who I expected to see out here."

Laz collected himself and shrugged as nonchalantly as he could. "You mean you're not here to keep tabs on me?"

"No." Sam wiped his face on the bottom of his shirt. "I don't have that much spare time."

"Yet you seem to be everywhere, whenever I turn around."

"Madison's like that," Sam said. "While it's true that Ulysses has been worried about you and wants to provide some kind of support system, this meeting is just a coincidence." He stepped up next to Laz, looking out at the sunrise. "After all, of the two of us, who has the well-known early morning running habit?"

The sweat was drying on Laz's body, chilling him further. "He's worried?"

"Yeah." Sam glanced over at Laz and waved one hand back and forth like he was weighing something. "You seem to be on an upswing, though."

Laz choked. "What?"

"It's been a couple weeks since you turned up at our apartment drunk at seven in the morning," Sam said. "You're going to work. You're forming a friendship with another human. These are signs of progress."

Laz didn't know whether to laugh or cry at that. He wondered how often Sam and Ulysses had discussed him. "Do you have any idea what I used to do?"

Sam probably didn't, but he looked unperturbed. "You'll figure it out."

Laz couldn't think of a response that didn't come off as either antagonistic or self-deprecating, so he stayed quiet, and for a few minutes they watched the sun creep closer to the horizon.

Eventually, though, he started to shiver and turned away. Sam jogged alongside him as far as the Union, then split off and took a diagonal line across Library Mall toward State Street.

That was Tuesday.

It was nearly lunchtime on Wednesday before he felt

ready to visit Eli's office, even though it was just around the corner. He waited a few minutes for the elevator, staring idly at the building directory: Greenblatt, Sobel, Conroy, Patrick, Rogers. Doctors on the third floor, lawyers on the second, and a big blank space on the first floor, home of something that had allowed its lease to lapse and moved out. The elevator didn't come and he jogged up the stairs, hoping Eli hadn't left for lunch yet.

He didn't have Ulysses's charm when it came to receptionists and secretaries, but the woman behind the desk took pity on him. Or perhaps it was just that the waiting room was empty of neurology patients. Either way, she vanished into the back for a few minutes before returning with Eli in tow.

He was wearing a white coat with *Dr. Sobel* stitched in red on the breast pocket, and beneath that a white shirt with suspenders and a striped bow tie. His eyes lit up when he saw Laz, but he didn't say much other than thanking the receptionist and a sort of, "Come along, then," to Laz.

He took Laz down the hall and around the corner to a small, windowless exam room, closing the door behind them like Laz was a patient. Maybe he was. It wasn't the room he'd done the suturing in, but it was basically the same, with a battered old exam table, a moveable light, and sundry other equipment.

"Take a seat," Eli said, digging through one of the drawers next to the sink. "I may have to fetch some scissors . . . ah, no, these will work."

Laz, finding himself without anything much to say, still decided to open his mouth. "Eli Sobel, huh? That's got a nice ring to it." He hopped up onto the table and lay down. "What's Eli short for? Elliot?"

Eli produced a pillow from a cabinet and stuffed it under Laz's head. "Elliot?" he asked, sounding slightly confused. There was a low pneumatic hiss as he hit something on the floor and the table sank a few inches. Laz didn't enjoy the sudden movement and tried his best not to show it.

"Isn't that your name?"

"Oh," Eli said, amused now. He came toward Laz's forehead with a small, sharp pair of scissors, and Laz had to be careful not to flinch. "No."

"So what's Eli short for?"

"Eleazar." He ran a finger over the place where the cut had been on Laz's forehead and bent closer. "Sorry, this may feel a bit peculiar, but it shouldn't hurt."

Laz ignored him. "Eleazar," he said. "And I thought my family was into classical names."

There was a quiet tick as Eli clipped something, and a slight tugging sensation when he grasped it with tweezers and pulled. He repeated the process twice more. Then nothing. "What do you mean?" he asked, dropping the removed bits on a tray. He stepped closer and pulled the light over to inspect the sutures past Laz's hairline.

"I mean, my brother is Ulysses and my father is Virgil. Hell, my aunt is Cassandra, which shows how deep this madness goes."

Eli pushed Laz's hair back and clipped a stitch. "But—all right, what's Laz short for?"

Laz closed his eyes as Eli gently tugged another stitch out, then ran his fingers over the newly mended skin. "Lazarus." When he opened his eyes again, Eli had a peculiar look on his face.

"Lazarus," he repeated. "Not Laszlo."

"No." Laz tried to frown at him without moving his forehead. "Lazarus Karl Lenkov. Why would I be named Laszlo?"

"It's a nice name. It's just—Lazarus is the same name." He gently placed his right hand on Laz's temple. "Stop moving."

"Sorry." He tried valiantly to be still. "The same as what?"

"Lazarus is the Latin version of Eleazar." He cleared his throat. "That is, they have the same root in Hebrew, Elazar."

"That's weird. Isn't that weird?" Laz moved his head to get a better look at Eli's face and the other man made a noise that was almost a growl. "Sorry!" Laz said meekly.

Eli grumbled under his breath, then added audibly, "I'm almost done."

Ten seconds ticked by. Fifteen. Laz took a deep breath. "I meant to get here earlier in the week," he said. "I just, uh." He was unsure of how to finish the sentence. How did he explain that sometimes the nightmares seemed to stay with him after he'd awoken, and it was bad luck or bad vibes to talk to anyone other than Ulysses on days like that (and Sam, because you could never fucking get one of them without the other)? It was—Eli was more likely to understand than anyone else, but Laz desperately wanted to keep him separated from all that for some childish reason. "Under the weather," he said when the silence grew too long.

"I'm sorry to hear that." Eli pulled back just enough to look Laz in the eye. "How are you doing today?"

"I'm better. I mean, fine. You know how it is." The naked compassion was almost too much.

Eli changed the subject. "Any leads on the men who attacked you?"

"I . . . maybe." At close range, Eli smelled like clean laundry and soap, which should have been forgettable but was actually quite pleasant. Laz didn't know what to do with that. "Ulysses is asking around."

"Why Ulysses?"

Laz started to stretch, meaning to put a hand behind his head, and then stilled himself. "He has more contacts in the magic community. I've been away for years."

"He . . . all right." Eli blinked. "So you think there was magic involved?"

He reached for the mala, stopped himself, then let the fingers of his right hand ghost over it. "I wondered if they were involved in a ritual of some sort. It doesn't take that long to steal a painting, if that was what they were after."

Eli was frowning. "Is their poor time management the only reason you think they were using magic?"

Laz shrugged. He wanted to say no, but what came out was, "There's something weird about the painting now. I don't really know how to describe it." Eli was still halfway bent over the table, but no longer rifling through his hair for sutures. "Are we done?" Laz asked quietly, hooking two fingers under one of the doctor's suspenders.

Eli looked at him unsteadily, then bent forward again and checked the formerly injured area a final time. There was a numb spot down the center where the nerves were messed up. Laz shivered, as much from the knowledge that Eli's fingers were combing over the area as from the odd feel of it. "We're done," Eli said, lowering his hands. There was a dull metallic noise as he set the scissors down on a tray.

Laz sat up slowly, giving Eli time to back away if he wanted to. But he didn't move, just kept his eyes on Laz's face with a curious expression. "Is this okay?" Laz murmured, leaning closer, barely able to hear his own voice over the ringing in his ears.

With him sitting on the table, they were about the same height. Eli rested his forehead against Laz's for a moment as though steadying himself, and then he whispered, "Yes," and kissed him, one hand gentle on the side of his face like Laz was something to be handled with care. No, like Laz was something to be treasured.

Savored.

He barely had time to consider that idea before Eli shifted closer, opening his lips against Laz's. Laz groaned. He wanted to touch Eli, press his body against the smaller man's and feel him respond. He wanted to push the suspenders off Eli's shoulders. He wanted—

He was jerking backwards before he understood what was happening. Eli made a surprised noise, and Laz wanted to apologize, even though he wasn't sure what was going on. Suddenly his racing pulse felt more like panic than pleasure, his body screaming at him that he should be running away.

Someone passing the exam room door out in the corridor had dropped a tray on the linoleum floor, and it hit with a loud clang. That was all. A noise. Laz covered his face with shaking hands.

"Hey," Eli said quietly. "Are you okay?"

He exhaled, then tried to force himself to do it again. "Yeah. Just . . . give me a minute."

Eli shut off the extra lamp he'd been using to see the stitches, then turned the room lights down as low as they would go.

"That's a nice trick," Laz muttered.

"A lot of my patients are light-sensitive." Eli was back near the exam table now, not crowding him but close enough to be comforting. "But you don't like loud noises."

"It's just sudden loud noises," Laz corrected. Also certain types of smells. A handful of places thousands of miles from here. Light had never really done it, but it probably could if the flicker pattern was right.

"Happy Veterans Day," Eli said dryly. Laz snorted.

He found he couldn't look at Eli and shut his eyes. This was almost as bad as having a nightmare in front of someone. Or the time he'd had an episode in front of this very doctor, which was definitely something he'd been trying not to think about. What the fuck was wrong with him, turning around and going after a guy who had seen him do that kind of bullshit? A repeat performance was not impressive at all, and Eli was going to come up with a way to very politely stop seeing him. It was—

"Lunch?" Eli asked abruptly.

Laz opened his eyes. "What?"

"Lunch?" Eli said again. "It's my lunch break, and I know you haven't eaten yet."

Laz rubbed his face. "How do you know that?"

"Because you taste like the coffee that seems to be your only source of nutrients." He slipped his white coat off. "Come on, we can go to Rennebohm's."

Laz nodded and hopped off the exam table, steadying himself for a moment while his legs remembered how to stand up. He was still wearing his coat, because he hadn't bothered to take it off for what he'd assumed would be a short procedure. Hell, it *had* been a short procedure—they'd been in there for fifteen minutes, if that.

He remembered Eli's warnings about the scar and tipped his head forward a little. "I forgot to ask," he said. "How does it look?"

Eli grinned and tugged Laz's collar straight. "You look perfect."

I T WAS THURSDAY, LATE enough that Eli was the only one in the office, when Ulysses Lenkov arrived.

He appeared in the doorway unannounced, leaning against the jamb with his hands in the pockets of his leather motorcycle jacket. Eli looked up from his charting, blinked, and then felt a quiet sense of doom settle over him like a blanket.

"Dr. Sobel," Lenkov said, cocking his head. "Sorry to disturb you. Could we talk?"

"Of course." Eli stood up. "Please, come in, Mr. Lenkov. Or is it Dr. Lenkov? Could I offer you anything? A spot of tea?" If he was going to be murdered by his boyfriend's brother, he was going to go out being as British as possible.

"It's Dr. Lenkov. But call me Ulysses." Lenkov settled into one of the guest chairs. "And no, thank you."

"Then please, call me Eli." He folded his hands across the blotter and looked at Ulysses. "What brings you by?"

Ulysses looked at him for a while without speaking. An uncomfortably long time, actually. "The stitches look good," he said finally. "Or I guess I should say the place where they were."

"It healed without any issues," Eli said. It was still too early to tell what the scar was going to look like, or if it would be visible at all, but he didn't feel like volunteering that.

"Do we owe you anything?"

We? Eli frowned. "No." After a moment, he added, "Your brother fixed my car."

"Oh." Ulysses didn't look totally surprised. "Well. Good." He took a deep breath. "Where are you from? I mean, obviously you're from the UK—"

"I'm English."

"Right."

"Oh my god, Americans." He sighed. "I'm from Northumberland. It's in the north, near the border with Scotland."

Ulysses nodded. "How'd you wind up here?"

"An opportunity came up." He realized what this was, or he thought he did. "Does Laz know you're here?"

"No."

"If I tell him, will he be upset?"

Ulysses considered this. "He'd probably rage at me for being overprotective, but we've been around that block before."

Eli smiled, barely. "So I'm being vetted?"

"Vetting suggests that if I provided a negative report, he'd listen to me." Ulysses scowled. "I just wanted to meet you properly."

"To meet me," Eli echoed. He tapped the blotter. "All right. Well. Have at it, I suppose."

"Where'd you go to school?" Ulysses asked, crossing his legs at the ankle and folding his hands in front of his abdomen.

"Oxford." Ulysses was wearing a ring on his left hand. Laz hadn't mentioned a sister-in-law.

"How old are you?"

"Thirty-two."

"Why neurology?"

"Brains are interesting," Eli said. "Just fiendishly amazing. Laz tells me you're a professor of magic?"

"Yeah," Ulysses said, just a hair uncomfortably, and cleared his throat. "Assistant professor." In his T-shirt, jeans, and leather jacket, he didn't look like a professor, but there were a lot of weird ones at UW. What *assistant* professor meant was an issue Eli decided to leave for another time. He waited, and Ulysses added, "It's a family thing."

"So I understand."

"Ah." And they'd come to the actual purpose of the visit. Eli could tell by the way the other man sat forward and he breathed a silent sigh of relief. "How much has he told you about that?"

"A bit. He said you talk to ghosts, for example. And . . . he said that he can see bits of the future." He hesitated. "I think I saw him do it when we were driving the other day."

"It wasn't part of one of his episodes?"

"No. I did see one of those, but he denied—well, I suppose I didn't think to ask if he was seeing the future during it. It's not really a standard part of the mental status exam." He tapped a finger on the desk, thoughts whirling. "Flashbacks have certainly been reported among combat vets, going back to the first world war. Shell shock, they used to call it. Now it's 'operational fatigue.' " He shook his head. "Sounds much less dramatic, doesn't it? But I've never heard of someone flashing forward during episodes of that kind."

"The things that are happening to him . . . there's no reference to it in any of the papers that I could find. But then, magic users are rarely in combat." Ulysses cracked the knuckles of his right hand while he thought. "It's not a magic-based problem, as far as I can determine."

"You mean the . . . operational fatigue is setting off the magic, rather than the other way around?"

Ulysses nodded. "Unfortunately, we don't know very much about the biological underpinnings of magic. It's speculated to be a dominant gene because of the way it moves through families. But the way it affects individuals varies wildly."

Eli licked his lips. "You probably know that we think different parts of the brain are responsible for different things. Language, sight, hearing. . . . What if we hypothesize that there's a region of the brain that handles magic? If it were adjacent to the region where the flashback is triggered, the excitement of the neurons might spread between them." He thought about the way electrical activity spread through the brain during a seizure, each area picking up the new rhythm from its neighbors. "It would be fascinating to research, honestly."

"How would you do that?" Ulysses cracked a couple knuckles on his left hand. "I mean, can you measure that somehow?"

"We have a machine called an electroencephalogram, an EEG, that picks up electrical activity in the brain. So ideally, we would hook him up and then trigger an episode somehow." Eli was tapping out a rhythm on the blotter now. "I don't know how we'd do that. He doesn't have much control over when he sees the future or when he has a flashback, as far as I'm aware."

They both considered that for a bit. Finally, Ulysses said, "What if we tied him to a chair blindfolded and threw tennis balls at him?"

Eli locked eyes with him. "That could do it."

"You busy Saturday?"

He had a few misgivings. It was always a bad idea to treat someone you were close to. But then again, there wasn't exactly another doctor he could refer Ulysses to who would carry out the experiment in his place. And there was a good chance they'd learn something interesting. Maybe something that would be helpful.

Eli spread his hands.

Chapter 6

Through some miracle, Eli finished all his notes by six o'clock on Friday afternoon and clattered down the stairs of the building at what felt like an indecently early hour to be breaking free. The dark street shone from recent rain, and the air smelled like wet leaves. It was the end of the autumn, but it was beautiful in its way. He appreciated the way the streetlights reflected off the pavement in amber puddles, and appeared as the fog creeping up on the Capitol lawn. It all made for a striking minimalist landscape. Or he was a besotted fool; that might also be possible.

Without thinking too much about what he was doing, he turned the corner onto State Street and wandered down to the gallery. That, too, felt unusually pretty. The door was set back from the sidewalk by several feet, creating a little alcove in between the shop windows. There was an old tin tile ceiling and a leadlight like a sunburst above the door. He still wasn't sure of its hours—none were posted, actually—but the lights were on and the door was unlocked, so he went in.

The gallery was one large room with a high ceiling, walls all painted white. Along the wall to his left was a series of bright abstract works with a sign above that said *Outsider Art*. Farther down were other landscapes, some more realistic than others, and at the far end, the painting.

It seemed odd to think of it like that, with a definite article, when obviously there were many paintings in the gallery, but it really dominated the space. Just the ornate gold frame felt like an overwhelming display of opulence because of its size.

A very tall, thin man, his height accentuated by a long black coat, stood directly in front of the painting. He had shoved his hands into his pockets and seemed deep in contemplation. Perhaps hearing the squeak of leather shoes on the wood floor, he turned and ran his eyes over Eli like he was another piece of art in the gallery to be examined. Then the man smiled. He had olive skin, pretty green eyes, and wild, wavy brown hair.

"Tell me," he said, "is there something odd about that painting? Does it seem strange to you?"

Eli looked. It was a landscape done in a style he'd not seen before, where all the objects within the painting seemed to phosphoresce. It was of a jungle, although he couldn't identify a single plant in it, with the ruin of a ziggurat or some other large, tumbled-down stone building, overrun with vines, drawing the eye to the horizon. The trees were out of scale, the flowers and fruit too big compared to the size of the bricks. Something with eyes lurked just beyond the lighted circle, and it was staring at him. If Laz was right and the painting had changed since the attack, what the hell had it looked like before?

Eli rubbed his eyes and looked back at the tall man. "It's a bit surreal," he allowed. "In the sense of being dreamlike."

The man's eyes were intense. "It doesn't make you feel weird or uncomfortable?"

"I don't know much about art." Eli looked again, frowning. "Is it supposed to?"

The man seemed amused. He dressed like he had money, and there was a sort of glow of good health about him. Eli wondered if he was just an unusually chatty art shopper until he said, "You're that doctor."

"I'm certainly *a* doctor," Eli said slowly. "Sorry, have we met?"

"Not yet. I'm Sam." The man's tone was cheerful, but he didn't offer a handshake. "I've heard a lot about you."

"That's a bit disconcerting." Eli glanced around, wondering where Laz was.

Before Sam could respond, they heard bickering voices, and an instant later Laz and Ulysses emerged into the main room of the gallery. They were speaking Russian, although as soon as he spotted Eli, Laz broke off. He scowled as he came barging across the space between them.

"Doc!" he said, and oh shit, Eli was in trouble. He didn't even know what he'd done. "Tell me about this experiment."

Eli said, "I can explain the idea, of course. What have you already been told?"

"Just that you want to take pictures of my brain while I'm having an episode." He turned and glared at Ulysses, who was lounging against the desk in the corner. "I'll be generous and assume this was his stupid idea that he somehow talked you into, and not that you met my brother and thirty seconds later revealed whatever mad scientist plans you have lurking in there." He poked Eli's forehead, making him blink.

"To be clear, are you upset about the proposed experiment, or my lack of subtlety?" Eli murmured, and heard Sam stifle a laugh. Laz glared at him, too, and he raised his hands and wandered over to Ulysses.

"Just explain this machine to me," Laz said, and folded his arms across his chest. He was wearing heavy black boots, jeans, and a burnt orange sweater, and Eli could see the tassel of that little rosary peeking out from the bottom of one sleeve. But he wasn't fidgeting with it today; annoyance had stilled his restless limbs.

Eli tried to gauge Laz's mood and whether or not suggesting they go somewhere to sit down would be well-received. Perhaps better to start where they were. "Have you ever had an EEG?"

"Obviously not."

"It's a way of recording what the brain is doing. You see, there are tiny electrical charges that change when things happen in your brain, and we can detect those—"

"Wait, wait." Laz was frowning. "Are you saying brains run on electricity?"

"Not the way a torch runs on batteries. But there are changes in electrical potential across synapses that happen because of chemical changes before neuronal firings." Laz nodded slowly, and Eli said, "You've never taken a physiology course, I take it."

"Too squishy, not enough circuits." He tilted his head. "Or so I imagined, anyway. But these must be very small charges."

"Right. They're mostly detectable because of the way the neurons are laid out all parallel to each other. The leads of the EEG really record an average change for whatever neurons are below. We compare each lead to another nearby one and subtract them from each other, then amplify the difference." He reached up and touched a spot above Laz's ear. "So we put one pair here to record changes in the temporal lobe . . ."

Laz shut his eyes. "Which does what?"

"Processing of sensory information, some receptive language things, visual memory. . . . I have a diagram in my office if you're interested. I did a fellowship in neurophysiology, so I can definitely talk about neuroanatomy at some length." He wiggled his eyebrows like Groucho Marx, and Laz finally laughed.

"And the electrodes are external?"

What had Ulysses been telling him? Eli glanced over, frowning, but Laz's brother was deep in conversation with Sam, who was perched on the desk. "We stick them to your scalp. My clinic doesn't have the facilities for anything invasive, and I don't think it would tell us anything more useful."

Laz exhaled. "All right."

"You don't have to do it. It's an interesting opportunity, but . . ." Eli fought the temptation to lower his voice. "I don't want you to feel pressured into it."

He stood for a moment watching Laz's curiosity and trepidation doing battle on his face. "If it helps," Eli added, "I wouldn't suggest it if I thought it would harm you in any way. Although I realize these episodes are emotionally distressing, which is—"

Laz shook his head. "I want to see this machine in action." Then, decision made, he shifted gears rapidly. "What are you doing here? Ulysses can't have called in reinforcements that quickly."

"I would have come earlier if I'd known he was going to make such a hash of things." He rolled his eyes. "I came by to see if you wanted to get a drink or something."

Laz nodded, a hesitant little smile curling up the corner of his mouth. "Let me lock up." He turned around and looked at Ulysses and Sam, who were still speaking quietly, heads together.

"Oi! Don't you two have somewhere else to be?"

"Nowhere in particular." Ulysses glanced at Sam. "You?"

Sam shrugged. "We could go grab dinner somewhere."

Ulysses nodded. "Webster Street Inn? Not too many students this time of night."

Both of them looked at Eli. He smiled uncomfortably and glanced over at Laz. "I don't want to intrude. I could—"

"No," Laz said to Ulysses, tone flat. "Fuck off. This is a private date."

"I have information about your case," Ulysses said, and Laz groaned.

"Really? Information you can only give me over dinner?"

They were doing this on purpose, Eli realized, watching them fling insults back and forth. It was some sort of bonding ritual. He glanced at Sam, who was fighting hard to keep his amusement hidden, and losing.

"Laz," Eli said quietly, "it's no problem. Let's all go."

Laz gave him a long look and then nodded.

Out on the street, Eli fell into step beside Laz, a few paces behind Sam and Ulysses.

"Sorry," Laz said. "I just—sorry."

"Don't worry about it. I'm pleased to have a chance to spend time with you, whatever the circumstances." He bumped his shoulder against Laz's.

"Don't say that, or he'll have us chasing through some cemetery looking for a lost cursed chess set or something," Laz fretted. "Don't look at me like that. It's happened before." Eli laughed, and grudgingly, Laz also smiled.

"Could I ask," Eli began, leaning closer to Laz to speak more quietly, "what your connection with Sam is? He didn't explain."

Laz sighed, his breath coming out as a white cloud in the cold air. "He's my brother-in-law."

Eli fixed his gaze on the back of Sam's coat. Ulysses was telling some kind of story, one hand on Sam's back, and Sam was laughing. He noted again Ulysses's silver ring, bright against the black wool, and tried to recall if Sam had been wearing something similar. "Oh."

"Yeah." Laz sighed. "They drive me crazy, and they've probably taken ten years off my life with the stress they've caused me. But they're joined at the hip."

"Why do I feel like they might tell a similar story about you?" Eli murmured.

"Because you've met me."

Another thought struck Eli. "When your brother showed up at my office yesterday, I thought he was there to do me some violence because I'd expressed an interest in you."

Laz made a face like he was genuinely weighing the idea. "It's possible," he said after a moment. "He can be pretty protective of the family."

Eli found that, far from being upset, he was glad Laz had someone on his side. "Noted."

T HE WEBSTER STREET INN was crowded and noisy. It was a Friday evening, and Laz was going to lose his mind. They all shoved into a booth together, Ulysses and Sam on one side, him and Eli on the other. His brother deployed a sharklike grin at Laz. He knew exactly what he was doing. Laz, on the other hand, did not.

It had been so long since he'd dated anyone, he barely recalled what one was supposed to do. Dancing seemed out, given how loud most bands were; maybe the movies? The competitive side of his nature argued that, while there probably wasn't one right answer, there was almost certainly a way that he could win. But he wasn't sure he could figure that out with Sam and Ulysses staring at him.

Eli was sitting close to him on the left, a warm and steadying presence in a dark suit and bow tie. He seemed at ease making small talk with Ulysses and Sam. More at ease than Laz was, anyway. After they'd ordered, Eli glanced around and then untied his bow tie and stuck it in an inner pocket, undoing the top button of his shirt along with it.

Laz must have made some questioning noise, because the doctor murmured into Laz's ear, "Just feeling a bit overdressed."

"You look fine," Laz said, and then realized that didn't sound quite right. He tried, "Actually, you look really good," and felt embarrassed at the confused look Eli shot him. "I mean—"

"Thank you," Eli said, and gently touched his shoulder. "You seem tense."

Laz exhaled and shut his eyes. It was still overwhelmingly loud, but at least without the visual he could focus on the bench beneath him, the warmth of Eli's leg pressed against his, the smell of burgers cooking somewhere in the back. He unwound the mala and flipped through the beads, not counting them, just feeling from one to the next. "I'm fine," he said, and then opened his eyes and said, "really. Just—long day."

"Does the painting bother you?" Sam asked abruptly.

The waitress arrived with their beers, and Laz waited until she'd left again before he said, "Bother?"

Sam looked around the room restlessly as he thought. "It feels cursed to me."

"What do you mean?" Laz sat forward a little.

Sam shook his head. "The nazar—it isn't hot, but it's warm." He glanced at Ulysses for help. "It's been useful in detecting malign magic before."

Laz digested this. "What does the curse do?"

Sam shrugged, and Laz looked at his brother. "Can you find out?"

"Perhaps." Ulysses turned the pint glass in his fingers. "Can I find out without damaging the painting? That's less clear. Usually you need a little piece of the cursed object that you can burn."

"We could clip a piece of the canvas off the back," Laz said.

"But if the curse only resides within the picture—"

"Yeah." Laz sighed. Eli was watching them both curiously, so he tried to explain. "The creation of cursed objects . . ." was as far as he got before finding himself unsure of what he wanted to say. "It's a big painting. If Sam thinks it's cursed, we should look into that. But what's actually cursed? Is it the canvas, the stretcher bars, the paint . . . only one layer of paint? The frame? I don't know. I don't think Carla will take it off display without more information, either. If it doesn't sell, she's out a ton of money."

Eli thought about this. "What could the curse do?"

Laz shrugged. "Curses are a wide and varied field." He glanced across the table at Ulysses. "He knows more than I do, but what with human beings being so awful, you can probably guess."

"I don't like the sound of that," Eli muttered. "All right. Is there any other angle we could come at this from?"

Ulysses cleared his throat. "I may have an idea for you there," he said, and handed Laz a piece of paper with an address on it. "It's your purchasers of the first painting. The Greenfields."

Laz raised his eyebrows, then tucked the paper away in his pocket. "Do I want to know how you got this? I couldn't reach her by phone."

"Dr. Ryan Greenfield used to work at UW. He was a professor of mathematics. Took a position at the University of Minnesota at the end of spring semester last year." Ulysses glanced toward Sam, who had some ridiculous secret smile on his face, then looked back at

Laz. "You could talk to the neighbors, see if there's been anything odd going on. And I can come by when the gallery is closed and take a look at the curse."

"Thanks." Laz sat back, looping the mala around his wrist again. The waitress appeared with their plates, and he found himself staring down at a burger and fries. He hadn't been especially hungry when he ordered, but now that he saw the food, he was starving.

Eli had fallen into conversation with Sam across the table, asking him about seventeenth-century pop-up medical textbooks. Sam was plainly charmed to find someone else who cared at all about books and excited to discuss this specific obscure type of object. Laz did not know anything about old books and wasn't following the conversation at all, but he enjoyed watching Eli talk. The man's face was quite expressive when he got excited. Not that he was bad-looking to begin with, but when he was engaged with something it transformed his features. He'd noticed it before when Eli was explaining the EEG, too. Laz gently pressed his leg against Eli's, enjoying the rush from the physical contact. The anticipation of further contact, sometime in the future.

Maybe Eli was right about this getting-to-know-you thing. It was exciting not to just fall into bed with someone. And he liked Eli. Really liked him.

Which led quickly to: What the fuck was he even doing?

Tomorrow, Eli was going to put electrodes on his head and discover exactly how big of a mess Laz was inside, and that would be the end of things.

But then again, he'd been through a lot of last nights. He made himself breathe through this one as well. Enjoy the ride, take the pain when it arrived; that was the human condition, and there was nothing to be done about it.

Ulysses, who had been enjoying the conversation as well, because he was also weirdly interested in old books, caught Laz's eye and made a little head motion toward the bar. Laz shut his eyes for a moment, then got up and followed.

"Are you okay?" Ulysses asked as soon as they were away from the table.

"People keep asking that." The bar was full of boisterous energy, and the smell of cigarettes and old beer was unexpectedly nauseating. *And* someone had just selected something new on the jukebox, adding to the general cacophony. If it was fucking Rod Stewart again, he was going to start flipping tables.

"You don't look great, Laz," Ulysses said quietly.

Laz pressed his fingers to his temples and glanced back at the table. Eli was laughing at something Sam had said, and Laz simultaneously wondered if this newcomer fit in better with Sam and Ulysses than Laz himself did, and if he could grab Eli and run. What types of things did people do that were at least date-adjacent and didn't include bars or exorcisms?

When he figured that out, could he somehow turn into a normal person who was capable of being happy in his partner's presence without losing his goddamn mind?

"I'm—I just can't—" He forced himself to stop and took a deep breath, because if he said everything in his head, Ulysses was going to try to give him advice.

A hand landed on Ulysses's arm, and a low voice said, "Lenkov, there you are. I need to talk to you."

It was Oran.

Ulysses appeared unsurprised by their presence. Or at least, he wasn't shocked the way Laz was. Maybe he shouldn't have been; he knew Oran was around in a general way, and it wasn't uncommon to run into people downtown. Madison just wasn't that big of a city. But to see them come up to Ulysses and ask him to speak with them outside . . .

Of course they knew Ulysses. Everyone did. But how *well* did they know him? Was he the reason they'd come to the gallery in the first place? Paranoia swam up in him, thick and choking, and he forced it down. Be rational. Ulysses didn't know anything about art. And Oran would have mentioned. A referral would have been—

Laz watched the two of them step outside. He was left hovering awkwardly in the space between the bar and the tables. After a moment, he went over to the bar and ordered a whisky on the rocks to soothe his nerves. Then he ambled back to the table, making a show of calm that fooled approximately no one.

"Who was that?" Eli asked as Laz slid back into the booth.

"A local magician." He glanced at Sam, wondering if he knew, if he had been a party to this conspiracy.

Sam nodded, apparently oblivious. "One of Ulysses's people, probably."

"He has people?" Eli sounded perplexed. "Like the Baker Street Irregulars?"

Sam shrugged. "I don't know what to call them. A loose assortment of magic users who come by if something weird is happening, and then we wind up dealing with ghost ships or cursed windows or, I don't know, getting chased by bats."

"What an interesting life you must lead," Eli murmured.

Laz shook his head and sipped his drink, watching Sam watch the door. After a minute or two, Ulysses was back, sliding into the booth, bringing with him a brief whiff of cold, fresh air.

"Oran found a stone circle in the woods out behind the limnology building," he said without preamble. "They're concerned."

Sam nodded and asked two or three well-considered, pertinent questions. Laz just sat back in the booth and drank.

Eli leaned closer to him. "Do you want to go?" he asked quietly, almost into Laz's ear.

Laz swallowed. "I can't stay here." Eli's fingers grazed his thigh and grabbed his hand under the table, squeezing his fingers and then letting him go.

"Let's check it out, then," Eli said. "Seems like an interesting time. And then we can see where things take us."

"Yeah," Laz agreed. He pulled out his wallet and thrust a random denomination of bill at Ulysses, who was signaling for the check. Then he downed the rest of his whisky and got up. "Let's do it."

Chapter 7

J UST LIKE BACK IN the gallery, Laz looked more comfortable after the choice was made. Maybe it was all those years as a soldier; once he had his brief, it was time to move out, regardless of his personal feelings. But he brushed against Eli's shoulder as they stepped out into the cool night air and smiled briefly when Eli looked over at him.

Laz ducked into the gallery as they went past and retrieved two electric torches, one of which he passed to Ulysses. They made their way down State Street, across Library Mall and past the Union and a big construction site for what Sam said was the new undergraduate library. As they went, Laz pulled out a pack of cigarettes, stared at it, and then returned it to his pocket.

"Trying to quit?" Eli asked quietly after the second time he caught this.

Laz shrugged. "I've been cutting down."

The road snaked around and terminated in a parking lot next to the lake. The limnology building, an inverted step pyramid of a structure made from steel and cement, crouched at the edge of it, looming over a stretch of sidewalk that led to the Lakeshore Path. They followed it, and then walked along the crushed limestone beyond until the sweep of Ulysses's torch discovered a trail tramped into the undergrowth leading away into the woods to their left.

"I think this is where the undergrads come to smoke weed," Ulysses said from somewhere ahead of them, and a moment later they emerged into a clearing.

"They need a special place?" Laz mused.

It smelled like Ulysses was right, and also like wet leaves and some sort of unpleasant dead fish smell from the lake, and underneath a sharp current of something he couldn't identify. Eli wrinkled his nose. Sam was looking around a little nervously, although neither Ulysses nor Laz seemed too bothered. Ulysses had gone off with his flashlight to look at a large standing stone—a menhir, for lack of a better term—on the edge of the clearing.

"Does this happen to you a lot?" Eli asked.

Sam, for god knew what reason, laughed. "Now and then." He strode to the edge of the clearing and pushed a tree aside. "Ulysses," he said, his voice a little tense, "shine your light over here, would you?"

There was another menhir.

Laz raised his flashlight and turned. The light reflected off the plants at the edges of the clearing that still had leaves, here and there catching a rock. "This shit shouldn't be here," he announced, voice tense.

Sam, from somewhere outside the clearing, called, "There's another back here."

Eli looked at Laz's face and found it worried. "You mean these were put here recently?"

"We would have known if there was a stone circle here." He looked across and discovered that Ulysses had stepped around behind the other menhir. Eli heard his voice as he spoke to Sam, though he couldn't make out any words. "We grew up less than a mile from here. We were all over these woods when we were kids. No way could we have missed this."

Eli fished his penlight out of his pocket. In the center of the clearing was an area that had once held a small fire, to judge by the charred spots. Around it were placed flat stones at oddly regular intervals. He bent over, shining his light more closely at one. It was smooth, dark gray, and it had something written on it.

He looked closer, but the figure was drawn in chalk and only small traces had survived the most recent rainstorm. The next one over was completely blank. And then the third—jackpot. Or was it? Looking closely, it seemed to hold a circle divided into even segments by lines radiating outward from the center. It wasn't quite a flower, but it seemed to imply one, somehow. Beneath that was a squiggly line, like a child's drawing of a snake.

That was an odd thing to find on a rock in the middle of the woods in Wisconsin. He reached out to pick it up so he could get a closer glance and—

Abruptly, Laz was back, one hand on his shoulder, one on his waist, yanking him up and away. Eli felt hot where they touched, despite his clothes, despite his embarrassment at almost doing something he shouldn't have. "It's a bad idea to go around touching stuff you can't identify, Doc," he said quietly. Then he squatted down, aiming his torch at the stone.

"What is it?" Eli asked.

"A sigil of some sort." He stood up and looked at Eli, eyes slightly wild. "This was for summoning something."

"This?" Eli licked his lips. The air tasted wrong, a little more acrid than air typically was, like vaporized acetic acid. Magic? Panic? "It's just paint."

"Stay clear of it," Laz advised, and stepped away, shouting, "Hey, U, come over here."

With the more powerful flashlight gone, Eli's penlight seemed inadequate, and he blinked into the darkness. It had begun to drizzle, and he could hear the drops hitting the ground around them, even though he hadn't felt them yet. And he could hear something else rustling in the undergrowth. He felt his breath catch unpleasantly in his throat.

He turned in that direction, fruitlessly shining his light toward the sound. There was nothing. Probably a squirrel.

A moment later, something jerked him off his feet.

L AZ WAS ON THE far side of the circle of standing stones when he heard Eli hit the deck. He whipped around, flashlight at the ready, but it still took a terrifyingly long time for the light to find the small man on the ground. He was struggling with a creature that looked like a giant snake. At least eight feet long and as big around as a man's thigh, dark on its back with flashes of red when it moved, it had wrapped itself around Eli up to the waist. Laz could see him struggling as it squeezed.

The worst part, though, was its head, which wasn't snakelike at all. It was long and blunt, like the skull of a crocodile, with too many too-long teeth shoved into its jaws, thin, needle-sharp, rows and rows of them, and its mouth seemed to open far wider than should be possible.

It was a nightmare come to life, and it was grinning at Eli.

Crossing the circle seemed to take much longer than the distance and his speed would indicate. Everything seemed to shift drunkenly as he threw his arms around the serpent right behind the head. He pulled as hard as he could, then punched it, which stung; it didn't seem to notice, so he turned the flashlight around and brought the heavy metal butt of it down in the center of the thing's nose.

"Ulysses," he shouted. "Sam! A little—"

The serpent shook itself and sent him flying into one of the standing stones. He met the muddy undergrowth with a painful thump. The damn thing was just one giant muscle. He pushed himself off the ground, heart pounding in his temples, and charged it.

Eli was still struggling. Sam and Ulysses were preparing a spell, a terribly slow process under the circumstances. Sam scrabbled at the creature's tail, shouting words that Laz couldn't hear over the roaring in his ears. Laz clasped his hands together and brought both fists down on the nightmare snake's skull. It turned to look at him with glowing red eyes, and—

Oh, shit.

One moment it was staring at him, and the next it was in his head. Eli was trying to tell him something, but he couldn't hear it over the hissing, the low gravelly voice speaking words he didn't understand that seemed to latch onto his insides. He could feel the creature in there, turning over his memories like it was at a rummage sale.

He still had his hands on its throat, although he was vaguely aware he'd stopped moving, too stunned by the intrusion. Eli, however, had not stopped. In fact, he'd managed to work an arm free and grabbed for Laz's shoulder as the serpent shifted.

The contact brought Laz back to himself. Let it search his memories and choke on them. He gave up on trying to move it directly, wrapped his arms around Eli's chest, and pulled, trying to yank him out of the serpent's coils. It was like trying to shift a boulder. In his mind, the serpent laughed. Eli had gone pale with fear or pain, or both. The first rule of rescuing an injured airman was to say something heartening to the guy to keep his spirits up. But that was never Laz's job; he flew the helicopter, he didn't talk to the patients. But—

"I've got you," he said, hating how useless a thing this was to say.

The serpent's maw moved closer, its hot-vinegar breath overwhelming Laz's other senses. He shut his eyes and gritted his teeth, burying his face in Eli's shoulder as he tried to find a new angle to pull at. The serpent moved forward with a twitch of its tail, shifting both of them into the circle, and suddenly Laz felt dislocated. He could still feel the chilly night air on his skin, the occasional raindrop that made its way through the trees, but he was also somewhere warm and humid, breathing air that smelled of dry dirt and something he couldn't quite place. Another flashback? Something from the future?

All the time there was a whispering in the back of his head. "You are going to die. Your bones will turn to dust and you will be forgotten. It is no more than you deserve." He wasn't sure whose voice it was.

He brought a knee up, hard, and hit the serpent under its lower jaw. It reared back, momentarily stunned, and they were back in the forest. He felt Ulysses's broad, solid form brush his as he leaned in to grab the Zippo out of Laz's jacket pocket. His brother said, into his ear, "Get clear," and the urgency in Ulysses's voice gave Laz a new burst of terrified strength. With a tremendous tug, he got Eli free and they stumbled a handful of steps across the clearing before an explosion pushed them both over into a heap.

It took a minute for Laz's vision to clear. He could hear again. He could—

He was lying on top of Eli. He must have flung himself there to protect the doctor from the flames.

Gradually the reports began to trickle in from his extremities—a knuckle stung, his back ached, there was a tender knot on the back of his skull. For some reason, his left leg had a few complaints. Nothing too severe. Across the circle, Sam and Ulysses were picking themselves up. Ulysses had the drained, keyed-up look of sudden magic expenditure. Laz turned his attention back to Eli.

"Hi," he said. His voice sounded rough, like he'd been shouting. He pushed himself up onto his elbows.

Eli's eyes were wide. "Hi," he breathed. He put one hand on Laz's shoulder and then paused, like he wasn't sure which direction he was going with that.

Laz wanted to kiss him. The feeling surprised him, his body reinterpreting the lingering terror and adrenaline as a different kind of excitement. "You still in one piece?"

"I think so." He turned his head, wincing. "That was . . ."

"Yeah." Laz realized he was still lying on top of Eli and forced himself to sit up. "Not how I envisioned the evening going."

Eli made an unhappy, slightly pained noise, but he seemed to be able to move all his limbs. "What's the bloody use of having foresight if you never foresee anything relevant?"

"I ask myself that a lot." He felt the amusement drain from him as he watched Eli run a hand over his own torso, wincing. "I assume that as a physician, if you were injured, you'd do your best to hide it from me."

"I see you've met our kind before." Eli steadied himself against Laz's shoulder. "I don't think I've cracked any ribs. I actually am fine. Or I'm more or less in one piece, at least."

"Good." Laz got to his feet and pulled Eli up after him. In the center of the clearing, Sam and Ulysses were conferring. Ulysses had an arm around Sam's waist, and Laz wasn't sure which of them he was trying to steady. "Where is it?"

Ulysses swung to look at him, eyes wild. "Gone." He tossed the lighter back, and Laz caught it with a fast, automatic motion.

Into the silence, Eli said, "Dead?"

"I don't know." Laz didn't like the way his brother's voice sounded. "That should have been enough to kill it, but there's no residue, so it may be . . . somewhere."

"Somewhere?" Laz echoed.

"We should get out of here," Ulysses said firmly. "It's injured, wherever it is, and we don't have the weaponry to do anything else to it."

"But it could hurt someone else," Laz protested.

"I think the circle keeps it bound to this spot." Ulysses looked around at the stones, like there was a warning sign they'd somehow missed. "It's not going to maraud around, menacing joggers. We'd have heard about that."

Laz glanced at Eli, pale-faced and trembling in the weak light, and gave up the fight. "All right."

The walk back to Eli's car was the longest of Laz's life, which was saying something. It started with Sam peevishly saying, "Why is there a henge with a giant evil snake in it in the middle of the city?"

"It's not a henge," Ulysses said. Sam was still half holding him up. "A henge is a circular earthwork. The presence of standing stones within it is optional. That's a stone circle."

"All right," Sam said, voice tight. "Why is there a stone circle in downtown Madison?"

With barely a pause, Ulysses launched into a wandering explanation of standing stones, their ritual properties, the liminal magical spaces they enclosed, and on and on until Eli said, "Is it related to what happened to Laz at the gallery?"

The silence that followed was interesting. Laz glanced over his shoulder and saw Ulysses looking pensive. He didn't answer for nearly a block, and when he did speak, it was to say, "I don't know. On the surface, I can't see a relationship."

It was drizzling steadily when they got back to Eli's car. Ulysses and Sam's apartment was only a few blocks farther—and so was the house on Pinckney Street, for that matter—but the two of them slid into the car anyway, Sam folding his long stork legs into the backseat. Laz examined Eli for a moment, noted his shaking hands, and took the keys, guiding him gently into the passenger seat. Eli exhaled softly and leaned back against the leather as Laz guided the car around the Capitol.

He'd expected to feel a certain grim satisfaction at getting through everything without freaking out. He'd kept his head. He'd probably saved Eli's life. Instead, he found himself adrift, wondering if he should be more shaken than he was, and if this was a new and different way he was broken now.

Ulysses and Sam left quietly. Laz still wasn't sure what had happened during the explosion, but it appeared to have knocked Ulysses around enough that he was holding himself stiffly, like his back hurt. Something to check on tomorrow.

Eli didn't say anything once they were alone, so Laz put the car back into gear and drove to Pinckney Street. It was five rapidly passing blocks, and there were about five million things he wanted to say before they got there, and he didn't know how to articulate any of them. Finally, he said, "I'm sorry about that."

Eli looked over at him. "I'm sure there are a lot of things in the world that are your fault," he said gently, "but that thing attacking me is not one of them."

Laz glanced sideways and caught Eli in profile. "I should have . . . I don't know. Protected you better."

Eli snorted. "You did punch it with your bare hands to try to save me." He reached over, grabbing one of Laz's hands off the steering wheel. With a gentle touch, he ran a finger across the skin of Laz's knuckles where it had split during the fight.

Laz shivered. "Don't tell me I need more stitches." He maneuvered the car into a parking space in front of the house and set the parking brake. When he turned off the engine, the silence was thick, but not oppressive.

"It's just a scrape." Eli smiled crookedly. "I was impressed, though. That was the most terrifying thing I've ever seen. And it was—in my head, it—" His voice cracked and he paused, looking down at his hands, at their still-intertwined fingers. Laz saw his shoulders move as he cleared his throat. "And you were very brave," he finished.

Laz opened his mouth to say something like, "I'm not brave," or "I would have done the same for anyone." Instead, what came out was, "Would you like to come in, Doc?" He shut his eyes.

He heard Eli take a deep breath, and then there was a long, thoughtful pause. "Yes," Eli said finally. "I think I would."

Chapter 8

ANY OF THE BIG old houses in Madison had been broken up into apartments. Eli wasn't sure why he thought that was the case with the place where Laz and his grandmother lived—it just looked too big for two people. So he was surprised when Laz opened the front door and they stepped into the broad foyer of what was clearly still a single-family dwelling, and one definitely occupied by more than two people. Laz left his shoes next to the closet and indicated that Eli should do the same.

It was a relief to press his muscles into motion climbing up what felt like an endless number of stairs, the exercise flushing the last of the adrenaline from his system. It was a relief to forget the churning terror and replace it with a knot of tense, pleasurable anticipation of things to come. Eli's knees felt watery as he finally reached the top of the last staircase, which ended in a little landing outside a heavy fire door. Whether the sensation was due to the retreating panic or the looks Laz kept shooting him was anyone's guess.

The room Laz let them into was large, former servants' quarters or a converted attic to judge by the ceiling, which seemed to follow the line of the roof. There was a large orange rug with hexagons on it and a bookshelf with a handful of books shoved onto it haphazardly—mostly small-engine repair guides and a few dog-eared mystery novels. The walls were bare, except for a small, bright still life and a variety of little snowflake-like circle-and-line drawings sketched over the white paint. There was a bed shoved into the room's far corner. As single men's rooms went, it was neater than most.

By far the most interesting part of it was a long workbench that ran along one wall and was covered with bits of motors and other mechanical objects. He drifted over to look more closely while Laz hung up their coats. A circuit board here and there, what looked like a disconnected blade, a rubber belt, a machine that clearly tested electrical circuits somehow, a soldering iron, a variety of screwdrivers and spanners, a sponge with little bits of metal melted to it.

"Not just brave, then," Eli said over one shoulder. "What have you been doing?"

Laz came up behind him and wrapped an arm around Eli's waist, pulling him against Laz's chest. Even with Eli's suit coat removed, his shirt was still sad and damp, spotted here and there with mud, serpent slime, and blood to break up the monotony. Probably not too pleasant for Laz to be pressed up against; he'd divested himself of his sweater, leaving him in just his vest. It looked good on him, to be sure, the thin material clinging to his chest and biceps. Eli could feel the warmth of Laz's body against his back. "That one is a blender," Laz said, pointing to a pile of shiny metal. "That's a vacuum cleaner motor. That's part of a dryer."

"Part of?"

"I couldn't bring the whole thing with me. That's the broken piece."

"This is what you do for fun?" Eli picked up a transistor and turned it in his fingers. It actually wasn't all that surprising; in fact, there was something grounding about Laz's obvious love affair with all things mechanical. It felt so very normal compared to evil snakes and sigil stones. "How did you get into this?"

Laz kissed the side of Eli's neck. He shivered. "It's really not very interesting."

"I bet that's not true."

Laz exhaled and then settled his chin on Eli's shoulder. "Babushka—my gran—needed her blender fixed." He reached out and took the transistor back from Eli, setting it gently on the bench. "And the day after, she went to this League of Women Voters meeting or something."

"Having met both you and Ulysses, I must say that seems a bit quotidian," Eli said dryly. "If you told me she was part of a coven, though . . ."

"I don't think she's part of a coven anymore." He plunged on before Eli could respond to *that* revelation.

"You know that thing they do where they're complaining but really not complaining?"

They both paused at this turn of phrase. "Bragging?" Eli suggested.

Laz considered the word. Eli felt him shrug. "Anyway, the next day there were two blenders and a vacuum sitting on the porch for me. After that, someone asked me to look at her dishwasher. Then I fixed a television and a fridge and now . . ." He waved at the bench. "People in the neighborhood just bring me stuff."

"Do you get paid for this?"

Laz said, "Sometimes," which was a funny way of putting it. "I got a bushel of apples a couple weeks ago."

"You're an old country doctor." Eli licked his lips. "What did you—"

"I gave them to Aunt Cass. I think she's making calvados with them." He grabbed Eli's hand and tugged gently, drawing him toward the far side of the room. Eli let himself be drawn.

"Have you considered opening your own repair shop or something?" He looked down, focused on unbuttoning his cuffs.

Laz snorted. "I have a job, Doc."

"But you must be so bored."

Laz sat down on the bed abruptly. "Is that what this is about?" And Eli realized with a twinge that he had made a misstep.

"I'm sorry," he said, sitting down next to Laz. "It's not about anything, per se. I'm just curious—"

"Yeah." Laz flopped back on the bed. "It's fine. No one gets it, I know. Ulysses has been on my case enough."

"I mean I'm curious about you, what makes you tick." Eli unbuttoned his shirt and dropped it on the rug, leaving him in a damp but mostly clean white vest. He hesitated and then lay down on his side next to Laz, propping his head up on an elbow. "Do you want to tell me about it?"

At least Laz's frown eased a bit. He folded his hands across his stomach, but he turned to look at Eli. "It's not bad. I have a lot of time to read. I manage the outsider art area. And I get to fix things."

Eli laughed, startled. "You what?"

"It's an old building, and it's not like Carla knows how to do any of that stuff." He shrugged. "If a lamp needs to be rewired, or a windowpane is cracked, or a pipe is leaking, I take care of it."

Laz's face said a lot, and Eli felt suddenly, savagely bad, because he hadn't been paying attention. "It's about being useful, isn't it." He groaned. "You even told me that."

"I did tell you that," Laz said quietly. "I tell everyone that. But you listened."

Eli leaned forward and kissed him.

It was a delight to lie there and kiss him in an unhurried way, letting the tension pool between them. Laz approached it with the same intensity he brought to everything, just shy of overwhelming but an amazing thing to have aimed at one. He certainly seemed intent on mapping the spots that made Eli writhe.

Their height difference was just enough that Eli was usually lifting his eyes to Laz. Lying down, chest to chest, it felt negligible. Eli's free hand landed on Laz's hip where his shirt had ridden up, and he traced the protrusive bit of the ilium with his thumb. Laz hissed and rolled onto his back, tugging Eli along until he was straddling the other man's lean pelvis.

Laz's body, when he shed his undershirt, was thinner than Eli expected, with ropy muscles. He still wore his dog tags on a skinny silver ball chain. He had a whole constellation of scars on the left side of his back that Eli discovered with his fingertips, and a curly tattoo over his heart that looked a little like the number six with calligraphic elaborations but probably wasn't, and tan lines on his neck and upper arms that hadn't yet faded. And he helped pull Eli's vest over his head with something like reverence that Eli thought was poorly deserved, because swarthy, skinny, and hairy were not exactly qualities that provoked the praise of poets. Laz, however, kissed the revealed skin, ran his hands down Eli's back, and gripped his arse as they rubbed together, arching in an unstudied way that made Eli's pulse race. But beyond the pleasurable friction, it was the soft sound of Laz's breath, hissing through his teeth like he was trying to keep himself under control, that left Eli full of an unfamiliar, overwhelming desire he didn't quite know what to do with.

Laz rolled them so he was kneeling between Eli's legs, kissed his ribs, his abdomen, moved his hands to Eli's fly, and then glanced up. "This okay?" he murmured.

"Yes, god, please," Eli said, and lifted his hips to help Laz tug his trousers off.

Things got more urgent after that. He tangled his fingers in Laz's hair and let the other man continue on his quest to take Eli apart. Eventually, he stopped thinking, and after that it was just sensations: Laz's mouth on him, Laz's erection through his trousers pressed against Eli's stroking hand, both of them fumbling for the fly of Laz's jeans, and then the rush of skin against skin and friction and heat and want.

He woke up the next morning with Laz clinging to him, his face pressed against Eli's chest, his eyebrows knitted together as though he were dreaming about something unpleasant. He had another tattoo, visible in the early morning light, down between his shoulder blades; Eli hadn't seen it the night before. It looked like a mountain, but made of curly letters in an alphabet he didn't recognize. None of the scars made it up that far, and Eli wondered what had happened.

But he knew, of course. Laz had told him, just not all at once. He'd been stationed somewhere in Thailand, so it wasn't as though he had stepped on a mine. His aircraft had been hit by flak. He'd said as much. The damage hadn't been bad enough to knock him out of the sky—he must have landed the plane despite his injury. How close had he come? Had he, like Lazarus, risen from the dead? He traced the tattoo with a finger and Laz jumped awake, pushing himself up, away from Eli. His dog tags swung absurdly in the space between them.

They stared at each other, and Eli felt unaccountably shy. But he realized after a moment that he was going to have to make the first move, because however he was feeling, Laz was clearly doing twice as badly, looking at Eli with wide, panicked eyes, body tense.

"Good morning," Eli said.

Laz licked his lips. Eli missed the warmth of his body. "This is going to sound strange," Laz began, "but could you say something I wouldn't expect you to say?"

Eli raised an eyebrow. "Something . . . ah, I see." He frowned, and then said, "Where did you get your tattoos?" After he said it, he realized the question was perhaps a bit expected and found himself mentally flailing. "Wait, no. That wasn't unexpected enough. I can do better. What's the value of the universal gravitational constant? What—"

Laz grinned. "That was fine, Doc. Don't hurt yourself." He relaxed back into Eli's side. "What time is it?"

Eli glanced around, then realized he was still wearing his watch. "Nine-ish."

"I never sleep this late." He buried his face in Eli's neck again. "You must've worn me out."

Eli chuckled. "It could have been that serpent."

"I feel we need further experimentation on this point. Maybe using the snake as a control group." He inhaled, and Eli felt the movement of his rib cage. "I'm never going to be able to sneak you out unnoticed at this hour."

"How upset is your gran going to be that you've brought someone home?" Eli asked uncertainly.

Laz groaned, and then started to laugh. "Whatever you're thinking, it's worse than that. She'll probably want to make you breakfast."

"Really?"

"I take it your family wasn't—that they wouldn't be—?"

Eli tried to smile. "My parents aren't that bad. The world has just changed a lot since their youths." He shrugged. "Intermarriage between Jews and gentiles is increasingly common, but they . . . well, it wouldn't be the first time I've gotten an earful."

Laz grumbled his feelings about that into Eli's neck, and Eli's heart clenched a little.

"Laz," Eli said, and then hesitated.

"You have a question. I can tell."

"I have a few questions," he confirmed.

"All right." Laz rolled onto his back and put his hands behind his head, a position that did interesting things to his shoulders. "I will indulge them. It'll be like question time with the Prime Minister."

Eli looked at him in amusement. "Did you get the BBC overseas or something?"

"Used to listen to the Empire Service when I was working in the shop." He grinned wickedly. "But I warn you. You get five minutes, and then I'm going to go shower. You can decide if you want to join me or not."

"Ah." Eli tried to get his mind back on track but found that Laz's bare chest was a distraction. He reached out and traced the little curly tattoo idly. "Where *did* you get these done?"

Laz examined him skeptically. "A temple near the base in Udon I used to hang out at. The monks do them. Actually, he did them." He gestured toward the bedside table, and Eli looked over to see a little framed snapshot he hadn't noticed the night before. In it was Laz, hair cut military short, wearing a black T-shirt and olive drab canvas trousers, sitting in a low plastic chair under a tree, gesturing with a bottle of Coke. Next to him in another chair was a stocky Thai man in orange robes. He had bright, intelligent eyes, and his expression was clearly amused.

"Who is he?"

"Phra Nok. Ah—phra is an honorific title for a monk, and 'nok' is a nickname." Laz cleared his throat. "He was a friend. We worked together for a while."

There was something different about the Laz in the photo, but Eli couldn't put a finger on it. His posture? The authority he wore? Eli was briefly sad that he'd never get to meet that stranger, who was so young and yet so weary. He decided not to ask what kind of work an American pilot might be doing with a Thai monk. "What do they mean?"

"They're supposed to be protective." Laz touched his chest with a couple of long fingers. "This one is the Buddha's third eye."

"And the one on your back that looks like a mountain?"

"It's a stylized version of Mount Meru, which is the center of the universe."

"I'm not sure that's cosmologically accurate."

Laz laughed. "It doesn't have to be. Every culture has its own ideas of protecting its people, right?" He reached out and carefully straightened the thin silver chain Eli wore, fingers glancing over the hamsa pendant he'd not been without since leaving home. "This is the same thing. The little—" He gestured at the little stick and ball drawings that dotted the wall beside the bed. "Same same. Apotropaic magic. Protect us from evil. It's very old."

"Does it work?"

Laz looked at him in an uncomfortably direct way. "Yes. But you have to be careful what you ask for."

Eli shook his head ruefully. "Isn't it always like that," he murmured, and Laz nodded. Impulsively, Eli leaned forward until he was pressed against Laz again, enjoying the way the other man's eyes went soft and out of focus when he brushed against him, trailed a hand down over his ribs and stomach. It was delicious—except that he could smell both of them, old cigarette smoke and acidic monster and dirt and sweat and semen. "Did you say something about a shower?" he asked, pulling back gently.

Laz grinned.

Chapter 9

L AZ DECIDED THE BEST tactic was to bring Eli down the back staircase to the kitchen. Babushka would probably hassle Laz a little, but nothing too heavy compared to what she'd do if he tried to sneak Eli out.

Mostly, he didn't want Eli to feel like Laz was ashamed of him. Somewhere amongst all the weirdness of the past two weeks, he'd decided that if he was going to do—whatever this was, going steady, god help him, or—if he was going to do this, he was going to do it right. He liked Eli too much for anything else.

He was in the closet buttoning a randomly selected plaid flannel shirt, the mala around his neck so he wouldn't forget it, when Eli came over, a towel wrapped around his hips.

"I, ah—" Laz watched with amusement while Eli folded his nervousness into some kind of extra-British armor. "I don't suppose you have any clothing I could borrow? Everything I was wearing yesterday smells like that snake, and if I'm to be presented at court, I'd like to make a good impression." He fell silent, perhaps considering whether being introduced to Babushka in Laz's clothes would actually accomplish that.

"You'll be fine," Laz said automatically, but found him a nice blue sweater and an old pair of fatigue pants. Laz was four or five inches taller than the doctor, but that was within US government manufacturing tolerances. After he was dressed, Eli frowned at his damp hair in the bathroom mirror until Laz drew him away. "I'm serious. Don't worry."

Eli made a face. "This feels like a big step, Laz."

"She likes to meet everyone who comes to the house." He tried to think of something reassuring to say, and eventually came up with, "She's not interested in what you're wearing."

"What is she interested in, exactly?"

"Magic? Fate? Something like that." He shrugged. "She never explained it to me. Not that I've ever brought anyone home before." Laz shut his eyes. "Shit, maybe this is a big deal."

Eli started to laugh.

Laz kissed him fast, then started across the room. "You're going to be fine. I'm sure you know how to talk to old ladies. That must be seventy percent of your job."

"Sixty percent, but the rest is largely paperwork," Eli said. He looked a little more relaxed. "All right, let's go."

Laz opened the door to the stairs. "Oh, hello, Tim," he said. The black cat looked up at him reproachfully.

"Tim?" Eli asked, crouching down and offering his fingers to sniff.

"He's Aunt Cass's." Laz crowded Eli out onto the landing and shut the door behind them. "It means they know you're here. I had been trying to think of contingency plans, but there's no escape. Tim's an informer."

Eli looked as though he wasn't sure if he should believe Laz or not, but followed him down the stairs. Tim trailed along behind them, keeping an eye on their six.

The kitchen was warm, quiet, and bright. Babushka stood in front of the stove, frying bacon. She was a bird-like woman with neatly bobbed white hair and the intense blue eyes she'd passed on to Laz's father and older brother. As they came in, she looked over at Laz and said, "There you are."

The way she said it felt a little too loaded for so early in the morning.

"Good morning," he said, and walked across the two-toned green linoleum floor to fetch coffee mugs for himself and Eli. "Babushka, this is Eli," he added, turning back around. "Doc, this is my grandmother, Ekaterina."

"Good morning," Eli said. He lingered in the doorway, his gaze on Babushka. She returned the attention, eyes narrowed. Laz saw Tim check the situation out, then hurry down the stairs to the back door, doubtless to find Cass and report.

Babushka finally shook her head. "Bacon and eggs, yes?" she said.

Eli cleared his throat. "No bacon, if that's all right."

Babushka scowled, but nodded. "No bacon."

She began cracking eggs into a bowl, whisking them ferociously.

It was galling to think that Ulysses must have managed to introduce Sam to her at some point, and probably with more grace than Laz was capable of. Ulysses was always charming. Ulysses was clever. Ulysses had followed her footsteps right into academic magic. Ulysses was the favorite grandchild. Ulysses—

He stiffened his spine. He was a goddamn officer, and he was going to get through this.

"Milk?" he murmured, passing Eli a mug of coffee.

"Yes, thank you."

"Sugar is over there." He gestured to where the counter stuck out like a peninsula into the room. There were stools underneath on one side and Babushka with her spatula on the other, and she was watching them. Two stools, because they were expected. Laz heard a door open and close somewhere else in the house.

"Come sit," Babushka said. Laz padded across the room and slid onto one of the stools, and after a moment, Eli followed suit. "Lazarus," she began, "this painting—"

Laz's brother-in-law Obe came in from the direction of the front door, carrying baby Lila tucked in the crook of his arm. She was six or seven weeks old, a tiny, bright-eyed thing who still seemed bewildered by the life she'd tumbled into. Laz didn't blame her. Babushka broke off and made a very un-Babushka-like noise, holding out her arms to take the infant. "This is

Lila," she said to Eli. "My great granddaughter. I watch her on Saturdays."

"She's adorable," Eli said automatically, and Ekaterina beamed as though this was somehow her doing.

Obe, meanwhile, was staring at Eli, a slow, mischievous smile curling the corners of his lips.

"What?" Laz asked, a bit more aggressively than he meant.

"Laz," Obe said, "you're making time with the neurologist?"

Laz got as far as, "What do you mean—" said, perhaps, at too high a volume, before Lila started to cry. Things devolved from there.

Ten minutes later, Babushka was cooking eggs with renewed aggression while Eli—Eli!—gave Lila a bottle.

"Celeste became worried because my hands shake," Babushka said. "I told her that for many years I have had this. Now it is a problem? They took me to the doctor, and he says I have benign essential tremor. It is nothing." She spat the last word like she was still annoyed at having her time wasted. "As I told her."

Technically, she was seventy-three. Laz always forgot that, because she was so lively, her eyes so bright. He sighed. "When was this?"

Obe was pouring himself a cup of coffee. "The end of September or the beginning of October?" He glanced at Eli for confirmation and received a shrug. "Celeste made the appointment and I took her."

"Nobody told me about this."

"We mentioned it in your presence." Obe came back to the peninsula and added an absurd amount of sugar to his coffee. "I told Ulysses about it right in front of you."

Laz rolled his eyes, but turned to the ostensible object of his affections. "So you met them both, and you didn't mention it."

"I didn't really—" Eli cleared his throat. "I met your grandmother once, for half an hour, over a month ago. Also, there's doctor–patient confidentiality to consider."

"My fate is always to be the last to know about these things." Laz made a face and his grandmother swatted at him across the counter with her spatula.

"Such a difficult life you have," Ekaterina grumbled, and set a plate of eggs, bacon, and toast on the counter in front of him. Eli got a similar plate minus the bacon, and she took Lila back.

Laz scowled, and Eli nudged him. Laz desperately wanted to rewind to an hour or twelve ago so he could properly panic about all the implications of these choices before making them. And then possibly have a more serious talk with Ulysses about his sudden sense that Babushka was far more deeply embedded in his life than he'd assumed.

"I was away for ten *years*," he said aloud.

When he looked up, it was to a lofty look on Babushka's face. "For this I will not accept blame," she said, nodding at a space somewhere between his right shoulder and Eli's left one. "You have brought it on yourself."

Eli muttered something that might have been, "That sounds about right," and Laz elbowed him.

"Is this why you and Ulysses are fighting? Are you to blame for Sam, somehow?" He wasn't even quite sure what he meant, but the troubled expression that crossed her face made him think he had hit something big.

"Dionysus Samuel Sterling is a problem that I could perhaps have prevented." She pressed her lips together. "Your brother is dealing with this knowledge." Eli shot Laz a slightly disturbed look. Laz shrugged, but he felt a sudden twinge of sympathy for Ulysses, who loved Sam, and who did not deserve to hear this kind of bullshit from Babushka, of all people.

Lila was dozing off in Babushka's arms. She frowned down at the child and carried her into the bedroom beyond the kitchen, then came back empty-handed. "Tell me about this painting," she said, leaning on the counter.

"It's just a painting," Laz said. "I've spent two weeks staring at it and nothing exciting has happened."

She looked at him more closely. "Does it set off your visions?"

"Not more than anything else." He had to look away from her stare.

"So little trust in your senses." She shook her head. "And you—" She turned to Eli, who was spreading jam on his toast with what seemed like excessive focus. "You have seen it?"

Eli nodded. "I didn't think there was anything odd about it." He frowned. "Not sure I knew what I was looking for, though."

"Mm." Babushka frowned at him. To Laz, she said, "What does your brother think?"

He crossed his arms in front of his chest. "Ulysses has his own problems."

"Such as?"

"Monsters," Laz said, and then they had to tell her about the stone circle and the remnants of the summoning.

"Ah, demonology." She sighed. "Reminds me of the bad old days."

Laz finally picked up his fork and took a bite of his eggs, then another. "Is that your insight?" he asked, sounding grumpier than he intended. "Nostalgia?"

She snorted. "Tell Ulysses to be careful. It is unusual for anyone summoning evil spirits to bother to erect a stone circle. Very old, strong magic."

Laz chewed thoughtfully on a strip of bacon. No one else spoke. Finally, Obe got to his feet and rinsed out his coffee mug. "I'd better be getting back," he said. "You have what you need?"

Babushka nodded. "You go. We will be fine. See you at four."

The door had barely swished shut when Eli said, "I should probably be going as well." Regretfully, or was that Laz hoping? To Babushka, he added, "Thank you for a lovely breakfast."

Laz got up. "I'll walk you to your car." But once they got out on the porch, he stared at his feet, trying to figure out what to say.

Eli beat him to it. "Do you still want to try the test with the EEG today?"

No. Not even a little bit did he want to give both Ulysses and Eli any further insight into everything he was desperately trying to paper over. There was no reason to think this was a good idea and a million reasons it could be a mistake. He took a breath and opened his mouth. "Sure," he said. "Let's do it. Why not? Light 'em up and all that."

Eli looked like he didn't really believe a word Laz was saying. But, on the other hand, he respected Laz enough not to try to talk him out of it. Before Eli could make a big deal about it, Laz stepped into his personal space and backed the smaller man up against the door they'd just come through.

Eli tipped his head back, looking at Laz's face for a long, lazy moment, and then grabbed the front of his shirt and pulled him into a kiss. It stole his breath and left him dizzy. When Eli let go, it was the closest thing to freefall Laz had experienced since he'd been grounded.

"What was that for?" he murmured.

"You're brave," Eli said with a laugh. "I admire that."

"Bravery has nothing to do with it," Laz said gruffly, and stepped back before he could take things too far. "What did we tell Ulysses and Sam, 1500?"

There was a pause as Eli converted that to civilian time. "Yes. We should have the clinic to ourselves."

"I'll be there."

It was past 1030 when Eli left. Laz, feeling inexplicably bereft, spent an hour tinkering with a toaster and then lay down on the bed. He woke up at 1450 and had to sprint for the Square, pulling on his coat as he ran out the door.

He was the last to arrive. He wandered through the silent waiting room and past empty exam rooms until he found a door marked "EEG LAB."

They were all inside, of course. It was a long room but not especially wide, and with four men in it, things grew a little crowded. A chair sat at one end next to a fairly large machine. There was an exam table in the middle, and on the far side a counter ran the length of the room, ending with a sink in the corner. In what had to have been a fit of perverse humor, someone had put up a handful of M. C. Escher prints and a trompe l'oeil still life on the walls.

Ulysses was sitting on the exam table when Laz came in, talking animatedly about an article he'd read. Eli stood next to the machine, adjusting the knobs and occasionally interjecting a comment. On the table sat a model of a brain and several diagrams of electrode placements, to which they were both occasionally making reference. Sam had dragged a chair over to the corner near the sink and was reading a novel with a bold green jungle on the cover.

Laz hesitated, then crossed the room to inspect the machine. It was pretty obvious how it worked now that he saw it. There were a lot of electrodes, but fewer writing arms, so clearly some of them got hooked together. He immediately began wondering how the signal was processed and analyzed.

Eli looked up, saw him, and grinned. The doctor was still wearing the sweater Laz had given him that morning with the cuffs turned back, and Laz, inexplicably, liked it. It was just a sweater, but it felt like a declaration of ownership. Something inside Laz cracked, just a little, exposing soft, gooey parts he liked to pretend weren't there. It had been so long since anyone had thought he was worth holding on to, and he hadn't thought he even wanted that, but apparently he did, very much.

He was never getting the sweater back.

"We should be ready for you in a moment," Eli said, oblivious to the fact that he'd suddenly acquired all of Laz. "Just let me finish this up, and I'll explain everything."

Laz nodded and grinned like an idiot, even though he was standing in front of Ulysses, who could no doubt read him like a book.

Eli did, as promised, go over the machine again and try to explain how the electrodes worked and how the signal was recorded—each channel was actually the result of two leads being compared and subtracted from each other, the difference being amplified in the output. Laz frowned. The whole system was ripe for digitization, if someone could invent a way to compress everything enough to fit on a storage tape.

The plan, as it was explained to him: He would sit in the chair and get hooked up to the machine. They'd blindfold him. Then Sam would chuck tennis balls at him in the hope of triggering his precognition, as indicated by his catching one. In an ideal situation, he gathered, they'd also record one of the episodes, but triggering one within the confines of the lab might be difficult.

That was somehow reassuring. He settled into the chair and sat quietly as Eli moved around him, measuring the distance between different points on his head and sticking electrodes to him with a pungent, sweet-smelling glue. His gentle touches were strangely intimate. And awkward, because Ulysses was hovering just behind Eli's shoulder, watching them.

"Sorry," Eli said, when he had to remove and reposition two of the electrodes. "I'm, ah—usually there's a tech who does this. I just read them."

"It's fine."

But maybe the awkwardness was catching, because he moved the next two as well. That was refreshing, to not be the only one going through everything, but also annoying, and he was about to order Ulysses to take his stupid stare out of the room when Eli stood back and said, "I think that's it. Unbutton your shirt, if you would. Just the top two or three."

Laz did as he was told. "What's this for?"

"Electrocardiogram lead," Eli said shortly, not looking at him. "It'll tell us what your heart rate is doing during all of this."

Laz wanted to ask how Eli was going to cancel out the effect of his presence on Laz's pulse, but Ulysses was scowling. "What's that?" he demanded, motioning at the unalom over Laz's heart.

"It's a tattoo," Sam said from behind him. "What does it look like?"

Ulysses turned. "Why do you know about this?"

"I didn't. But he was in the military for a decade." Sam unfolded from the chair, stretching. "It's not exactly a surprise that he'd have a tattoo."

Ulysses walked away, grumbling something about sigils and skin.

"I'm gonna catch hell later," Laz whispered to Eli.

Eli shrugged. "I think it looks nice."

"Thank you." Laz wanted to run his hands through his hair, couldn't, so settled for nervously clasping them in his lap. "Are we ready?"

"Mm. We should be. Let me get everything going." He heard a series of clicks, then an electronic hum.

"Do you need me to think real hard about something?" he asked.

"I need you to not speak or move." Across the room, Ulysses snorted. Laz rolled his eyes, and Eli prodded the back of his neck.

"I'm concerned about movement artifacts," Eli said suddenly to Ulysses. "If he moves to catch the ball, that's going to be relatively large magnitude waves, and what we're looking for is probably pretty small."

"The precognition should precede the movement," Ulysses said, coming back over. "But we could strap down one of his arms. Would that reduce the artifacts?"

"A bit," Eli said. "Laz, are you okay with that?"

"Sure. Delighted." He got a worried, skeptical look from Eli, but they strapped him down anyway, with another strap across his chest for good measure.

After a minute or two listening to the scritch of the pens, Eli seemed satisfied with whatever Laz's brain was doing. "Let's try it with the blindfold," he said from his spot beside the machine, just behind Laz's left ear.

It was Ulysses who brought it over, so there were no last-minute requests for confirmation that this was still okay with Laz or that he was doing fine. It wasn't that Ulysses didn't care about Laz's feelings, but he was philosophically in favor of getting on with things, and Laz was absurdly grateful.

Being blindfolded wasn't as bad as he'd expected. He could still hear Eli adjusting knobs, humming to himself, occasionally taking sips of tea. The movement of the pens, the whirr as the paper advanced. And across the room, the sound of Sam's feet shuffling as he fidgeted, and Sam and Ulysses whispering to each other.

After a while, Eli said, "That seems like a good baseline. If you're still doing fine, Laz, we can begin."

Laz wanted to nod, but he remembered the warning about movement artifacts, so he just stiffened his spine. "Yeah. Let's go."

Chapter 10

LAZ HAD BEEN BRACED for the worst, but the initial shots were fine. The balls were mostly off to his right, hitting the ground or the wall with a soft pock. He breathed. The fourth ball hit him in the chest. Someone coughed. The fifth ball hit his shoulder.

There was a pause.

The vision was of a ball hitting him hard in the face. Blood. A bright burst of pain. Sam's surprised gasp. Eli turning, about to insist they end the experiment early.

He managed to get his hand up in time and catch it. Someone across the room let out a relieved breath.

After that, things went downhill. There were more balls and two more visions, and then he realized how similar this felt to flying the Phantoms, the endless dodging of tracers and surface-to-air missiles, chaff, debris, all the monitors screaming, and he started to tense up.

He caught three in a row and knocked the fourth away. Two went wide, and he was practically straining forward in his seat for the next one. There was a long silence. He could feel his heart beating in his fingers, in his ears, in his stomach. Something was coming, he just didn't know when, and it was the waiting that killed him.

The next throw hit him hard, and then while he was still focused on the stinging in his bicep, there was a gasp and the wet, crunching noise of something breaking.

Laz jerked and screamed.

THEY UNHOOKED LAZ. SAM and Ulysses shifted him over to the exam table while Eli powered down the EEG. Laz was combative, like he'd been in the grocery the day they'd met, until Ulysses grabbed a wild swing and growled something in Russian; then he settled down. Eli suppressed a little spike of jealousy at that and tried to make himself useful, turning down the lights and finding a blanket and the broom and dustpan.

At that point, Sam took his elbow and guided him out of the room before he could sweep up. "Let's give them a minute," he said gently.

Eli leaned against the wall, feeling useless, and closed his eyes. After a minute or two, Sam cleared his throat.

When Eli looked at him, Sam essayed a tentative smile. "Primum non nocere, eh?"

"I tried." He sighed. "I didn't do it on purpose."

"But you feel bad about it."

"Wouldn't you?"

Sam stuck his hands in his pockets. He was wearing a suit, even though it was a Saturday, and he looked impossibly tall and lean, like a model from some magazine. "Probably," he said thoughtfully. "Have you seen one of the episodes before?"

"I have." Eli waited a moment and then threw his innate politeness to the wind. "Had you?"

"Oh, yes." Sam looked toward the door of the lab, then shook his head. "They were very bad when he first came home. Stronger and more frequent, or that was my impression. He was angry all the time. And he was drinking a lot, which seemed to make them worse. I don't know that he felt he had a lot to live for."

Eli forced himself to nod in acknowledgment and swallow a host of follow-up questions. He could imagine Laz like that all too easily, slipping across the gentle divide from a sort of ironic insouciance to nihilism and passive suicidality. "That sounds dreadful."

Sam nodded, and then said, "You care about him."

Eli stared at him for a long moment, trying to parse that. "Could I ask you a question?" he said eventually.

There was a pause. "If you want."

"Ekaterina called you a problem she failed to prevent."

Sam raised both eyebrows. "Did she?" He glanced over his shoulder again as though he could see into the room. "She's probably not wrong. My grandfather was a very powerful magician, and as a result of his experiments, I was a god, briefly. I'm sure she would have stopped him, if she could have. For all I know, she did try. And yet." He spread his arms.

Eli stared at him. "That is not the explanation I expected."

The door to the lab opened and Ulysses stepped out, the sharp scent of acetone wafting behind him. He looked tired, but not excessively concerned. "He wants to see you," he said to Eli.

So Eli went in. Laz was stretched out on the padded exam table in the dim room, and Eli felt like he was looking at an ancient king on a bier. Then he shook his head and it passed. "Hello," he said softly.

Laz opened his eyes. "Hey."

For a moment, they stared at each other. Eli remembered that morning, lying in bed together and watching Laz trying to hide his anxiety. And now here they were, a different bed between them, and Eli was awash in guilt to the point that he was hoping Laz would rescue him, which hardly seemed fair.

He prodded Laz's legs slightly and hopped up onto the table next to him. "How are you doing?"

Laz shrugged. "I don't blame you."

"You do, at least a bit." Laz looked at him sharply, and Eli shrugged. "It was a very ill-timed error."

"But it was an error."

Eli nodded. "That was my favorite mug."

Laz sat up and turned himself sideways, dangling his legs off the side of the table. He was sitting all of two inches away from Eli, but the distance felt like an unbridgeable gulf. "I suppose you already had an inkling of how this could go. God knows I did." Laz paused. "You have the right to know what you're getting into."

"Laz . . ."

Laz hunched forward, resting his elbows on his knees, fingers tangling in his own hair. "Show me what you recorded."

Eli looked at him closely. "All right if I turn the lights back on?"

He pulled the long strip of paper off the EEG and showed it to him: the normal brain activity before the test had begun, the small movement artifacts from when he was hit early on, the odd activity in the T3–T5 lead just before he caught the ball, how it repeated, and meanwhile Laz's pulse was escalating, and then there was a mass of activity starting in the P leads when Eli had dropped the mug.

Laz ran his fingers over the paper gently. "So the broken circuit is . . . somewhere over here," he said, and reached up to touch the right side of his head above and behind his ear.

"This isn't quite that straightforward," Eli said, "but if you want to visualize it, that's not a bad way to do so." He carefully folded the paper and put it back on top of the EEG machine. "Unfortunately, there are limitations to the way we're gathering data. Ideally, we'd try this again with the leads clustered differently . . ."

"But you'd still have the sensitivity of the electrodes, and the fact that you're trying to map a three-dimensional object onto the surface of a sphere," Laz said. He sat, looking at his folded hands for a moment. "Think I'll pass for now." He carefully peeled the detached cardio lead off his chest and buttoned his shirt.

There was one electrode left in his hair. Eli carefully removed it. "Are you upset?"

"Upset," he said thoughtfully, "no." Eli felt relief, followed almost immediately by a renewed feeling of terror as Laz walked across the room to retrieve his coat. "I need time to think."

He turned and gave Eli a last glance. Eli wasn't sure if it was meant as a farewell of some sort, or what Lazarus might have been searching for in his face. Laz nodded, then turned and walked out of the lab.

L AZ DIDN'T HAVE ANYTHING to do and he didn't especially feel like seeing anybody, so he went home, disassembled the Goat's carburetor, cleaned it, and rebuilt it. It was a task he'd been putting off for a while, and it should have been satisfying to complete. But by the time he finished, it was well after 2100, fully dark, chilly, and spitting rain, and he didn't feel anything but tired and numb. He sat on the porch and smoked a cigarette.

He was starting to hate the smell and taste of them. But the chemicals calmed his brain down and gave him a few moments of peace.

He was going to have to find some new vice.

The thought drove him inside. No one was around. Of course not; it was a Saturday night. Babushka had cooked something for dinner—he could smell it, but someone had already put the leftovers away. He had a vague memory of Virgil touching his ankle a few hours ago while he was still under the car.

It was fine. He hadn't moved back in because he wanted to be coddled. He'd . . . just thought he shouldn't be entirely alone.

Heating up food seemed like a monumental task, and his stomach didn't feel quite right anyway. There were places he could go, bars up on the Square. It was only a handful of blocks to walk. He could get a burger, listen to whatever band was playing and tune out for a while. He could go across to Ulysses's pad, spend the evening taking up space on the sofa while Sam tried to feed him. He could call the operator and get Eli's phone number.

Instead, he poured himself a glass of scotch and took it upstairs.

On Sunday, Laz decided to go see about the other oil painting that had been weirdly menaced. It was either that or hang around Madison all day waiting for someone to come check on him, and that felt a little sad and pathetic. He was up by 0600, the Goat was in tip-top shape, and Edina, Minnesota, was only about three hundred miles away.

He took a thermos of coffee and set out just as the sun rose over the lake, which put him in the Twin Cities by noon. Edina was a suburb of Minneapolis, full of winding streets overhung with old trees and large stately homes hidden behind big yards and elaborate gardens. The Greenfields lived in an older section of town, in a colonial-style place, all dark shutters and white clapboard siding, with a vast white porch in front.

Laz drove past slowly and parked out of sight around a bend in the road, then got out and went back on foot. It was about ten degrees cooler here than it had been in Madison, and he pulled the fleece collar of his jacket closer around his neck, wishing he'd brought a hat.

There didn't seem to be anyone at home at the Greenfield house. There were no signs of life when he rang the bell, not so much as a dog barking. Well, it was a Sunday. How long did church go? He rang it two more times just to be sure, and then started back down the driveway.

He'd gotten four steps before the door swung open behind him. He turned around to see Mrs. Greenfield looking at him, more mean than curious. She was on the tall side and had a kind of lanky, bohemian look about her—slim black pants, black turtleneck, long hair loose around her shoulders. Blandly pretty, although he recognized his response was colored by the way she looked at him, as though she'd scraped him out of the gutters. But the pale skin under her eyes was purple with fatigue she couldn't disguise, and her lips were tight and strained. "Good afternoon, ma'am," he said, coming back to the door. "I'm sorry to bother you. You're Mrs. Greenfield? From Madison, Wisconsin?"

She nodded slowly. "Evie. But I don't have anyone in Vietnam, if you're coming here to tell me there's been an incident."

Did he look like—But they did those visits in uniform. He exhaled. "You must have me mixed up with someone else. I'm—I understand you recently purchased a painting by the artist S. Rochester at a gallery here in town."

Evie Greenfield's face didn't change, but Laz fancied he was hearing some level of hell freeze over. "Where did you get your information?"

"The gallery gave it to me." He chewed on the inside of his cheek. "If they got their wires crossed—"

She shivered. He was reminded of a small, nervous dog, just before it lunged. "No, we have it." She fell silent, inspecting his face. "What is your interest in it?"

"I'm studying the painter. He's not very well-known; how did you happen to choose that particular work?"

"We're collectors, and one of my husband's colleagues . . ." She stumbled to a halt. The expression on her face was somewhere between fear and surprise, and then that was gone and she glared at him. "I don't see why it's any of your business."

"Just curious," Laz said. He paused and waited a moment. "Is it possible I could take a look at the painting? I'd love to see the rest of your collection, too—"

Something in her face went rigid and her voice flattened. "It's not for sale." She smiled in a way that did not move anything higher on her face than her nose.

"Oh, I'm not interested in buying it. I'd really just like to see it." When she didn't say anything, he cleared his throat and went on. "I wouldn't take long. Just in and out."

Evie Greenfield stared at him for a long moment, eyes moving back and forth over his face. "My husband's not home," she said abruptly. "This is all a nightmare. And there's the insurance and the—I'm sure you understand. I've been having these dreams. I just can't—" She broke off and looked at him, eyes a little too wide. He had just enough time to wonder where the self-assured woman who had opened the door had got to before she stammered, "I'm sorry," and closed the door in his face.

Laz stood there for a moment, distinctly nonplussed.

Up the street between the Greenfields' place and his car, he heard the crunch-swish of someone raking leaves from the backyard. Laz hesitated—talking to Evie had been enough for one day—but then again Phra Nok had taught him better than to leave a job unfinished when you were already in the neighborhood, so he went over.

"Good afternoon," Laz said when he got within hearing range. "Have you seen the Greenfields today?"

The man shook his head. "If they're not answering, I don't know what to tell you. Thought they might be out of town. Weren't at church this morning." He leaned on his rake. He was middle aged and portly, nose and ears red from the cold air and exercise. "They expecting you?"

"Yes, sir," Laz said, leaning into the Georgian drawl he'd heard his favorite sergeant use when he was trying to be charming. "Mrs. Greenfield is a friend of my mother. When she heard I was moving here, she offered to take me around and show me some places that were on the market." He hoped that was the sort of thing normal people did for each other. His mother Mariah's friends mostly lived in places like New York, London, and Amsterdam, where they did performance art and avant-garde theater. They had offered to help him buy drugs and potentially find invitations to night clubs if he was ever in need of companionship, but real estate felt a little beyond them.

The neighbor was looking at him with a little interest now. "Around here, you say?"

"Yes, sir. I've got a job with Honeywell."

The man looked harder at Laz, and he wished he'd worn something that looked a little more professional. "Doing what, if I might ask?"

"It's classified." He dragged up an apologetic smile. "I'm an aerospace engineer."

"You?" The man scratched the back of his neck. "Air Force or Navy?"

"Air Force."

The man nodded. "Seems to me you boys are doing a hard job out there." Laz nodded and mumbled something he hoped sounded appreciative. "You're looking for a house here in Edina?"

Laz shuffled his feet. "I heard it's a nice place to live."

The man nodded. "It is at that." He paused for a long moment, like he was studying Laz's features. "Listen, you're not Jewish, are you? I mean, it don't mean nothing to me, but a lot of the houses around here still have covenants." To Laz's blank expression, he added, "In the deeds," as though that explained it.

"I'm Buddhist."

The man blinked, probably trying to decide if that was some protestant denomination. "That's fine," he said after a while. "I don't think there's anything about that."

"Well, thanks for the advice," Laz said. "I'm gonna head back to my hotel."

"Best of luck. They've been gone a lot lately. I hope nothing's wrong."

Laz managed to keep himself together until he was back at the car. Probably good that he hadn't brought Eli. What an asshole.

He'd barely gotten back on what felt like the main drag when he spotted a diner, and was suddenly starving.

Inside it was like his childhood, black and white linoleum, red vinyl booths, and a guy making milkshakes behind the bar. Absurdly, he remembered visiting—not Rennebohm's with Mariah on one of her visits, but—a place called Sabai 59 he had gone to a handful of times in Bangkok, the low plastic stools, the metal tables on the sidewalk, the iced coffee, the warmth of the day as the sun sank below the horizon.

He slid onto one of the stools and ordered a burger and a milkshake.

When the waitress brought them, she stood drying coffee mugs for a bit, making curious eyes at him. She was five foot nothing, young enough that she looked very young to Laz, with blond hair and brown eyes, freckles, hair pulled back in a ponytail, wearing some unpleasant uniform that was the same color red as the booths. Her name tag said Cindy. "Haven't seen you around here," she said at last, which was true enough.

"I'm just visiting some friends," he said. "Or I was supposed to be. They stood me up. I'm up from Madison."

"Oh yeah?"

"Mr. and Mrs. Greenfield. You know them?"

She tilted her head. "I know him. Think I met his wife once or twice." The expression on her face was professionally unreadable. "How d'you know them?"

"Not well. Distant friend of the family. I was coming up here for other reasons, and my brother suggested I pay them a visit." It was a reasonable lie because it was so nearly not one, and he thought he delivered it pretty well. Or she was so ready to gossip she didn't care to look too hard at it.

"Is he okay?" she asked, which was so unexpected that Laz couldn't stop himself from raising his eyebrows. She must have noticed, because she rushed on. "I only know him because he came in every morning for a cup of coffee, and we'd chat. But he stopped real suddenly."

Laz nodded, trying to project sympathy. "When?"

She shrugged. "A week or two ago. I saw him when I was coming out of the bank on Friday, but either he didn't recognize me, or . . . I don't know." The corners of her mouth turned down as she relived some old hurt. Laz wondered if there was some other piece of the story she wasn't telling him, something that had transpired between the businessman and the diner waitress. "It's not—we were friendly," she added awkwardly, as though sensing the drift of his thoughts. "That's all."

"I'm sorry to hear that," Laz said.

She leaned on the counter, looking at him. "Don't tell him I was complaining about him if you see him."

"I won't."

"I know you won't," she said, and then someone at the back of the diner raised a coffee cup and shouted, "Hey, Cin, could I get a refill?" and she had to go.

Laz missed Eli abruptly, with the same surprising ferocity with which he missed Asia. It was unexpected. There was a giant seething mass of feelings in his chest that were probably best left unexamined, because he wasn't angry, not really. He was just exhausted. After yesterday's disaster of an experiment, Eli had certainly realized what a mess he was, and it was better to distance himself. But also he wanted to spend five hours in the car with the doctor, having the sort of meaningless conversations you had on road trips. He wanted to know what Eli's childhood had been like, and if he missed his sister, and if he liked dogs and who his favorite composer was and what movie he'd been obsessed with when he was fifteen and what he ate if he couldn't have bacon. All the stupid bits of trivia that made up a friendship, a relationship, a life.

Of course, Laz had walked out on Eli rather than talk, so where did that leave him?

He left some money on the bar and walked out, letting the cool Minnesota breeze soothe his heated skin. There were two things he wanted back. Maybe he couldn't have either of them. Maybe he was just going to have to make peace with losing things.

Maybe it was worth trying before he gave up.

Naturally, his foresight didn't have any advice for him. He tried tapping the side of his head, as though his brain were a goldfish, but it did nothing. He was going to have to figure this out for himself.

He laughed aloud, baring his teeth into the wind, there in the parking lot.

Then he got back in the Goat and drove home.

Chapter 11

T UESDAYS WERE MIGRAINE DAYS. Eli didn't remember telling Catherine, the secretary who kept the schedule, to do it that way, but somehow he had wound up running a mini clinic once a week. Migraine patients tended to be complex cases with lengthy neuropsychological histories they would unload at the slightest provocation. On the positive side, sometimes the medication actually helped them.

He charted through lunchtime, then waded through another eight patients before the waiting room was finally empty. He was exhausted and starving. It was well past six o'clock now, and he still had two more charts to write before he could leave. He was going to have to talk to—

There was a knock on the door. "Sobel, you still here?"

Eli looked up from his desk to see Alden Conroy, the practice's other neurologist, looking around the corner of the doorframe at him. "Clearly." He sat back, capping his pen. "As are you."

"I wanted to pick your brain." He hesitated, and added, "If you're not busy."

"Of course." It had been a while since they'd had time to chat. Alden had been young and single when they'd met in San Francisco three years ago, and now he was married with a newborn. Eli liked the man, but he always gave off the sense that he was late to an appointment he'd only just remembered. Eli gestured to Conroy to sit. "What's up?"

"I have a patient, male, late sixties, with marked bilateral bradykinesia."

Eli frowned. "You can't be asking me about a Parkinson's patient."

Conroy shook his head. "No tremor, no muscle rigidity. Just the slowing of movement."

"No history of stroke?"

"No. No evidence of a tumor, no changes in mental status, and all his blood work is fine." Conroy spread his hands. "I'm stuck."

"No depression?" Eli scratched the back of his head. "You could give him L-dopa, see if that helps," he suggested, a bit doubtfully.

"He won't take it. He's one of those damn magic people." Eli tried hard not to raise an eyebrow; if Conroy noticed, he didn't remark. "Sorry. I guess I'm trying to find something that I can treat."

"Why did he come in?"

Conroy picked up a tuning fork from the corner of Eli's desk and turned it over in his hand. "His wife made him. She got tired of all those herbs they're into not working."

"She's not a—"

"No, mixed marriage. She decided his problems arose because of the herbs, and wanted me to convince him to stop." Alden Conroy had a guileless smile, that was the problem. He deployed it now in Eli's direction. "You wouldn't want to see him, would you? See if I'm overlooking anything?"

Eli thought about his current patient load and shrugged. "Sure," he said. "I'd be happy to."

"Great, I'll have Catherine set it up." Conroy got to his feet and made it as far as the doorway before he hesitated. "Do you mind seeing magic people? Some people find them troublesome."

Translation: *Alden* found them difficult.

Eli immediately felt bad about the thought. "The ones I've met have been lovely." After he said it, he wasn't entirely sure that was the right word for Ekaterina, but—well, he'd just never mention it to her.

"Lovely," Conroy repeated, and grinned. "I'll let Catherine know."

Eli sat for a while after that, staring at the open chart but trying to discern what he'd just agreed to.

In some respects, he was happy for the distractions. Since Laz had walked out of the lab on Saturday, his own emotional state had been unsteady.

It was a difficult situation. He didn't necessarily think he'd done anything wrong, but Lazarus was upset, and he wanted to make that better. Ulysses had suggested giving him some time to think; it seemed like good advice, but how much time? Should Eli approach Laz at the end of it, or was he to wait until Laz came back?

He felt like he might be waiting for a while, if he went that way.

Ayala had once observed to him that Americans were very free with their affections. It had definitely been a rush to be on the receiving end of that. He and Laz had been in the middle of this thing practically before Eli had known they'd begun.

The problem with affection easily given was that it was also easily taken away. That was the painful reality of—well, America, probably. And while in theory, two days was not a lot of time to see if it would be the case with Laz as well, in practice . . .

It was enough time to realize how attached he'd grown. And to understand exactly how well he'd buggered everything up.

The worst part was that while the EEG had confirmed many of their suspicions, it hadn't provided any insight into treatment. It certainly appeared that Laz's combat fatigue or what have you was mixed up with his foresight. But there was no chemical model for transmission of the signals from one area of the brain to another, probably because no one had tried to locate foresight in the brain before. On that point, the experiment had been a resounding success, and Ulysses was very excited.

But.

Even armed with the most basic hypothesis of how the triggers and the episodes and the foresight were bound up together, he hadn't a clue how to fix it. Tranquilizers were the most obvious option to interrupt the episode to foresight bridge, but he suspected Laz would probably reject that out of hand. He didn't seem like the sort of fellow who would be interested in secobarbital, if indeed he hadn't yet tried it.

Eli sighed and set down his pen, resting his forehead against the heels of his hands.

He shouldn't have gotten involved. Or perhaps not that, but once he was involved with Laz, the experiment had become a bad idea. He needed to do a lit search. He needed to finish his charting and eat something. He needed a stiff drink.

"You busy, Doc?"

Eli's heart skipped a beat. He looked up to see Laz lounging against the doorframe, hands in his pockets. God, he was an attractive man, and those amber eyes were striking. The light of his office made them look yellow-orange, and his posture was almost vulpine. Eli felt abruptly like prey.

"What's on your mind?" Eli asked, trying to sound casual. He thought his voice came out a little choked.

"I thought we could go for a drive. The Leonids are happening. . . . Well, my sister told me they happen sometime in November, so maybe we'll see some." He favored Eli with a little half smile. "I made sandwiches."

Eli's stomach growled loudly in the small room, and he felt himself flush. "I don't think I'm physically capable of saying no to that," he said. "Can you wait a few minutes while I finish these?"

"Sure." He settled into the chair opposite Eli. Eli looked at the top chart, trying to make sense of what he'd already written. A moment later there was a rustle of paper; when Eli looked up again, Laz was frowning at a magazine. The title wasn't visible, but the page he could see was mostly math equations.

When Eli finally put down his pen and shoved the last chart into the out basket, Laz perked up. "Ready?"

"It seems so." He got to his feet, stretching. "What are you reading?"

"*The American Journal of Applied Mathemagics and Engineering*," Laz said, shoving it back into an inside pocket.

Eli nodded. "Sounds heavy."

Laz had located Eli's coat and held it out to him. "Eh. It's no *IEEE Transactions*," he said, and then gave Eli a sly look that suggested he had made some kind of complex joke.

"What are you interested in?" Eli looped his scarf around his neck and followed Laz out into the corridor.

"The paper is called 'A Mathemagical Approach to Miner's Rule.' It's about calculating material fatigue from cyclic loading."

Eli spent a moment trying to parse this. "Why?"

Laz paused, hand on the door to the stairs, and waited while Eli locked the office. "Back when I was in school, magic was usually discounted as pretty useless in engineering applications," he said eventually. "Magic is fussy, sacrifices don't scale well, there's issues with power. I was curious if that had changed at all over the last decade."

"Huh." He followed Laz down the echoing staircase. "Has it?"

Laz made an equivocal noise. "Somewhat. At least there are academics in U—in our generation who are starting to do research in the area. It's all very cutting edge."

Eli slid into the passenger seat of Laz's car. "I'm surprised no one has looked into it before."

Laz shrugged. "All the scientists want to pretend they're better than that. And the magic people feel exactly the same way."

He pulled away from the curb, taking them around the Capitol and down East Washington. Eli relaxed as they went, passing pedestrians walking quickly along the sidewalks, then various businesses. A few blocks down Laz turned left and headed toward the lake. "I stopped by the house yesterday," Eli admitted after a while. "An older man told me you weren't in."

"Probably my father," Laz said. "I went to Minnesota. Thought I'd look in on those people who bought the other painting."

Eli raised an eyebrow. "That's a long drive."

"Worth it if you find out something useful." Laz looked over at him, face rueful. "Unfortunately, I did not."

"I'm sorry."

"Yeah, well." He made a disgruntled noise. "The wife was not forthcoming. Talked to a few people who said both of them had been acting odd lately. Neighborhood didn't feel like a great one for a stakeout. I got the feeling it was only just barely not a sundown town anymore."

Eli blinked at that. "Jesus."

They drove on for a while in silence. Eli had a hundred questions, but Laz seemed to be thinking, and he didn't want to interrupt. "It's an interesting mystery," Laz said eventually, "but I'm not sure it matters that much."

"What do you mean?"

Laz parked, and Eli got out of the car. They were in a park at the edge of Lake Mendota, the dark sky spread out above them, the city lights glittering around the edges of the water. Laz opened the boot to retrieve a blanket and a small cardboard box. Eli took the former and found a patch of grass by the shore to spread it out on.

"What I mean," Laz said finally, sitting down on the blanket, "is that nothing much happened. The guys who jumped me didn't steal the painting. No one got killed." He shrugged. "It's a puzzle. But how much energy is it worth to solve it?" He opened the basket and stared down into it. "Ulysses is worried. But Ulysses has a large capacity for worry."

Eli sat down beside him, nearly shoulder to shoulder, and received a waxed-paper-wrapped sandwich. "He, ah, thought it was cursed, didn't he?"

Laz pulled a bottle of wine out of the box and then felt around for a corkscrew, frowning when he couldn't find one. Eli took the bottle and fished out his pocket knife. Laz said, "Sam thinks it's cursed." The distinction was apparently meaningful.

They were sitting just out of the reach of the nearest streetlight, and neither the twinkling stars above nor the houses on the opposite shore were especially bright, so Eli wrestled the cork out of the bottle mostly by feel, somehow not removing any fingers or spilling wine everywhere in the process. "Did you bring glasses?"

There was a dull clinking noise, and Laz produced two mugs. "I'm not completely uncivilized."

"Tell the French that," Eli muttered, and poured them each a cup.

The wine was a dry red, with a lot of tannins and a strong black cherry flavor. The sandwich turned out to be brie and butter on a baguette. "This is delightful. Reminds me of a school trip to Paris. Have you been to France?"

"My mother is French." Laz took a drink. "She lives in Paris."

"Please thank her from me for teaching you to make sandwiches, because this is delicious." He took another bite and thought back to their conversation. "Are you saying you don't believe the painting is cursed?"

"I don't know anything about that. Just—I'm the only one who's been hurt so far. And I don't—"

Eli cleared his throat. "Lazarus, if you say something like you don't matter, I'm going to be quite cross."

"No." Laz looked away. "But I can decide how much energy is expended on my behalf, surely."

"I suppose." Eli chewed thoughtfully. "If you've reached a dead end in your investigation, it makes sense to take a break and see what happens."

Laz took a long drink from his mug. "Did you and Ulysses make any amazing discoveries about my brain after I left?"

Eli sipped his wine, feeling suddenly sheepish. "I wouldn't say amazing," he said. "In fact, I'm rather afraid to tell you." He drained the cup and set it down on the grass beside the blanket. It was chilly out, around forty degrees, but between the alcohol and his coat and Laz's body pressed against his side, he wasn't especially cold. And then Laz shifted away, just a hand's breadth. Just enough to notice.

"Am I that badly broken?" Laz's voice was thin.

"You're not, and that isn't what I meant either." He ate the last bite of his sandwich and folded the paper carefully, considering his words. "People with intrinsic magic, like you and your brother, tend to avoid the healthcare system. It's not clear why. But that means there aren't very many studies, let alone case reports, on a variety of things ranging from how magical brains work to how to fix them. A bit like your engineering problem,

I suppose." He sighed and wished he could lean against Eli's shoulder. "Your EEG may be the first time someone captured an episode of foresight that way."

Silence for a moment. "Wow."

"Ulysses was very excited. He wants to write it up for some journal." He looked out over the lake, then up at the glittering sky. "The problem in my mind is that we put you through a lot of discomfort, and we have nothing that would be immediately helpful to you. I could study this and come up with some theories about dopamine and magic, perhaps, or some other hormone. We could test some drugs. But I don't want you to feel like a lab rat, and I don't want to make suggestions that would bring you more pain." He hesitated, waiting to see if Laz had any questions, then continued on. "From talking to Sam, it sounds as though your episodes have been improving over the last two months, so I'm not sure how beneficial treating you is going to be."

There was a silence, and then Laz said, "I'm always going to be broken, you mean."

"No." He elbowed the other man. "Don't be a prat."

"I'm not—I just—" He huffed. "Sorry, this is hard."

Suddenly, Eli understood. "You left on Saturday because you were embarrassed. The same way you tried to get rid of me as soon as you came back to yourself that first time."

Laz made a noise halfway between a groan and a laugh. "Is that so surprising?" He was silent for a long moment and then drank the last of his wine in a sudden violent swig. "This is all—once, I was a captain, and I was in charge of a whole flight of men. I flew missions, and I gathered intel, and I was good at it. And then one day, we got hit, and I got us back and down safely. And the brass gave me a goddam medal, but everything went fucking haywire inside me, and that was it." He took a deep breath. "You never think that one day is going to be the last day you get to do something you love until it's in the rear view mirror. And now everything is different. I'm past my use-by date. When I was a kid, I spent my time running around with Ulysses dealing with ghosts and finding lost watches and cursed books, and that felt important. But he's got Sam for that now, and anyway what good is dragging someone like me into a fight if there's an even chance I'm going to wind up curled up on the ground shrieking?"

"Lazarus," Eli said, "stop."

Laz looked over at him.

"There's more to life than being useful. You are more than what you do or what you produce."

Laz didn't reply right away, and when he did, it was tinged with irony. "Those are radical ideas, Doc."

"Not that radical." He took a deep breath. "Look, Laz, you're a lovely person. And I know we were all hoping there would be some obvious way to help you." He stopped, because Laz had gone absolutely rigid, but he didn't say anything, so Eli went on. "If you want to continue doing tests and maybe trying out some other treatments, I can ask my colleagues for someone who has experience with magic people. I'm sure there's someone, the dearth of published cases notwithstanding."

Laz shifted farther away from him. Eli felt suddenly at sea, convinced he'd erred in some way but unable to see where it was.

"It's unethical," he said, grasping at straws. "It's not personal. Well, I suppose it is personal, in a way. I'm just—I'm too attached to you to be objective. I probably shouldn't have agreed to do the tests in the first place, but I'd only just met you, and I didn't realize things would change as quickly as they did, but I—"

"What?" Laz was staring at him now. "What are you saying?"

"I can either be your doctor or your boyfriend," Eli said. "And if I have to choose, I don't want to be your doctor."

Laz tackled him to the blanket and kissed him with a suddenness that left Eli stunned and speechless.

"I thought you were working up to dump me," Laz admitted when he pulled back.

"Why would you—" Eli went over his words in his mind again and didn't see it. "No."

Laz kissed him again, and Eli relaxed into him, his heart racing. The ground was cold underneath his back, but Laz was heavy and warm against his chest. He snagged one of Laz's belt loops with a finger, trying to tug him closer. Laz shifted obligingly, pressing Eli down into the blanket from hips to shoulders. Eli looped one leg around the back of Laz's thigh to keep him where he was. He heard Laz's breath hitch with the contact and shifted a little, trying to roll his hips up into Laz's, seeking—warmth, friction, reassurance, something.

Laz was kissing the side of his neck now. It seemed one of them was going to have to make a decision soon about whether the park was the best place to be doing this when his house was actually only a few blocks away and had the dual advantage of being much warmer and free of any possibility of arrest for indecent exposure. Eli was finding it hard to focus on asking the question with Laz's breath hot on his neck, his hands on Eli's coat buttons and the top buttons of his shirt, Laz's mouth tracing his suprasternal notch. Eli untucked Laz's shirt and ran both hands up his back.

Laz yelped and jumped back. For a moment, Eli felt like he was in free fall, stomach twisting as he sat up. Then Laz was laughing and grabbing his hands.

"What the hell, Eli? You're ten degrees colder than the ambient temperature."

Eli looked at their entwined fingers and started to laugh himself. "I have poor circulation." He cleared his throat. "Didn't realize it was that bad."

"What say we get you somewhere a little warmer?" Laz grabbed his mug and threw it back in the box, and Eli added his own.

"Want to come back to mine?" he asked, trying to sound casual. "It's not far." He could see well enough to know Laz was looking at him without being able to decipher the expression in his eyes. But he saw his nod.

Eli lived in a little brick house on the other side of the isthmus from the park. It was bordered on one side by the Yahara River and on the rear by Lake Monona. Laz pulled into the driveway and sat for a moment, looking at it.

"This place?" he asked, in that unnecessary American way that meant he was working up to something.

"You're not going to tell me that it's haunted, are you?" A few weeks ago, it would have been a joke. Now he wasn't too sure.

"Not my department." Laz set the brake and turned off the engine. "My sister Celeste and Obe live a block or two that way." He gestured vaguely over his shoulder.

Eli wasn't sure what to say to that. "Well, it's a nice neighborhood." He tried to consider the situation from Laz's point of view. "Or do you mean we would have met eventually, even without that day at the Superette?"

Laz looked at him for a moment, then shook his head, smiling. "That's Madison for you." He paused with his hand on the door handle. "Any roommates or anything I should know about?"

This was—what did the military call it? Operational intelligence or something. "I live alone," Eli said. "Come on in, I'll show you around."

Laz lowered his eyelids halfway. "I'm not really here for the tour, Doc."

Eli grinned broadly at him. "Then perhaps I have other things that might interest you inside."

Chapter 12

E LI'S HOUSE WAS QUIET in the early morning darkness. It was only 0530 when Laz woke, but Eli had already gotten up. Laz turned on the lamp and glanced around a room he hadn't paid much attention to the evening before. In addition to the double bed they'd slept in, he saw a dresser and doors to the bathroom, the hall, and a third he hadn't been through that proved to beg a closet. There was an armchair in the corner with a floor lamp next to it. Eli had left a handful of novels stacked on the floor in easy reach. One eight-by-ten black and white photograph of a beach with the Golden Gate Bridge in the background adorned the wall. The space was a bit minimalist, but Laz found it unaccountably charming.

He'd slept fitfully but without nightmares. The world felt solid under his feet. It was nice.

Laz found his undershorts and pants on the floor of the bedroom, then stepped shirtless into the hall, skin prickling in the cool air. A few doors stood open, so he peered in—another bathroom, a spare bedroom with a slightly frilly bedspread, and a room filled with bookshelves and a desk that appeared to serve as Eli's study.

He turned on the light and stepped into this last one. Eli's imprint was much stronger here. A little glass-fronted cabinet in the corner held a few animal skulls about the size of a rabbit's or smaller, a piece of rock with a fossilized fish in it, a chunk of a geode, an antique pocket watch that wasn't running, a small bird made from welded-together springs and gears, a postcard with a photograph of the Taj Mahal, a few small disks he recognized as Chinese chess pieces. On the walls Eli had hung several framed plates that might have been pulled out of books, gorgeous drawings of plant cells, skeletons, and birds. There were papers and books stacked on the desk. The space was comfortable and well-loved, but Laz felt like he was intruding, so he withdrew and went downstairs.

He found Eli reading a journal article at the kitchen table next to an empty mug with the string of a tea bag sticking out. The kettle on the stove was steaming but not actually boiling; Laz inspected it.

"I think the burner might have a short in it," he said, holding his hand next to the metal heating element. "It's cycling on and off too rapidly to heat the water effectively."

Eli looked up and blinked, eyes widening slightly as he took Laz in. "I thought it was taking a while," he murmured.

Laz shifted the kettle to a different burner. "I'll take a look when it's cool, see if I can fix it."

"You don't have to be useful to stay."

Laz met his gray eyes. "I'd like to."

Eli got up from his chair, still looking at him. "Then I suppose the polite thing for me to say is thank you." He took a step closer and wrapped his arms around Laz's waist. "You're tense," Eli muttered, pressing his forehead against Laz's shoulder.

Laz wound his arms around the smaller man's shoulders and willed himself to relax. "It's been a decade since anyone hugged me on a regular basis," he said finally, feeling like it was a vast, terrible thing to admit. But also, it didn't cost him as much to say that as he'd expected.

"Really?" Eli pulled back far enough to give him a concerned look. "That's awful."

He shrugged. "I lived."

"I guess that's one metric." Eli was wearing threadbare blue pajama pants and a soft white T-shirt. Laz ran a hand up his back, then remembered his quest.

"Have you seen my sweater?"

Eli gave him a sly little smile. "I ought to hide it, just to force you to go around like that." But he retrieved the garment, along with Laz's undershirt, from the table. "I meant to bring them up as soon as the water boiled."

Laz looked at the shirts, eyebrows drawing together. "Have you been up long?"

"Since five." He looked a little sheepish. "It's a habit from my training days."

Laz nodded, pulling on the T-shirt. "I've been through that training too."

The kettle started to boil and Laz stepped out of the way. He went to sit in one of the other chairs and inadvertently dislodged a gray cat with yellow eyes. "Would you like a cup of tea?" Eli asked over one shoulder, pouring water into his mug.

"I—sure." He watched Eli retrieve another mug and tea bag and pour steaming water into it, frowning as though this were a task that needed a lot of concentration. The cat stalked across the room to its food dish and crouched down. "What's your cat's name?"

"Luria." Eli set the mugs on the table and busied himself with finding an extra spoon, the sugar dish, the milk container, and a small saucer. Laz had never realized how many accoutrements tea required. "Are you weird about cats?"

Laz folded his arms across his chest. "Only cats that aren't cats." As soon as he said it, he realized how it sounded. "I'm pretty sure that Tim is actually a gremlin of some sort that Aunt Cass bound to that shape."

Eli sat down in the chair opposite him. "In anyone else, I'd wonder if they were experiencing some kind of delusion. But knowing what I know about your family . . ."

Laz shrugged and smiled.

"Could I ask you a question?" Eli asked, playing with his spoon. "You needn't answer if you don't want to."

"That's promising," Laz muttered. He wanted to take Eli's hand, but that felt maudlin, so he grabbed his mug instead. It was hot against the pads of his fingers. "What?"

"I was just curious. I know you saw some kind of vision when you had your episode on Saturday. What was it?"

"Ah." Laz gazed down into his still-brewing tea. "Nothing coherent. Running somewhere in a jungle. The feeling of terror, the inability to draw breath." He sighed. "I had something similar, back at the Superette." Very reluctantly, he added, "This time, I thought I was being pursued by that serpent."

"I see." Eli considered this for a moment. "What does the change mean?"

"It could be that I'm seeing different points in the same event. Or it's a . . . I don't know. A brain thing." Eli made a noise, and Laz knew he'd piqued his interest. But Eli didn't say anything, and after a moment, Laz went on. "Having these episodes can be like going through a door in my head to escape the panic, and sometimes I wind up in places that don't make sense." He looked down. That was more than he'd told anyone about it, including Ulysses. "It's not very helpful. When I'm not having an episode, sometimes I get a strong feeling, like 'wait for a moment' or 'take evasive maneuvers,' but most of the time I see two or three seconds entirely devoid of context. That's why I don't talk about them much."

"I see." Eli looked at the mugs. "Do you take milk and sugar?"

Laz also looked at the mugs. "Sure."

"You're not really a tea drinker, are you?"

"No." He tapped his fingers on the table. "Babushka used to read tea leaves. It put me off."

Eli smiled. "The tea bag seems like an excellent innovation to prevent that." He fished them out of both mugs and set about doing whatever it was one did to make tea taste good.

Laz looked around the kitchen. It had a lived-in feeling—the cabinets could have used a fresh coat of paint, there was a large burn on the linoleum next to the stove, but everything was clean and tidy. It was the sort of place belonging to someone more interested in function than in aesthetics. There was an avocado green phone hanging on the wall with a notepad tacked up next to it, and a few photographs on a corkboard: Eli in front of the Grand Canyon; Eli and a dark-haired young woman, both wearing black gowns and mortarboards, on the steps of some ancient stone building; Eli and the woman next to the Golden Gate Bridge; the woman and two people who looked a little like Eli—a short, dark woman and a man with pale skin and curly hair.

"Is that your sister?" Laz asked.

"Ayala. Yes."

Laz looked at the woman again. She was roughly Eli's height, with dark hair worn pulled back from her face, high cheekbones, and small wire-rimmed glasses. "Did you say she's a doctor?"

"She's an orthopedic surgeon." He finished whatever he was doing to Laz's mug and pushed it across the table to him. "She's pretty busy, but she visits occasionally. And I go down to Chicago when I can. I'll introduce you sometime, if you want."

"If you think I wouldn't embarrass you too badly." Laz took a tentative sip of the tea; it was still very hot, milky, sweet, and smoky, with an undercurrent of something slightly citrusy.

Eli was giving him a look that was half-fond, half-aggravated. "Laz, of course you wouldn't."

Laz hid his smile with his mug. "What were you reading?" he asked, gesturing at the discarded journal. "I interrupted you."

"Oh." Eli held it up so Laz could see the title: *Brain*. "It's about how patients with certain types of brain damage performed on spatial visualization tasks."

Laz bit the inside of his cheek. "Sounds exciting."

Eli shrugged. "Danger of the job, I'm afraid. The paper should be here soon if you want to read that."

Laz found that he didn't. He glanced at the clock on the stove. It was barely 0600. "What time do you usually go downtown?"

"Sometime between eight and nine." Eli looked down at the journal, dog-eared a page, and then looked back up at him. "Why?"

"I figured I'd offer you a ride back to the Square, since we abandoned your car there last night." He set his mug down on the table.

"Oh, thank you." He cleared his throat. "Do you need to be downtown earlier?"

"No." He looked at the mug again. It had squiggly lines on it that he now recognized as an EEG, with very small squiggles on one side and big squiggles at the other end. It was clearly some kind of neurology joke, possibly related to the effects of the beverage within the mug on the drinker's brainwaves. "This is a different side of you," Laz murmured.

"Is it?" Eli asked, looking up from the article. "Really?"

"You don't have to look like I've pronounced a death sentence on you just because it seems you have a soft side," Laz said, gesturing to the cat, the kitchen, the everything.

"What are you talking about? I'm all soft side." Eli's eyes twinkled. Laz had thought, somehow, that Eli was reserved when they'd met. Formal. Now he didn't know where he'd gotten that idea.

"My mistake." Laz sat back, tilting his head slightly. "It seems that we have a fair amount of time to kill before we have to leave."

"Yes," Eli said, checking the clock. "Well, I have to shower, I suppose."

Laz nodded. "I probably should as well." He picked up the sweater he hadn't put back on yet and folded it. When he looked back up at Eli, the other man had set his mug down and was watching Laz carefully. The attention was unsettling, and Laz had to force himself to hold on to Eli's gray-eyed gaze. "I don't suppose you'd want to—"

"God, yes," Eli said, getting up and grabbing his hand.

Laz parked the Goat and bounded into the house only to be hailed by a voice from the kitchen before he could vanish up the stairs to his room.

It was Ulysses, of course. Sitting on a stool at the kitchen counter, drinking a cup of coffee and reading the paper. He smirked, running an eye over his brother.

"Late night?"

Laz rolled his eyes. "Not especially." He grabbed a mug and poured himself a cup of coffee. "You're here early."

"Not especially." He got up and followed Laz up the stairs, taking up a sentry position in the bathroom doorway while Laz tried to determine whether it was worth shaving. "Eli have anything else to say about your brain?"

"No more than he told you." He rubbed the week-old scruff on his chin, decided he wouldn't especially enjoy kissing himself, and dug out his electric shaver.

"Any interesting info on the Minnesota painting?"

"Not really." The shaver was pretty loud, so Ulysses could only stare at him unnervingly. When Laz had finished, he added, "It was a long drive just to hear a diner waitress say Mr. Greenfield stopped buying coffee there a few weeks ago." He brushed the head of the shaver with his fingers to get the loose clippings out, then bent and blew over the top of it. "I talked to the wife for all of three minutes. She shut me down. Wouldn't let me in to see it." He set the shaver on the edge of the sink and examined the fresh planes of his face. "Do we know if Greenfield was part of Army Math?"

Ulysses shook his head. "I'll ask Sam."

"Sam?" He turned on the water and washed a few extra bits of hair off one cheek, then buried his face in the towel for a long moment before facing his brother.

"He's got a friend in the math department. She was the one who recognized the name." Ulysses's eyes had gone serious. "Ellen will know, even if it's not in the obituaries."

Laz's heart stuttered unpleasantly. "Obituaries?" he echoed.

Ulysses nodded slowly. "They were in Edina, right?"

"Why?"

Ulysses held out a newspaper clipping from that morning's *Wisconsin State Journal*. The headline read *EDINA COUPLE FOUND MURDERED*.

Nauseated anxiety rolled through Laz. He scanned the article, eyes lighting on unhelpful phrases like *may have been* and *police sources suggest*. "They're not naming names," he said, barely hearing his own voice over the roar in his ears. "It could be anyone."

Ulysses snorted. "Bet you it's not."

"How much?" He pushed past Ulysses, stripping off his sweater as he went.

He heard Ulysses say, "It'd be a shame to take your money," as he tugged on a clean sweater. When he came back out of the closet, Ulysses was shaking his head. "I'm going to call the Edina PD this morning."

Laz grunted. "Why bother?" he asked, even though he knew he sounded petulant and tired. "We're not going to get any more information out of them, unless you've taken up necromancy."

"Wow, you're in a mood."

Laz reclaimed his coffee cup and started down the stairs to the kitchen, Ulysses in his wake. "I didn't especially like Evie Greenfield, but I don't like to see her dead," he said eventually.

Ulysses shrugged. "Maybe you'll get lucky, and it'll just be some random idiots who got themselves whacked by the Minneapolis Mafia."

"Minnesota being a well-known hot spot for mob activity these days." Laz pulled his jacket back on and followed Ulysses out onto the front porch. The crisp, cold air was delightful, and he suddenly wanted to—what did regular people do in the fall? Go apple picking? Have repeated conversations about the weather-forecasting abilities of woolly bear caterpillars? Watch the geese fly south? He sighed, his breath condensing in the air in front of him, and stuck his hands in his pockets. "If we have to make the trip, give me enough warning that I can tell Carla ahead of time."

Ulysses glanced sideways at him with a little half smile that he hid as soon as he thought Laz was looking. "I'll do what I can."

ON THURSDAY, ELI RUSHED through his last chart of the day so he could be strolling through the door of the gallery just after six o'clock. It was warm inside—whatever Laz had done to the boiler was obviously working quite well. Laz was standing behind the desk in a rust-colored jumper, slightly scruffy, frowning down at a periodical of some sort. When he heard Eli's shoes on the wooden floor, he glanced up, smiling when he realized who it was.

"Didn't expect to see you today," he said, voice just rough enough that Eli knew he was pleased.

Eli shrugged. "I hoped that if I got here early, you might not have any plans for the evening."

Laz leaned forward, resting his elbows on the desk. "What are you proposing?"

"Dinner?" Eli tried to sound nonchalant. "My colleagues tell me there's a new French restaurant on State Street that's rather good."

"That sounds nice." Laz glanced down at himself skeptically. Eli couldn't see anything wrong with what he was wearing. "Am I supposed to pretend I'm very in demand? I don't want you to think I'm too easy."

Eli thought about the word easy as applied to Laz and snorted. "I don't think I should worry about it, if I were you."

"You could ask him to buy a painting," a woman said, coming out from the back room. "Really, Laz. Remember where you are."

Eli glanced over at the gallery's offerings. There were a few smaller pieces on the *Outsider Art* wall that looked nice—but before he could say anything, the woman was in front of him, still speaking. "This isn't a lonely hearts event. I don't know what the point of having you standing around looking like that is if you're not going to attract people who are interested in art." Despite the fact that she wore very large glasses, she still seemed to peer at Eli over their tops.

Laz rolled his eyes. "Carla, this is Dr. Eli Sobel. Eli, this is Carla, my boss."

"Oh! You're the one who stitched our boy up," she said, offering a hand. She had a firm handshake. "Thanks for that. I'm sure it healed much better than if he'd been allowed to leave it alone."

"It was nothing," Eli said.

"As I understand it," Carla began, but he never found out what she understood, because Ulysses came banging through the door. He strode across the gallery, Sam in his wake.

"There you go," he said, slapping a newspaper clipping on the desk in front of Laz. "Greenfield, right? I told you."

Laz bent forward to inspect it, then straightened. Eli caught the dismay on his face, quickly hidden. "That doesn't mean that their deaths are related to the painting, U."

Eli reached forward. "May I?" Laz nodded, and he grabbed the article. Headline: *Edina Police Name Murdered Couple as Investigation Continues.*

Ulysses was saying, "I've been in contact with the detective in charge of the investigation. They'll let us take a look at the painting if we come by the house tomorrow."

"Do we need to look at the painting?" Laz muttered. He was watching Sam, who had stopped halfway across the room and was staring at the big Rochester uneasily, one hand pressed to his breastbone. Eli looked at it as well, but it was unchanged since he'd last encountered it. A jungle scene, with a ziggurat in the background, and two pairs of eyes. He glanced at Laz.

Wait. Two pairs?

He looked back and there was only one pair of eyes, very faint, just behind a large leaf. It looked like a monstera plant. Very droll.

Eli thought of how warm and peaceful the jungle looked, and how terrifying it would be to be stalked through it by something well-camouflaged ... something that moved almost silently over the leaves ... and then he remembered wrestling the serpent. He'd had a strange sense of transposition to somewhere—somewhere humid, with a distinct smell of recent rain and—

There was a thump, and he jumped and turned away, distracted. Laz had slammed a palm down on the desk, arguing with Ulysses about going to Edina. Apparently they'd skipped straight to the part where they shouted at each other in Russian.

It was like a summer thunderstorm, over almost as soon as they'd gotten started. Laz turned away, pinching the bridge of his nose. "Did you at least find out if they're related to Army Math?"

Sam nodded. "They are. Or he was, I mean. Ellen thought he was a true believer."

"Sorry, a believer in what?" Eli asked.

"The war."

"But they moved away before everything happened," Laz said. He didn't sound happy.

Another missing piece. "What happened?"

Sam blinked. "Army Math was a facility on campus that was—"

"It blew up," Laz interrupted, turning back to look at Eli. "And some of the jerks who worked there tried to kill us a few weeks ago. So this looks awfully—"

Ulysses waved a hand. "Not everyone at Army Math was part of Stricker's group."

Laz pressed his lips together and didn't say anything. Instead, Ulysses looked over at Eli and said, "Hey Doc, what are you doing tomorrow?"

"He has a name," Laz said.

Eli frowned. "I have a holiday, actually. I agreed to take call over Thanksgiving, so this week I have a three-day weekend in lieu of that."

"Perfect." Ulysses grinned. It was like looking at a shark. "Would you like to come with us—"

"Ulysses, he doesn't want any part of your hare-brained schemes," Laz snapped.

"He can speak for himself," Ulysses said, glaring at his brother. "Now, as I was saying, we'll head out early, do our thing, get back by teatime—"

"You don't know when teatime is—"

"And you'll have the rest of the weekend to yourself." He shot Laz a quelling look, and the younger man threw up his hands.

"What do you want my help with, exactly?" Eli asked. "This can't be a social call."

Laz said, "He wants you to look at the bodies." His own body was oddly stiff, enough that Eli wanted to put a hand on his back or something, though that would probably make it worse.

"I'm not a pathologist," he said, wondering if that was why Laz was upset.

Ulysses was undeterred. "No. But you've had more medical training than the rest of us. And you can *talk* to the pathologist."

Eli started to say that if the coroner was any good, they could just explain in plain English what they thought had happened, but Laz preempted him.

"It's a ten-hour round trip *if* the weather holds. It's going to be miserable. You don't have to do this."

Eli shrugged. "Neither do you."

They stared at each other, and then Laz shut his eyes, a helpless expression crossing his face. Eli looked over at Ulysses and nodded. "I'll go."

"Great." Ulysses glanced between the two of them, smirking. "See you tomorrow morning, then."

He and Sam swept out of the gallery together. Eli watched through the front windows as they paused to confer. Ulysses still looked triumphant, but away from an audience there was strain in his face. It was evident around the eyes, and in the way he held his shoulders. Sam gestured at something up the street, and Ulysses nodded, and then they had stepped out of sight.

When Eli looked back at Laz, Carla was standing in front of him, arms crossed.

"—represents a substantial investment—"

"I know, Carla."

"And I'm not about to just—"

"I know, Carla." Laz sighed and bent forward, resting his elbows on the desk and his forehead on his folded hands. "It's very vague, I agree with you."

"Go find out what's going on, then," she said. "When you get back, we can talk about it."

"That's very reasonable of you." He straightened up. "I'll see you Saturday."

"Now get out of here, and take your doctor with you," Carla said, with a gesture toward Eli. "Don't want him cluttering things up for actual buyers."

Laz cocked his head at Eli and strode through the door to the back of the shop. Eli followed him down a short hall, hands in his pockets.

"You know," Eli said, leaning against the doorway of the back room while Laz pulled on his bomber jacket, "if you told him no, he'd find a different way to get to Minneapolis. You don't have to do what he says."

Laz was facing away from him, but Eli saw his shoulders slump. "I know." He sighed. "He's right that it seems related to my case, and if I can avoid someone else getting hurt . . ."

"If you don't want me to come," Eli began, feeling less sure by the moment that he'd read the situation correctly.

Laz straightened. "It's not that," he said, turning back toward Eli. "I—you're not going to enjoy it."

"Maybe not. But it will be fine. I've done worse things than take a spontaneous road trip to Minnesota to look at a dead body."

"Like what?"

Eli trawled through his memory and came up with: "Once some mates and I skived off class to go wander around the catacombs in Paris."

Mild surprise registered on Laz's face, followed by amusement. "So . . . a road trip to look at a lot of dead bodies?"

Eli put his hand on Laz's arm, felt the tension thrumming through him. "Ulysses doesn't scare me. Come on, let's go get something to eat."

Laz's amber eyes were troubled, but eventually he nodded. "On your own head be it," he muttered.

Chapter 13

B Y NOON ON FRIDAY Laz was back in Edina, where he didn't want to be, this time with both Eli and grave misgivings about getting him involved in this nonsense. To say nothing of Ulysses and Sam.

As they proceeded up the long walk to the house, Ulysses glanced over at him and said, "You couldn't have shaved?"

"I shaved Wednesday."

Ulysses rolled his eyes. "I can tell."

"What's the problem?"

"Just try to act professional." He went on ahead.

"What did you tell them about me?" Laz called after him, but he was ignored.

Inside, they were met by a harried-looking woman. She wasn't in a police uniform; she wore a neat, rather conservative pantsuit beneath her winter jacket, her hair pulled up. Not an officer. Possibly a secretary of some sort.

"Dr. Lenkov?" she asked, glancing at Sam questioningly, and Ulysses stepped forward, suddenly all business and charm.

"Nice to meet you, Ms. Andersson. Thank you so much for taking time to assist us. May I introduce the rest of my team: Dr. Sobel, Mr. Sterling, and Captain Lazarus Lenkov."

Laz tried not to react, though he felt Eli twitch beside him. Andersson didn't appear to notice. Her eyes were fixed on Sam, who—despite his attempt to hide it under a fancy suit and long coat—looked like a goddamn Grecian statue come to life.

Laz sighed. He'd always assumed somehow that if he ever returned to civilian life, being a captain would give him a certain amount of cachet. It sounded good to civvies. Dashing. Instead, he was playing second fiddle to his brother's husband.

"Whatever you told Chief Lennox impressed him. He's sorry he can't be here today to greet you personally, but I'm sure you know how it is." Andersson gestured them into the house. Laz read between the lines on both sides as Ulysses reassured her that it was fine: She had probably been sent as a subtle slight against the out-of-towners. Regardless of her abilities, most men would probably look askance at being greeted by a secretary rather than a cop. The chief wanted Ulysses to know he thought Ulysses was a crank without insulting him too openly in case all those fancy titles in their group came back to bite him in the ass.

It was a miscalculation, but in their favor. Ulysses would no doubt prefer to fly as under the radar as possible, making Andersson the perfect person to show them around. And in Laz's experience, secretaries tended to know the score better than anyone else. Laz had no idea what favors Ulysses had called in to get them through the door, or what lies he'd told. Now he was telling Andersson that they'd like to look around, and especially to examine the S. Rochester painting. She gestured to the hall leading out of the foyer.

It was a large house, with a high entryway. Laz had been too preoccupied trying to maneuver his way to the painting to try to look past Evie Greenfield's shoulder when they were chatting, so it was all new to him. It was impressive in a bourgeois sort of way, if you wanted to live in a house that might be showcased in *Architectural Digest*. Andersson led them through a well-manicured sitting room, down a hallway past the dining room on one side and the kitchen on the other, and into a spacious study. Large windows lined one side of the room, which was flooded with November sunlight. Above the fireplace hung a portrait—Laz recognized Evie Greenfield standing next to a brown-haired man with a blandly handsome face. There were two heavy leather and chrome Bauhaus chairs arranged in front of it.

It was a pity the portrait was clearly supposed to be the centerpiece of the room, because the rest of the art was amazing. The walls were covered with paintings in the manner of a nineteenth-century gallery, and he spotted Jackson Pollock, Mark Rothko, Gustav Klimt, Elaine de Kooning—Helen Frankenthaler, for god's sake, the works jumping out like an auction catalog come to life. And yes, Laz was spending a lot of his days staring at a painting worth $25 grand, but wow. There was well-heeled and then there was—whatever this was.

In amongst all of these was the S. Rochester. It was smaller than Laz had expected—about twenty-four inches wide by the same in height, and hung at hip height. It was definitely not being shown off to its best advantage, squeezed alongside the bright verbosity of the Frankenthaler and the calm stateliness of the Rothko. It was another jungle landscape, almost a warm-up for the one back in Madison, with the same feeling of surreality to it, and a piece of stonework in the background that looked an awful lot like a corner of the same ziggurat in the other painting. But this one felt different. It didn't trigger his weird paranoid sense that he was being watched, for one.

Sam and Ulysses immediately crowded around the S. Rochester. Andersson spent a minute watching the two of them confer, but it wasn't very interesting, and she drifted over to the wall Laz was busy holding up.

"From what the Chief said, he's here to look at the bodies," she remarked, nodding at Eli. "And those two are magicians, clearly. So what's your part in all this, Captain?"

"I'm the art critic," he said dryly, and she laughed.

"What do you think of the gallery?"

He glanced at her and at Eli, who also seemed interested. And then, uncomfortable, he looked around, trying to come up with something. "I can't say I think they've hung it well, but the collection is worth a lot of money."

"Really?"

"Oh yes. Probably a million at least, if these aren't prints or forgeries." Eli let out a low whistle and Laz grinned, feeling more confident. "Honestly, it's a little odd that they have the Rochester, since they seem very interested in abstract expressionism."

"Can you tell if they're real?" Eli asked.

Laz shrugged and went over to the wall. The Pollock was hung at eye level, so he leaned closer to inspect it. The paint drips certainly looked authentic, and there were tiny bits of grit embedded in it. There was a signature that looked reasonably correct. He glanced over at Sam and Ulysses, but they weren't paying any attention to him, so he lifted it off the wall.

As he'd expected, there were stamps from various auction houses on the back of the canvas, and a sticker from an exhibition. There was also an envelope with the provenance documents in it, tucked into the back of the frame between the canvas and the stretcher. It was a terrible place to keep that kind of document for several reasons, not the least being that yahoos like Laz could get their hands on it.

Not that it made any difference to the Greenfields now.

He opened it.

A minute later he put it back and rehung the painting. "Either that's the real deal, or it's a very well-done fraud," he said, walking back to them.

"What's it worth?" Andersson asked.

"I can't appraise it, but some of his paintings have sold for hundreds of thousands of dollars." He fell silent, looking at the painting again. It was mostly black and white, gray where the drips had mixed together, and he wasn't sure what the attraction was unless they'd bought it as an investment. He tried to imagine having enough money to spend five or six figures on something like that. Better to give the cash to Oran and ask them to paint more dragon fruit. At least he'd want to look at that every day. He took a deep breath. "There's two reasons why rich people buy art. One is because they like art and they want to have their names in a museum with the phrase 'by generous donation of' above it."

Eli was leaning toward him, eyebrows raised. It was adorable. "What's the other reason?"

"Money laundering."

Eli scoffed, and Andersson said, "No, that's true. I was just reading about it." Laz grinned encouragingly at her, and she continued, "You can anonymously buy and sell things through the big auction houses. So you buy a painting with the dirty money and then resell it, and the money you get back is now legitimate."

Laz nodded. "Are you training to be a cop?"

She gave him a weird little half smile. "I've been taking some classes."

"Seems like you'll be good at it."

She blushed, pale Nordic skin going a delicate pink. "The department's never had a female officer before."

"High time they started, then," Eli said.

Sam had produced a pair of white cotton gloves from one of his pockets and was running his hands along the edge of the frame.

"Do you want to take it down?" Laz asked, crossing the room to them.

Ulysses glanced over. "I'm not sure it would make a difference." But he nodded to Sam, who lifted the painting off its hook.

"It's heavier than I thought it would be," Sam muttered, resting the frame on the ground.

Laz crouched down to look at the back. Unlike on the Pollock, there was only the sticker of the Minneapolis gallery that had sold the painting and one from the dealer. Still, the dealer sticker looked like the one on the big S. Rochester painting, and the work was signed across the back of the canvas in the same way. He shrugged, getting to his feet. "What do you guys think?"

"It's cursed," Sam said immediately. "The nazar is warm."

Laz waited, but Ulysses nodded like that settled everything. So Laz had to be the one to say, "Do we have anything more conclusive than a magic necklace?"

Sam frowned at him, stung. Ulysses said, "Smell it."

Despite himself, Laz leaned forward until his face was just inches from the canvas and inhaled, eyes closed. He smelled linseed oil, pine, varnish. But there was something else, something sour—it wasn't quite right. It smelled like . . .

He sniffed again.

Like rotting leaves.

It was gone almost as soon as he identified it. He sat back on his heels, not quite trusting himself. "That's weird, but it's not much."

Ulysses grumbled, "I'd hoped it was going to be more straightforward than this."

Sam shook his head. "It never is."

Laz moved around to the other side and looked hard at the image. It was the same as it had been. Unsurprising, since finished paintings rarely changed. Although up close, he thought he could see a single yellow eye behind some of the foliage. It wasn't *not* weird, but there wasn't a specific thing he could point to and say, "Look, that, there."

Ulysses said, "We'll do the Griswold test. Do you have a spare button?"

Laz knew when to retreat. He pointedly did so, without asking what the Griswold test was or why they couldn't have done it to the painting in Madison. Perhaps they had. He didn't want to know.

Eli was talking about migraines to Ms. Andersson when Laz returned to where they'd stationed themselves next to the windows. Laz took up the spot to Eli's left, trying to discreetly position himself between Ulysses and Andersson. She was focused on Eli, who was holding up one hand as though cupping a brain in it, and pointing at it with the other. Laz listened with half his attention, trying to summon equanimity about whatever the hell Ulysses was doing behind him. Part of him felt like he was a child again, standing lookout while Ulysses did something that was going to get them into trouble. Phra Nok would have said that was Ulysses's problem; Laz couldn't mitigate his karma for him. Cultivate ubekkha—equanimity.

There was a click and a little flash of green light, enough to attract Andersson's attention, and sure enough she squawked angrily. "None of that," she said loudly, and marched across the room. "You promised the chief—"

Ulysses immediately shifted into some explanation. Laz shoved his hand into his pocket, where he'd left the mala. Eli looked slightly disgruntled to have been cut off mid-explanation. "How much more time do we need for kibbitzing?"

"Anxious to get to the morgue?" Laz murmured.

Ulysses, apparently having talked his way out of whatever trouble he'd gotten himself into, turned around and grinned. "Bored, Doc?" Before Eli could answer, Ulysses was looking at his husband. "I've seen enough," he announced. "Sam? Then let's rehang this thing and go."

The Hennepin County Medical Examiner's office was an ugly industrial building in downtown Minneapolis. A light snow was falling by the time they followed Andersson into the parking lot. Laz frowned as they got out. The Goat didn't handle especially well in wet weather, and it wasn't like they needed another thing to make the trip home longer.

Andersson led them through the front door and down a hall to an office whose door stood open, revealing a balding man sitting at a desk, rough skin florid across the cheekbones and nose, a cigarette dangling from the corner of his mouth as he perused the top of a stack of papers.

"Dr. Rubble," Andersson said, knocking at the door. "Some gentlemen here to see you."

He looked up. "Are these the boys from Madison?"

"Yes, sir," Andersson replied. "We have Dr. Lenkov, Dr. Sobel, Captain Lenkov, and Mr. Sterling." She stepped back into the hall. "Unless you fellas need me, I'll be on my way."

Ulysses went with her. Meanwhile, Eli took charge with the pathologist.

"We were hoping we could take a look at the autopsy reports on the Greenfields," he said, and Rubble bristled.

"You can't," he said shortly, scowling at Eli.

Laz watched the man's jowly face for a moment. "You haven't got them yet?" he guessed.

The man tapped his own ruddy nose with one blunt finger. "We've been waiting all week to get permission from their next of kin to cut them up. Now we've got it, but my assistant is out." He shoved back his chair with a screech and shouldered past them out of the office. "Come on."

Eli fell into step beside the man, asking a couple of questions that were answered with grunts.

The morgue was a cold, ugly room with a row of refrigerator drawers on the far wall. White cabinets, white floors. Rubble checked a clipboard and led them across. "Here you go, take a look."

What had he expected? Ryan Greenfield looked dead. Not the calm and ironed-over type of dead that was showcased at Christian funerals, but the unfortunately dead, the newly dead, the unpretty person who had become meat. The same bland face from the portrait, but somehow all wrong.

Laz swallowed, his stomach turning over. They hadn't stopped for lunch yet, and he was suddenly glad. It had been a while since he'd had to look at a dead body, and although this was a stranger rather than a friend, it wasn't any easier.

Eli was saying something about marks on the man's neck that sounded like it was coming from a long distance away. Rubble was finally looking at the doctor with more interest, but the ringing in Laz's ears was getting louder. He was sweating now, breathing faster to try to push away a wave of nausea.

Shit, was he going to have an episode?

A firm hand came down on his arm, and Sam murmured something, drawing him away and back toward the parking lot.

Ulysses, on his way in from seeing Andersson to her car, met them in the vestibule. Laz saw his lips move when he spoke to Sam but couldn't follow the words, and then Ulysses went in and Sam steered Laz out.

Stepping through the doors was like jumping into a lake. There was a bench next to the entrance, and Sam gently pushed him down onto it, then sat next to him while the cold air and freezing metal pulled him back into the present.

He opened his eyes and looked at the damp sidewalk, unable to recall how long it had been since he'd shut them. Sam was humming tunelessly to himself, fingers laced together around one knee. If he was cold, he didn't show it.

"Sorry," Laz said, and clenched his teeth. He was shivering.

Sam shrugged. "Don't apologize. It's not your fault."

Laz wanted to laugh. "Isn't it?"

"Only in a very convoluted way." The corner of Sam's mouth turned up. "No one blames you. Anyway, that medical examiner was something else. I don't blame you for almost passing out. No warning, just, 'Hey fellas, take a look at this here body.' How . . ." Sam searched for a word and finally settled on "unceremonious."

Laz snorted. "I'm sure his patients don't mind his bedside manner."

"Did you see his face?" Sam shrugged. "If he's not three sheets to the wind every day by the middle of the afternoon, I'd be very surprised."

Laz considered that for a while. "Was it obvious that I was . . ." The words caught in his throat.

"Freaking out? Nah." Sam offered him a little smile. "I only noticed because I've spent enough time hanging out with people having bad trips that I know the symptoms." He hesitated, and added carefully, "I'd wondered if the bodies were going to be a problem, so I kept an eye out."

Laz couldn't decide if he liked that or not. He was still embarrassed that it had happened at all, and ashamed that he'd needed to be extracted. But then again, that Sam of all people would do that for him . . . that meant something. "Thanks," he said, voice low.

Sam waved this away. "Laz . . . we're family."

Ulysses came back then and did not at all notice that Laz was just sitting there, gutted. Or if he did, he was good enough not to let on. "Eli is going to help Rubble with the autopsy," he announced, sounding grudgingly impressed. "I don't know exactly how he talked him into it, but they're scrubbing in, or whatever you call it."

Laz nodded. "How long does that take?"

"A couple of hours."

Laz took a deep breath, then coughed at the cold, dry air in his lungs. "What do we do in the meantime?"

Ulysses glanced at Sam. "Let's go grab some lunch and talk about it. The Griswold was ambiguous. Andersson couldn't let me see the case file, but she gave me a few interesting leads we might want to follow up on."

That sounded exhausting and miserable, but better than sitting around on a bench overlooking a morgue parking lot and gradually becoming a snowman. Laz hauled himself to his feet, taking a moment to note that he was still a little shaky but no longer about to collapse.

"Let's go."

Chapter 14

LAZ, ULYSSES, AND SAM picked Eli up at 1700. It was snowing and Laz was tired, the kind of bone-deep weariness without the possibility of relief that he remembered from his time in Vietnam. Nothing to be done about it but push through. No quitting in the middle of a run. At least there wasn't anyone to force go pills on him.

None of their exertions had produced a smoking gun; that was the best part. Ryan Greenfield had been a mathematician at the University of Minnesota Twin Cities, so Ulysses had dragged Sam and Laz to campus to see if anyone in the department had insight into who he was as a person. The professor in the office across the hall, Kowalski, had been happy to talk. Laz even understood the first few minutes of the explanation of Greenfield's actual work on fluid mechanics; then, sensing they were being too comprehensible, Kowalski had started on a more complete discussion of what Greenfield had actually been up to with the Navier–Stokes equations and totally lost Laz.

At any rate, during the last few weeks of the fall term, Greenfield had started keeping to himself more. He had barely shown up for classes, leaving his TAs scrambling to cover. When he did appear, he looked exhausted, and moved like he was waiting for something to jump out at him. Kowalski displayed a mix of disapproval and retroactive sympathy. They didn't really understand what had happened; they wished Greenfield had said something. Kowalski said the whole department assumed Greenfield had been worried about being targeted by anti-war activists in the wake of the bombing in Madison.

After that, Ulysses had decided to try to track down the mysterious Frankie Argent, and so it was off to the Minneapolis gallery that the painting had come from. They were lucky enough to find the docent Laz had talked to on the phone. She thought the man who had come to see the painting and locked her in a closet sounded a lot like Laz's attacker. However, it had been months, and Laz knew better than to put a lot of weight on a witness account after so long.

When Eli joined them, his report wasn't much more helpful. Ryan Greenfield had died of a cardiac arrest sometime Monday evening. How both of the Greenfields had managed to wind up dead within such a short span of time was unclear. Rubble hypothesized that Ryan had died first, his sudden collapse triggering some calamity Evie was predisposed to—an aneurysm, perhaps. Eli was unconvinced. But they'd only had time to perform one autopsy, so the question remained open.

Eli had delivered his report while eating a bagel and lox sandwich they'd brought him from a deli near the university. Then he wiped his fingers on his handkerchief and almost immediately fell asleep, slumped against the door.

In the backseat, Ulysses and Sam continued to talk quietly for a while. There were rumors to follow up on in Madison. But all in all, the day had not been what anyone had been hoping for.

Eventually the discussion in the back trailed off. When Laz checked the mirror, Sam was asleep, wedged nearly sideways across the space; the car felt considerably smaller for having a man his height in it. Ulysses was gazing out the window at the snow-streaked median. Traffic was bad along I-94 heading back to the state line, and when Laz checked again a while later, his brother was also asleep.

A warm peace settled over the car. It was going to be a long drive. He fiddled with the radio until he found a station playing quiet classical music and tried to relax.

They were enjoying the first winter storm of the season and people were driving pretty cautiously, so he had the chance to sneak occasional looks over at Eli. He caught glimpses of the man's sharp nose and thick eyebrows, the tiny lines around his eyes as the skin went gray, then pale, then dark in the changing illumination of street lamps and passing car headlights. He had a kind face, although Laz was willing to admit he was biased in his assessment. When they'd picked him up at the medical examiner's office, he'd glanced briefly at Laz as though reassuring himself that everything was fine, and then they'd moved on. No tedious questions about the episode. Laz desperately wanted it to go unremarked, and Eli was willing to give him that.

Laz didn't quite know how to deal with that kindness. But he was grateful.

He pulled into a truck stop in Osseo, about ninety miles past the Wisconsin border. It had taken them more than three hours to make it to almost the halfway point, and the storm wasn't getting any better. Laz's hands were cramping where his fingers clenched the steering wheel.

Eli stirred when he turned off the car, but didn't wake up. Laz got out to fill the tank as quietly as he could.

A few minutes later, he went into the little convenience shop to try to find caffeine and sugar. Fortunately, they had both. He picked up a box of donuts and the biggest cup of coffee available. If he was going to have to vacuum the Goat later, he'd at least make it worthwhile.

As he stepped up to the counter, the cashier was turned away, speaking on the phone. Laz caught a string of syllables that sounded like 'Khun yak arai khrap?' *What do you want?*

Suddenly, he felt dislocated in time. He remembered walking into a convenience store somewhere outside—where the fuck had they been? Near Aranyaprathet, on the way to the Cambodian border.

They could have flown, but Phra Nok had claimed it would be too conspicuous. Laz could also have requisitioned a Jeep, but for some reason, that was out too. So they'd taken a bus. The kind of tiny local bus with chickens in cages on the roof and old women coming up to the windows to sell peanuts when they stopped, which was frequently. Laz suspected Phra Nok had chosen it on purpose. He was being tested in some way he didn't really understand.

It was the hot season, 1969, and the smell of dust and diesel exhaust stuck in Laz's nostrils as he made his way into the store and picked up a couple of Cokes. He recalled being vaguely surprised that there was electricity to keep them cold so far from Bangkok.

Knowing Phra Nok was watching, Laz had gone up to the cashier and asked to pay for the bottles of Coke in the politest Thai he could summon. The man rewarded him with a quizzical look and said, in English, "American, hey?" Behind Laz, Phra Nok laughed.

Somewhere cold, Laz said, "Ah . . . phom yak kafae, khrap," feeling like all his language skills had deserted him. *I want coffee, please.* Good start. "Su dai mai?" *Can I pay?*

The man said, "Sorry, I don't speak German," and Laz was solidly back in Wisconsin.

The cashier in Osseo was tall and Nordic, blond, with skin so pale it was almost clear and deep purple bruises under his eyes. He was wearing corduroy pants and a plaid shirt, one sleeve neatly pinned up at his shoulder.

Maybe that was what had triggered Laz's memory; the man in Aranyaprathet had been one-armed as well.

"Sorry," Laz said, and set his purchases on the counter. "Forgot where I was."

The cashier frowned at him. "You okay, man? You tight?"

Laz gripped the edge of the counter for a moment, trying to let the mortification roll through him. "No, sir," he said automatically. "I just sometimes get these . . ."

The man looked around the shop, which was empty—it was after 2000 during a snowstorm—and said, "Nam?"

Laz nodded slowly.

"Yeah," the man said. "I get that." He nodded with his head toward his left side.

Laz nodded solemnly and said, "I'm sorry," because it was the first thing that came to mind. The man laughed.

"Yeah, well. You know how it is."

Laz found that he did. "How are you doing?"

"Sometimes better than other times. The government's done fuck all for me since I got out of the hospital. But there ain't no magic cure, so I just . . ." The man shrugged and cleared his throat. "Which way you boys headed?"

Laz turned around to see Eli through the shop windows, stretching his legs next to the Goat. "Madison," he said.

"You got a blanket or anything in there?"

"Hmm?"

The man snorted. "You been away too long, man. You gotta keep a blanket in case you have a slide-off. Here." He came around the counter and went down an aisle, coming back with a wool camping blanket. "Take that."

Laz nodded, bewildered. "We had gas, too. Ten gallons."

"Sure." The man pushed a few more buttons and Laz gave him some money.

"You stay warm out there. Temperature's dropping, it can get real slick real fast."

Laz gathered up all his things. "Thanks, I will."

ELI WAS LEANING AGAINST the car feeling sorry for himself, hands shoved deep in the pockets of his coat. He had no idea where they were—some place called Osseo, for god's sake—and it was cold and windy and damp. They'd already been in the car eight hours, which was a good seven hours longer than he ever wanted to spend in a car again, even with Laz as his charming chauffeur. His back hurt. He was getting too old for road trips.

Laz came out of the truck stop carrying several disparate items: a box, a folded blanket, and a cup of coffee held somewhat perilously against the side of the previous two items. Eli could tell even in the bad yellow light from the street lamp that something wasn't quite right. Laz's normally mobile features were tense, his face pale.

Eli stepped forward and took the box from him. "What's the blanket for?"

"In case we wind up in a ditch," Laz said. "Roads aren't great." He looked down at the blanket as though he couldn't quite believe he was holding it. Eli couldn't quite believe it either. It didn't seem like the sort of thing truck stops sold. It didn't seem like the sort of thing Laz would think to buy, either.

"Is something wrong?"

Laz shrugged, taking a sip of his coffee. "Nothing fixable," he said with a sad smile, and went around to the driver's side door.

Once they were back inside, Laz seemed to be in no hurry to get going. He tossed the blanket into the backseat and cast about, fishing a pen out of the glove box. "Do we have a notebook or something?" he asked Eli, still searching.

Eli had a small one in his pocket and passed it over.

"Thanks." Laz traded him for the coffee. After a moment, he said, "Sometimes I have these memories." He bent forward and started to scribble, the notebook braced against the steering column.

"When you say memories," Eli began.

Laz's mouth was a straight line. "The source of all life's problems." He cleared his throat. "Things can remind me of . . . you know. Over there."

"Traumatic things?" Eli wanted to reach out and put a hand on Laz's shoulder, but he was drawing small precise lines, and disturbing that felt unconscionable.

"Not always. I'll remember walking into a convenience store in—on the border. That sort of thing."

Eli waited, but Laz didn't say anything else. "They're very vivid, these memories?"

That got him a long pause, but eventually: "Yes."

"But you don't get them confused with reality."

"Typically not." Laz appeared to be writing out equations now. Eli was familiar with some of them from the physics he'd taken at university; others were new and interesting. He leaned closer. Laz smirked, the corner of his mouth just barely turning up. "You gotta hold on a sec, Doc." After another twenty or so seconds, he said, "I've been thinking about magic since I got back."

"You said as much," Eli said. He opened the box and breathed in the sugary donut scent. "That's not too surprising. You're surrounded by it here."

Laz started to draw something else—a marvelous little schematic. "The source of all life's problems."

"You just said that about memories." He could see Laz labeling his diagram in the wan light.

"Lotta problems." He sat back, frowning at his work.

Eli wasn't entirely sure what to do, so he took a sip of the coffee. It tasted like battery acid. Laz had added about fourteen sugars and five creams, but it didn't help. He took another sip. "What have you been thinking about magic, then?"

"There are a few people out there who are trying to meld magic and engineering," Laz said, adding another equation to the page. Eli heard him take a breath. "I was remembering a man I met. He'd—" Laz paused. "He'd lost an arm. I don't know how, exactly. But I was struck by . . . there wasn't a good prosthesis for him. He just had his shirt, you know, pinned up." Laz turned the diagram and added another few lines. It was an arm, Eli realized. The arrows and equations were describing its motion. "The guy in there, he also—"

"From Vietnam?"

Laz didn't look over at him. "Yes." He sighed. "He gave me the blanket when he clocked me." He handed the notebook back to Eli and took his coffee.

"It's all right," Eli said. Laz shut his eyes, his expression suggesting he'd somehow filleted himself and offered up some messy internal bit. "Laz. It really is."

Eli looked down at the notebook. Laz had filled up two pages with his scribblings; it appeared to be a concept for an arm prosthesis that used electrodes similar to those in the EEG to detect nerve signals. There were also channels that fed backward from the fingertips, letting some types of sensation run up the arm. That was where the magic came in. "This is amazing, Laz. I've never seen anything like it."

Laz rearranged himself in his seat. "Powering it is going to be the trickiest bit." He took a sip of the coffee and leaned back. "Batteries are heavy."

"Could you run it on magic?" Eli asked.

Laz frowned. "Sure. Once. And then you need a new sacrifice." He took a donut.

"What if the spell was the battery, and you recharged it by plugging it into the wall . . ."

"We'd have to ask the professor," Laz said, gesturing to the backseat. Eli blinked; he'd forgotten there was anyone else in the car with them. He glanced back. Sam was asleep, half folded over with his head in his husband's lap, but Ulysses's eyes glittered just a little when his gaze met Eli's.

For an uncomfortable moment, Eli held his breath. But Ulysses just said, "If it's posed as a small series of transactions rather than one really large one, that could be workable." He reached forward, careful not to bump Sam, and Eli passed him a donut.

Laz finally shoved the rest of his donut into his mouth so he could reach up and fasten his safety belt. After a second, he took a long swallow of his coffee and handed the cup back to Eli.

"Three more hours to Madison, if we're lucky," he said, turning the key.

"You know, one of us could drive, if you'd like," Eli offered, knowing before he said it what kind of look it was going to earn him.

Sure enough. "If I'm bleeding out," Laz said easily, and put the car in gear.

Hours later, Laz had dropped off Ulysses and Sam at the Baskerville building and crept slowly across the isthmus to Eli's house. The snowstorm had come south with them, with two inches or so already on the ground and what seemed like a lot more in the air. Occasionally, they passed a plow or salt truck, but the city seemed largely abed, asleep and unconcerned by the weather.

Eli looked up at the dark windows of the house and at the strange Midwestern sky, pink where the light pollution was reflecting off the clouds. "Laz," he murmured, not quite sure how to frame the invitation to sleep over when it really was just about sleep, or if they were even at that point in this thing he continued to insist was a relationship yet. "Would you like to come in? You—don't drive back across the isthmus."

"It's only two miles," Laz said, looking down at his hands on the steering wheel.

"So? You're knackered," Eli said. It occurred to him that perhaps, deep down, Laz just wanted to be told what to do. There were probably a lot of reasons one joined the military, but the idea of following orders was something they drummed in pretty hard. Laz clearly had plenty of his own ideas, but maybe his sense of being at loose ends was—what had Kierkegaard said? The dizziness of freedom?

For an instant, the pieces seemed to align, but then Eli lost the image again. For the time being, he decided to rephrase his request, because he really did not want Laz to talk himself into driving anywhere else, even if it were only two miles. "Come on, then," he said, and got out of the car. He was still carrying the mostly empty box of donuts. The air was cold and humid, which made the chill more pointed. It was refreshing after so long in the stale, warm car.

A moment later he heard the click and thump of the driver's side door being opened and shut, followed by the crunch of Laz's boots on the snowy driveway, and Eli grinned to himself.

Chapter 15

L AZ SLEPT DREAMLESSLY, A relief after everything that had happened, and woke up after 0800. For a while he lay staring at the ceiling, enjoying the half-awake feeling of having no thoughts in particular to chase around.

He hadn't really meditated since the day he'd been wounded. He'd seen Phra Nok a few times between getting out of the hospital and being sent back to the States, but he hadn't been up for any prolonged sitting. Now, though, his stamina was basically normal again, and he could . . . He could probably go down to the university and see if there were any other Buddhists, maybe even find a new achan . . .

He had a lot of feelings about that idea, so he closed his eyes and breathed until they went away. It seemed disloyal to replace Phra Nok, who had been with him through so much. Although he knew how the monk would react if he said that aloud—with that story about a monk foolishly carrying a raft around long after he'd crossed a river. Don't hold on to things that don't serve you anymore. As though it was so simple.

There was a groan and a movement in the bed beside him and Laz came all the way awake, suddenly realizing that he wasn't at home or alone. Eli buried his face in his pillow, muttering imprecations into it.

"Sorry, I didn't catch that," Laz said, shifting onto his side. After a moment's hesitation, he gently pressed a palm into the hollow between Eli's shoulder blades where his T-shirt bunched and pulled as he moved.

"We should have stopped at a motel," Eli groused, still mostly into the pillow. "My entire body hurts. I bet Sam will never walk again after being forced into the backseat all night."

"Sam will be fine. I'm sure he was up and running this morning like nothing happened." He slid his hand to Eli's shoulder and tugged gently until he turned onto his side facing away and Laz could curl up around him. "I'll get you an aspirin if you tell me where you keep them."

Eli said, "You might just get a car with some kind of springs in it. What do you call them? Shock absorbers."

"The Goat has shock absorbers." Laz kissed the back of his neck. "We can take your car next time if you'd like."

"I'd rather there wasn't a next time."

Laz pressed his forehead against the back of Eli's shoulder, forcing down the pang that elicited. "That's fair. I enjoyed having you along, though."

"Did you?" Eli asked, voice lighter.

Laz realized that he hadn't done much besides lecture about art in the most boring way possible, leave Eli alone to cut open a dead man in the presence of a drunkard, and then cut himself open, metaphorically speaking, so that Eli could take a look at all the twisted viscera within. "Sorry," he said after a moment, toying with the sleeve of Eli's shirt. "I guess it wasn't a very good time for you."

"Not a traditional date, certainly," Eli said. "But I think you are discounting how much I enjoy autopsies."

Laz licked his lips and then propped himself up on his elbow so he could see Eli's face. "You're making some sort of complex British joke, aren't you? Like wine gums."

"Wine gums? Who have you been hanging around with?" Eli rolled onto his back and looked Laz full in the face, smiling indulgently. "Laz, it was fine. I told you I did a fellowship in neurophysiology, didn't I?"

"*Neuro*physiology, not—" He gestured at the rest of his body, and Eli started to laugh quietly.

"It's true that we had to examine the entire corpse rather than just the brain, but—" He broke off at Laz's expression, laughing in earnest. "Really, Laz, it's fine. I'm just kvetching. Even riding five hundred miles in a Pontiac GTO was not really a problem."

"You're weird," Laz muttered. "You should—you should be dumping me over this, not—"

Eli's face gradually grew serious, and then he shook his head. "Laz, this is shared suffering. You also had a cruddy time, right?"

Laz nodded. "But that doesn't—"

"It does matter. This wasn't you being intentionally cruel. Just poor circumstances." Before Laz could protest further, Eli reached up and put a hand on the back of his neck, tugging gently. "Come here."

He kissed Laz very sweetly for all that they were lying in bed together in their underwear. It was one of those things, like being hugged, that Laz wasn't very good at. Intimacy. All the squishy, sappy things that went along with seeing someone. Laz tried to untense himself and almost thought he was succeeding until Eli made a little noise between a huff and a laugh and tugged Laz over until he was braced above the doctor on his elbows.

"I feel like you're having fun at my expense," Laz muttered into the hollow of his jaw.

"You're so very highly strung sometimes—say, did you have an embarrassing nickname back in the service?" Eli gently grasped Laz's dog tags where they hung down and brushed against his chest. "Was it Flinch or something?"

"No," Laz said, sounding a little defensive, even to his own ears. "I mean, I had one. It wasn't Flinch." He kissed Eli's shoulder.

"What was it?"

"Jitterbug." Eli bit his lip in an attempt to stop himself from laughing. Laz tried to look severe, but in the end his grin won out. "Yeah, all right. I'll admit, it's funny." He looked at Eli, trying to judge if the moment had been lost. But Eli was grinning and rolling Laz over onto his back, and it turned out that some moments were never really lost, just delayed a little.

He stayed to shovel Eli's driveway, and then they had breakfast together, so all in all it was past 1100 by the time Laz stumbled down State Street and through the door of the gallery. So late, in fact, that Carla was already there, and she had sold the painting.

"You what?"

"No shouting, Laz," she said. "I sold it. My guy is coming to get it this afternoon. I need your help to crate it up before then."

He forced himself to take a deep breath. Everything had been going so well. Of course this was happening. "I thought we had decided not to sell it until Ulysses completed his investigation into it possibly being cursed." He tried to keep his voice under better control, but it rose as he got to the end of the sentence.

"People do not walk in every day looking to spend twenty-five thousand dollars on a painting," she said. "So tell me, how is the investigation going?"

He didn't wince, but it was a near thing. "It's inconclusive."

"Really?" she said dryly. "Any leads on the elusive Frankie Argent?"

Laz took another deep breath. It didn't help. "We have a few leads to follow up on."

"Do you have anything concrete at all?" She looked at him over the tops of her glasses.

"The Greenfields died suspiciously," he said. "Doc—Dr. Sobel did the autopsy, and—"

Carla waved a hand. "How long did they have the painting before that happened?"

"A few weeks. Six, maybe."

"Then you've got some time. And in the meantime, you and I will be safe from these alleged horrors, although I don't suppose that means anything to you." She smiled tightly. "Come on, the packing crate is in the back room."

The new buyers lived in the Highlands, a neighborhood on the west side of Madison full of wealthy professors and judges and other motherfuckers Laz was not interested in getting to know. The buyers, Nadine and Fred Foster, lived in a large white house on top of a hill. At some point in the past, it might have offered a view all the way down to Lake Mendota, a few blocks to the north, and the Capitol, some six or seven miles northeast, but now the neighborhood was filled with tall trees that blocked the sightlines. Laz helped Carla's mover, a guy who'd introduced himself as Mack, maneuver the crate into a large sitting room and crowbar it open.

Hanging the art was technically the customer's responsibility, but Laz offered anyway, just as an excuse to stick around and keep an eye on things. Together, he and Mr. Foster lifted the canvas into place. Then Mr. Foster tipped Laz and Mack each a dollar and waved them out.

The house was at least on a scale that meant owning a painting of that size wasn't totally absurd. Unfortunately, its hilltop position was going to make it rather difficult to watch, should it need watching. The rest of the neighborhood was wooded, and probably lushly green in the summer, but the area directly surrounding the house was bare—and anyway, most of the leaves had fallen.

He waved off Mack's offer of a ride back downtown and walked along South Highlands Drive until it met Old Middleton Road. It was a pleasant neighborhood, similar to Mansion Hill, where he lived, but the houses were all single-family homes set on huge, golf-course-like plots of land. One, far from the road, had a sign out front that said Brittingham House. He wondered if he was supposed to know its significance.

He turned right on Old Middleton and walked until he found a butcher shop with a payphone outside about half a mile down the road.

He called Ulysses and Sam, but no one answered. Fine. Then he realized he didn't know Eli's number and called directory assistance; unfortunately, Eli wasn't answering either. So Laz carried on walking down Old Middleton in the direction of the Capitol.

He made it about another half mile, thinking of nothing in particular but the smell of the wind and the crunch of the sidewalk under his boots and how pretty the few large drifting snowflakes were. Then he heard the sound of tires on pavement and turned, sticking out his thumb. To his immense surprise, the car was a green BMW 02 series, and it came to a screeching halt in the middle of the road just after passing him by.

He took a few seconds to compose himself before he went over and opened the passenger door.

"Laz?" Eli looked as confused as he felt, which was somewhat steadying. "What on earth are you doing out here?"

"Walking," Laz said, and slipped inside. "Carla sold the painting."

"Oh dear."

"I was just assisting with the delivery." He fastened his seat belt because Eli was giving him a *look*. "What were you doing?"

"Picking up firewood from a chap in Middleton." Apparently catching Laz's confused glance at the small backseat, Eli added, "It's in the boot."

Laz nodded. "Whip a shitty and I'll show you the buyer's place."

Eli stared in mute incomprehension. After a moment, he cleared his throat. "I beg your pardon?"

"Make a U-turn." Laz tilted his head.

Eli finally put the car in gear. "What was that majestic piece of Midwestern vernacular? Whip a shitty?"

Laz rolled his eyes.

The neighborhood felt equally like a problem on his second trip through. It had one road that formed a loop, both ends leaving from and returning to Old Middleton Road, so there was little through traffic and no tucked-away places to park. And unlike the cheerful chaos of downtown, here no one parked on the street—they all had adequate driveways and large garages. He pressed his lips together.

"You look like you're casing the joint," Eli said, looking sidelong at him.

Laz half grinned at the slang. "I'm trying to figure out where I'd watch the place from."

"If you were that serpent, you mean?" Eli glanced at him, brow furrowing. "Oh my god, that's not what you mean."

Laz shrugged.

⤜⤜⤜⤜ ⤛⤛⤛⤛

ELI DROVE THEM BACK downtown. Although he offered to drop Laz at the gallery or at his place, they fetched up at Eli's house again, as though it were a sort of natural island in the flow of the city. They unloaded the firewood, Laz stacking it with a sort of careless efficiency against the house next to the back door. When they were done, he squared his shoulders, looking down the driveway toward the street with the expression of someone about to do something mildly unpleasant.

"You off, then?" Eli asked, sticking his hands in his jacket pockets.

"I better." Laz's face was pensive. He looked down at the toes of his boots. "I feel like if I don't go now, I won't."

It was shockingly close to an admission of positive emotion, the second that day, and Eli jumped at it. "You don't have to, you know. I like having you around." Laz frowned at him, and he sighed. "It's not a riddle, Laz."

"No." The corner of his mouth quirked up. "Monday, maybe?"

"Yeah," Eli said. He gave in, reaching out and grabbing the soft collar of Laz's jacket. "Come by the clinic?"

Laz nodded, and then a moment later he was gone. Eli waited outside until he couldn't hear the sound of his boots on the pavement anymore.

Then he went inside and made tea.

Luria was inside a paper bag he'd left to hold the old newspapers. She poked her ears out curiously when he came in and put the kettle on, then crouched back down.

"You and me, kid," he said to her in his best Bogart impression. She didn't emerge, not even when he dumped a scoop of food in her bowl.

Laz was going to report his findings to Ulysses, no doubt, and be dragged off on some strange trek through the underworld as thanks.

Perhaps that wasn't fair. Madison didn't seem like the sort of place that had much of an underworld. Most of what he'd seen was hippies and wannabe communists. Campus had changed since the shooting at Kent State and the Sterling Hall bombing, or so he'd been assured. The anti-war movement was different now. Everything was a little more tentative; people were afraid to push too far lest the tension explode into open violence.

Still, if there was a dangerous part of the city, he had no doubt that Ulysses knew where it was. Eli was beginning to come back to his original feelings about Ulysses, which were definitely in the neighborhood of suspicion. Yes, the man was protective, and he and Sam had clearly been doing their best with a relatively limited arsenal of tools to help Laz get back on an even keel. But he didn't have Laz's best interests at heart when it came to the case.

"I should have seen it when we did the EEG," Eli told Luria's paper bag. The kettle started to boil and he poured hot water into his cup. "He was far too focused on the findings rather than what harm we might be doing."

He moved around the kitchen retrieving the milk bottle and a spoon. Luria poked her head out of the bag like a prairie dog, then hopped nimbly out and made her way over to the food dish.

"Am I wrong? I know I was also caught up . . ." Luria's ears twitched, but she didn't turn her head. Perhaps that was for the best. Talking to cats set a bad precedent, and it made the cats think they were important.

Eli sat down at the table and stirred a lump of sugar into his tea, frowning at it. The problem was that he liked Laz a lot. He felt protective of Laz now too, and if his purposes were counter to Ulysses's, they were all going to have a rather bad time of it.

Chapter 16

S OMEONE WAS KNOCKING ON the door of his hooch.

No, his room. Laz opened his eyes and stared up at the distant plaster ceiling. His bedroom. No more hooches.

"What?" he called, just to make the knocking stop, and apparently Ulysses took that as permission to come in, Sam at his heels.

"Get dressed," he said, waving a garment bag at Laz. "We're going to a fundraiser."

Laz, halfway sitting and still groggy, said, "What?" again. He'd fallen asleep in his undershirt and jeans partway through getting ready to shower. Now everything felt faintly surreal. It was evening, nearly 2000. "What are you—"

"We brought you a jacket," Ulysses said.

"A sports coat," Sam corrected. He took the bag and hung it on the armoire, then unzipped it and removed the unfortunate garment itself.

"Jesus fucking Christ," Laz said.

Ulysses rolled his eyes. "It was the best we could do on short notice. I figured you didn't want to wear your dress blues."

As coats went . . . well. It was a mustard yellow and navy blue plaid, with very wide lapels. "That's the best you could do? What was the worst?"

"Candy stripes," Sam said in a firm, slightly prissy tone, as though this argument had already happened. "Believe me, if we'd had time . . . but we didn't."

Laz shook his head. Sam was wearing a rather nice gray suit, but that wasn't unusual—Sam had to be pried out of those monkey suits, probably. Ulysses had on a brown tweed blazer with leather patches on the elbows that *must* have been someone's idea of a joke gift, and a white button-down. No tie, which was all that prevented Laz from pinching himself to make sure he was awake. "What are we doing?"

"Fundraiser," Ulysses said, and then he started in on a long explanation that Laz tuned out as soon as he got the gist: rumor was that Frankie Argent was also known as Francis Burnsides, under which alias he might be working as a waiter for a catering company. They were going to scope out the situation at an event that evening. They needed Laz along to determine if Burnsides been present for the gallery attack.

There were a lot of unknowns, but from an operational perspective the plan seemed passable. "Give me fifteen minutes," Laz said, and went into the bathroom, cutting

Ulysses off mid-stream by closing the door between them.

He came out eight minutes later with a towel wrapped around his hips, primarily because he knew the sight of his tattoos would piss Ulysses off again.

Ulysses and Sam were sitting on the love seat when he came out, Sam in an elegant sprawl with his arms spread along the back, Ulysses leaning forward, elbows on his knees, saying something in a low tone. Sam was listening intently. As Laz turned around, heading for the closet, he heard Ulysses make a choked noise.

"I know," he said over his shoulder. "Enough already."

Ulysses cleared his throat. "That's not . . . Laz, are you all right?"

He'd forgotten the scars. He'd *forgotten* all those goddamn scars. "I'm fine," he said shortly.

"What happened to you?"

Laz sighed. "I don't want to talk about it with you."

There was silence. He waited it out. "Do you talk about it with Eli?" Ulysses's words were even and unrushed, but his voice was low and crunchier than usual.

"I don't talk about it." Laz turned on his heel and went into the closet, shutting the door behind him.

It proved his point, somehow, but it did leave him stuck alone in a small, dark space that lacked an overhead light. It was like being cocooned. He stuck his face into a stack of undershirts and forced himself to breathe until his racing pulse was under control.

When he thought he could talk to Ulysses without making a Brando-esque scene, he opened the door just enough that he could see what he was doing and got dressed. By the time he stepped out in black slacks and a black turtleneck, Sam had apparently talked Ulysses off the ledge too, because when their eyes met his brother just nodded and got to his feet.

The fundraiser was in one of the upstairs rooms at Memorial Union he'd never entered. Laz wasn't a UW alum, but he'd spent his share of summers drinking out on the Terrace anyway. The building itself was from the days in which colleges thought of themselves as august institutions devoted to educating young elites and all the buildings had that neo-Renaissance look with Grecian columns and ivy crawling up the outside. The interior matched, with lots of marble floors and high, vaulted ceilings covered with filigreed frescoes that would have been nice if they hadn't been dulled by years of cigarette smoke. The party room itself had big windows on the back wall overhung with a banner that said *Welcome, Class of 1955*. There was a fair amount of art on the walls, portraits of former university presidents done in the same boring pseudo-Rembrandtian style.

A band was parked in one corner, all wearing powder blue tuxes, the lead singer crooning a Sam Cooke cover. The attendees were exactly what he would have guessed if Ulysses had told him the guests of honor ahead of time: largely white, most of them in their late thirties or early forties, women in cocktail dresses and pearls, men in two-button suits. There were a fair number of faculty in circulation as well, notably older than their one-time charges and more carelessly dressed. Laz watched Ulysses accept a cocktail meatball from a uniformed waiter with a tray of them and vanish into the crowd. When he looked back, Sam was gone as well.

Laz collected a glass of wine off the tray of another passing waiter and made his way to the farthest corner from the band. It wasn't bad, watching the swirl of the crowd without really being a part of it.

He'd been there for a few minutes, watching the crowd grow denser and the waiters sneak in and out between them, when a voice next to his ear said, "You look like someone scraped a beatnik out of a lint filter and stuffed him into a—what do you call that thing you have on?"

"A mistake," Laz said. He glanced over at the man who'd joined him; he had the upright bearing and crew cut of someone who had come through the army, a cane hooked over one arm suggesting he'd seen combat, and a bushy mustache suggesting he wasn't under any regulations anymore. "You look about as excited to be here as I am."

"My wife," the man said, gesturing with the glass he was holding toward a knot of people that had formed around a woman with red hair and a vibrant laugh. "She was the '55 class secretary." Laz nodded like that meant something to him. The man examined Laz again, then glanced out at the assembly. "Which one's yours?"

"Oh, I—my older brother is a professor. He dragged me along." He glanced down at the coat again, as though he'd forgotten it somehow. "The jacket was his idea."

The man laughed, head thrown back. "You sure he likes you?"

"Not so much now." Laz took a swig of his wine. It was some kind of pinot and very oaky. He watched a waiter make his way out of the crowd and through a curtain that was partitioning off part of the hall. A few moments later, another waiter came out with a new, full tray. How many staff would they have at an event this size? There had to be at least a hundred and fifty people standing around now, with some still trickling in. He tried to calculate how many deviled eggs one tray could carry. Over in one corner, Sam was speaking with someone significantly shorter than him; Laz couldn't see the person's face. Where Ulysses had got to he wasn't sure, but he occasionally heard a familiar laugh cutting through the din.

"What are you in?" the man asked, and Laz blinked, recalled to himself.

"Fine art," he said, which was sort of true. "On the sales side. What about you?"

"Defense." The man offered him a crooked smile. "Went into engineering after I got out, one thing led to another . . ."

"Sure," Laz said. "You here on campus, or—no, you must be in from out of town."

"No, no," the man said. "I'm with Convair. We're out by the base."

Laz nodded. The Air National Guard had a large installation at the Madison airport. "You fly them too?"

"Just fix them anymore." The man sipped his drink, which was half full of something that looked like a brandy old fashioned. "Mind if I ask how you got into the art business?"

Laz shrugged. "No real mystery. I got out"—he hesitated—"not long ago and I was staying with my grandmother. She decided I needed something to do with myself and a friend of the family needed a hand." He frowned at the memory. "My mother is in the arts, so it feels pretty familiar, even though I'm an engineer by training."

The man chuckled. "Here, let me ask you something. A guy I know here at the university put a bug in my wife's ear about this painter, name of Rochester. Says he's very modern, a real up-and-coming guy, and his stuff's a solid investment. You ever hear of him?"

Laz fought the temptation to wave his handkerchief like a semaphore flag, requesting help. He had the strange feeling of pieces starting to click into place. "What's your friend do?"

"Math."

"Must pay well." Laz watched the man's eyebrows climb. "S. Rochester is big now and getting bigger. Your friend isn't wrong about that. But will they be worth anything twenty years from now?" Laz waggled one hand side to side. "My feeling is, yeah, you could drop a couple grand and get something to hang over your sofa. Then when you die, your kids can donate it to a museum and maybe they'll put a little tag on it with your name. But on the other hand, if you're not overly concerned with status symbols, you could go to a gallery, find a piece by someone local you like, and then give them the money to paint something for you. Like—I don't know, a portrait of your wife. You know she'll like that, you'll like looking at it, and it'll be something your family can cherish afterward." It was the most Laz had said in some time; he didn't even think he'd come up with that many words when he was trying to convince Eli to sleep with him. Of course, in the end Eli had needed less convincing.

"That makes a lot of sense," the man said after some consideration. He clapped Laz on the shoulder. "Thanks. I needed to hear that." He reached into one pocket and pulled out his wallet, from which he removed a business card. "Look, if you ever decide you want to get back into engineering, give me a call. I could use a guy like you."

Laz watched him limp off. A moment later, Ulysses materialized out of the crowd and shoved a little paper plate of cocktail meatballs into Laz's hand. "Who was that?"

"I don't—" He looked down at the card. "Adom Morris."

Ulysses shook his head. "Doesn't mean anything to me." He took one of the meatballs. "They've lured a lot of junior faculty here. I guess they want the donors to feel like there's something going on here, intellectually speaking. More than football and beer."

"Is there?" Laz picked up one of the meatballs and tasted it. It was edible; better than C-rations, anyway.

Ulysses snorted. "Depends on where you're looking."

They fell silent, watching the crowd circulate. Laz wondered if there was going to be a dinner as well. He hoped they didn't have to stay for it. "Who told you he might be here?" Laz asked after a bit, mostly because he wanted to hear what seedy magician bars Ulysses had been hanging around at.

Ulysses was looking at Sam on the other side of the room, but Laz was pretty sure he just did that by default these days. "The intelligence came from multiple sources," he said.

"Such as—oh!" Laz shut his mouth abruptly. That face. . . . He watched a man offer a cluster of women refills of their wine, alarm bells ringing loudly in his head. Blindly he reached over and grabbed Ulysses's arm.

"Is that . . ." Ulysses looked where Laz was looking. Then he carefully removed his forearm from Laz's grasp. "I'll get Sam."

Before they returned, Laz saw the man he'd met as Frankie Argent, possibly also known as Francis Burnsides, hand off the bottle of wine to another waiter and leave the room. Laz followed. The man seemed oblivious to the tail as he went down the grand staircase and then through the union, emerging onto the Terrace. It was a wide open space without anywhere to hide.

Nowhere for Argent to hide either. Laz went out after him, trying to come through the door nonthreateningly.

Either he'd accomplished it, or Argent was unconcerned by his presence either way. The man pulled a pack of cigarettes from his back pocket and lit one, staring out at the dark mirror of the lake and the constellation of lights marking Maple Bluffs and Waunakee. It was cold, and Laz's breath steamed out into the air in tandem with the smoke the other man exhaled. Laz watched jealously as Argent took another drag.

Argent was about Laz's height, but burlier, slightly barrel-chested like he'd spent time doing physical labor. The way he lit his cigarette and let the match chew through the cardboard almost all the way to his fingers before he waved it out spoke to that too—he was familiar with pain and unafraid of it. He had sandy blond hair, cut short, and a turned-up nose. He looked like a cross between some Massachusetts politician and a construction worker.

"You want one?" Argent asked over his shoulder without turning.

Laz shook his head, then said aloud, "I'm trying to quit."

Argent made a derisive noise and took another drag. "If you're here to beat me up—"

"I'm not." Laz felt a little surprised when he realized he was telling the truth. "At least, if you leave me alone, I'll leave you alone. I just want to know what's going on."

"Hmm." Frankie Argent glanced over at the shadowy bulk of the theater wing where it stuck out behind the rest of the Union and made a fast motion to someone in the shadows. It was some kind of infantry hand signal, but not one that Laz recognized. 'Cover me,' maybe. Or 'don't shoot him yet,' if he was lucky. "What's going on," Argent mused. He turned around and looked Laz over. "You're the guy from the gallery on State Street."

"Is Frankie Argent your real name, or are you Francis Burnsides?" Laz asked, crossing his arms.

The man shrugged. "Frankie Argent wasn't meant to turn up again. Burnsides is more of an ongoing nom de guerre. But feel free to call me whichever you prefer." Laz followed the bright cherry of his cigarette as it moved to his mouth, then away. "What do you want to know?"

"Why did you jump me?"

"Sore?" Argent—Burnsides—took another drag. "I won't tell anyone you're not as tough as you thought you were."

Laz felt his hands curling into fists and tried to force himself to uncoil. "But what was the point? What did you need?"

"Ten minutes alone with the painting and no additional questions to answer." Burnsides tapped the ash off the end of his cigarette. "You know how it is."

"Expedience?" Laz managed. "What did you do to the painting? You could have taken it and sold it. It's worth—"

"Who gives a fuck what it's worth?" Burnsides bit out. "The rich sons of bitches who buy things like that aren't worth the time it takes to scrape them off your shoe."

"Sure," Laz said, struggling to keep his tone level when what he really wanted to do was pop the guy one right in the face. "I get that. I just don't understand how this ended up with me getting cracked over the head."

Burnsides gave him a long look. "Sorry to have damaged your self-esteem." He made a motion, and two of the individuals Laz had assumed were around appeared out of the darkness on either side to grab Laz's arms. Laz let them. Still two missing. Burnsides continued, "Do you really care why we were there? If I apologize, are you going to turn around and leave?"

"Not until I get an explanation." The worst part about the two holding his arms was how on-edge they were. He could feel the tension coursing through them. The situation was still under control, but it balanced on a knife's edge, like it could turn at any moment.

Burnsides took a step toward him, cigarette between his lips. Laz tried to relax his shoulders, keep the anger out of his face. And then Burnsides reached out and grabbed for his neck.

Instinctively, Laz flinched, tried to twist away, but the two holding him were strong. Burnsides pulled the dog tags out of his collar and stared at them, an unpleasant smile on his face. "I see." He stepped back, taking a drag from his cigarette. "You must be *just* back. What did you think, soldier?"

"I—what?" Laz squinted at him through the smoke. "Of what?"

"You ever think that maybe our puppet masters deserve some sort of comeuppance?" Burnsides brought the cigarette back to his lips. "All those boys downtown at the Hanoi Hilton, all those poor suckers camping in the Delta in the rain . . . they're all pawns, being used to fight a war they don't agree with against people they have no quarrel with, all while the ruling class grows rich. That doesn't bother you?"

Laz frowned. "Are you accusing the Greenfields of war profiteering? Wasn't he a mathematician?"

"You don't see the connection?"

The woman holding Laz's right arm snapped, "Loose lips, man." She had the precise, clipped diction of every military nurse he'd ever had the misfortune to meet.

"Jimmie." Burnsides made a vague, dismissive motion. "Cool it."

The man on Laz's left said, "I don't want his blood on my hands. He didn't do anything." He sounded worried.

Sweat prickled between Laz's shoulder blades. He wondered where the other two were. Still upstairs? Somewhere else entirely? He'd expected to see them by now. "It's all groovy, man," he said, aware that he sounded like the type of man for whom nothing had ever been groovy. "I don't wanna start anything. Just thought we could have a little chat."

"So you can drop a dime on us?" Jimmie said. "I don't think so."

"I don't want to—" He tried to hold up his hands, forgetting that they were pinned. "Come on."

"Let's take him over to the circle," Jimmie said. "He already knows too much."

"No," Burnsides said. "He's one of us. If we can convince him—"

"He's not one of us. I bet he's wearing a wire." Jimmie tugged Laz's ugly jacket down his arms. "We don't know if those are his real tags."

Burnsides made a sound like he was about to object, but the guy on the left yanked Laz a couple of steps to one side, twisting his arm up behind him, forcing him to bend forward until he smacked face first into one of the bright enameled tables with a hard, sudden clang. He blinked away an orange starburst of pain. "Ow," Laz said loudly. "Shit, that hurt."

"Shut up," Jimmie said, and frisked him.

Laz was carrying: a wallet containing twenty bucks and his driver's license, a Zippo with the words *Kiss My Ass* carved into it, the mala, his keys, his dog tags. No weapons, not even a jack knife. If Ulysses ever found out, he'd call Laz six kinds of fool. And he would be right.

The mala was ignored, the ID inspected, compared with the dog tags, and then dropped. The debate began again; Burnsides thought he'd be sympathetic to the cause, while Jimmie thought officers were not to be trusted. Ever. Under any circumstances, apparently. Laz forced himself to take as deep a breath as he could and exhale, focusing on the cold metal against his skin, the breeze coming off the lake that was ruffling his hair. Somehow he still felt like he could salvage things. There was time to pull up before he crashed. There had to be.

The guy holding him down wasn't participating in the fight between Jimmie and Burnsides—maybe he didn't have a settled point of view. Laz thought about trying to sweet-talk him, but what was he going to say?

"Hey, uh. What's your name?" No answer. Laz hadn't really expected one. "It's not Kevin, is it? You sound like a Kevin." He couldn't see the guy's face, but he felt a momentary change in pressure.

The guy said, "Not Kevin."

"Don't suppose you could let me up? I have a bad shoulder." It wasn't exactly true, but the man eased back, enough that Laz could bend his knees and get his hips stacked better. If he could get a moment of surprise, he could bust out. His heart raced. He felt like he was standing on a precipice, just about to tumble over the edge. He had to keep it together or he was done for. He needed to get off the Terrace, find somewhere more populous.

Jimmie and Burnsides reached some sort of accord, although Laz could tell she was not happy about it as she stalked back to where Not Kevin was holding him down.

"He thinks you're trustworthy," she said, jerking a thumb over at Burnsides. "Me, I think you're suspect as hell."

"I'm not—I just wanted to know why I got beat up." Laz tried to sound hard done by. It didn't take much of an effort. "Just let me go, and I'll scram—"

"You're gonna bring the fuzz down on us."

"I don't know anything about you!" Laz protested. "I've barely seen your faces."

"You recognized Frank easy enough," Not Kevin said.

"He's the one who hit me!" Laz tried to flex his fingers discreetly. "No hard feelings, by the way, but I had to get stitches."

Burnsides cleared his throat. He was standing somewhere behind Laz and to the left, where Laz couldn't see him. Between Laz and the way out, in other words. "What we're going to do," Burnsides said, "is give him a chance to prove himself."

Jimmie turned around. "How?"

Laz heard the door to the Terrace swing open and knew before Burnsides opened his mouth. "No, man, I can't—"

"We found these guys lurking around," said a voice that sounded unfortunately familiar. "What do you want us to do with them?"

The other two guys Laz had been wondering about had arrived. They were standing on the step just beyond the door; one was holding Ulysses's hands pinned behind his back, the other Sam's.

"Friends of yours?" Burnsides asked Laz.

"No. Never seen them before in my life." His pulse raced uncomfortably with the lie, and even his scalp was prickling now. The situation was spiraling out of his control, and he wasn't sure he could obey the voice that was screaming, 'Pull up! Pull up now!' He tasted metal and realized he'd bitten his own tongue. The pain washed in a moment later and he tried to focus on it, ground himself down into it.

"Then you won't mind helping us deal with them." Burnsides was circling closer; Laz heard him pick up his Zippo from where it had been discarded, the low snort as he studied at the words on it.

Laz took another deep breath. "What do I get if I do?"

"You can join us." He heard the click of a lighter as Burnsides lit another cigarette. "You don't, we'll drag all three of you up to the circle and let the snake take care of you."

Laz let the words settle over him like a bad prophecy. He said, "Let me up."

Chapter 17

I T WAS STILL FAIRLY early, as these things went, for a Saturday night: around ten p.m. or so. At one time in Eli's life, he would have been out and about at such an hour, sitting in a jazz club or drinking in some pub. Now he was reading in bed, tired but not ready to turn in, like someone who was, well, old and boring. He hadn't thought of it like that until he'd met Laz; he'd just been a normal adult keeping normal adult hours.

There'd been a bit of a dearth of normal adult hours since he met Laz. But that would probably settle down at some point.

What happened with Laz, who was a bit of an adrenaline junkie, when things got quiet? Was he going to be content to sit in front of the telly of an evening? Go to a film?

A car door slammed outside, and the sound pulled him out of his thoughts. With the lake behind the house and the river on one side, there wasn't much passing traffic here; he'd become used to the quiet street, despite the years he'd spent in San Francisco.

It was probably the neighbors coming home drunk, he decided, and was about to go back to his book when he heard voices bickering.

In Russian.

Shit.

Eli hauled himself out of bed, wide awake now. He wrapped himself in his dressing gown and hurried down the stairs. He could still hear the voices, Laz's and two others that he was growing familiar with; from the sound of it they were standing in his driveway. And that was the tableau when he opened the door: Laz on the bottom step, turned back and shouting at Ulysses and Sam, who were still on the sidewalk.

"Gentlemen," Eli said, crossing his arms. They all turned and looked at him, and he was suddenly aware that he was wearing a tatty old dressing gown over his pajamas. "Can we avoid waking the entire neighborhood?"

Laz looked sheepish. All three of them had been in a fight sometime earlier in the evening, that much was obvious—there was a scrape on Laz's forehead and a smear of blood along his upper lip, and Ulysses was both scuffed and standing a little oddly, as though he was protecting his ribs. But Sam . . .

Sam was wearing only his vest. He looked wan and cold under the streetlight, and he had white cloth—his shirt?—wrapped around his forearm, the limb clutched protectively against his body.

Ah.

As the three of them made their way inside, he thought of his brief interview with Ekaterina when she'd visited his office as a patient. She'd mentioned in passing that she hadn't seen a physician in ten years, not since an occasion when she had cut herself cooking badly enough to require stitches. His research suggested that magic users avoided medical clinics. He wondered why, and if there was a way to change that

It was clear, by the time he got everyone to the kitchen, that Sam was really the concern—or at least that's what the Brothers Lenkov had decided. More blood than Eli would have liked was seeping through Sam's makeshift bandage, and it had left a dark smear on his white vest. Ulysses pushed Sam into a chair and hovered behind him, a hand on the back of his neck. He looked exhausted and in pain, but Sam was worse off, skin too pale, thin body curled around his injured limb.

"All right," Eli said, and put the kettle on to give himself some time to think. "What happened?"

"We tracked down the fucker who attacked me," Laz said, voice tense. "He goes by Francis Burnsides."

"And you picked a fight with him?" After a moment's pause, Eli added, "Or he did with you." The word "again" hung unsaid in the air. He got down four mugs and set them on the table. Then he fetched the larger teapot as well and rinsed it out.

"They had knives." Laz was standing between the back door and the sink, looking unsure where he should go. Eli paused, assessing him; the scrapes were nonlethal and he didn't seem to be concealing anything worse, but his body was rigid when Eli's fingers grazed his back, and he was breathing in an odd, intentional way, like he was barely holding body and soul together. Eli pushed him toward one of the other kitchen chairs. A cup of tea would doubtless help. "We only went to take a look at him."

"Five of them again?" Eli asked lightly, turning his attention to Ulysses.

Ulysses nodded. "A nasty little coven." He paused, like he was going to exhale sharply and then thought better of it. He wasn't actively bleeding, as far as Eli could tell. "We did discover that Francis Burnsides works for a catering company."

Eli motioned for Ulysses to spread his arms out, but he didn't move. "Is that significant?" he asked, and made the motion again.

"No." Ulysses deflated somewhat. "It bothers me that no one I've talked to knows who he is. No one in the magic community has heard of him. He's just some vigilante." At Eli's look, he shook his head. "I'm fine. Take care of Sam."

Eli scowled. "I will. Let me finish my triage so I can be confident I'm starting in the right place."

Ulysses stared back at him for a long moment, face hard. Then he shook his head. "My ribs hurt. It's nothing."

Eli decided to take that as the concession it doubtless was and stepped away. He found a bag of peas in the freezer. "What happened?"

Ulysses took too deep a breath and coughed, wincing, his left elbow clutched against what must have been the painful side. "Someone got in a lucky kick. Don't worry about it."

"Of course." Eli wrapped the peas in a clean tea towel and passed it over Sam's shoulder to him. And then Eli turned to Sam. Normally he would have crouched down to be face to face with a frightened patient, but their height difference put him almost at the right level already. "Could I see your arm?"

Sam hesitated. "I don't want to bleed all over your kitchen," he said a little apologetically, but he did extend the limb. Eli thought again of magicians and medicine. Sam was—no, he'd said he'd *been* a god, implying he had somehow been cured of it. As though any of that made any sense at all. But he was certainly acting a lot more tentative than most people when injured and faced with a doctor.

"Are you a magician?" Eli asked casually as he unwrapped the makeshift bandages.

Sam gave him the ghost of a smile. "No. I married into magic." Ulysses had a reassuring hand on Sam's shoulder, and he squeezed gently as Eli revealed the cut.

Sam's forearm had been nearly filleted right along the anterior side, the cut deep enough to display the subcutaneous fat beneath, and he hissed when the air hit it. "I see," Eli managed, keeping his expression as blank as he could. "That looks painful. Can you move your hand and fingers for me?"

Sam's face was tense, but he did as Eli asked.

"It's going to leave an impressive scar," Eli continued.

"We should have gone to the ER." Ulysses's tone was that of someone reopening an argument that had been settled.

"It'll be fine." Sam sounded surprisingly dismissive for someone who was still actively bleeding. "I heal pretty well."

Eli wanted to ask what "pretty well" meant, but perhaps it wasn't the moment. He looked up from the wound and saw Laz breathing slightly too fast. Whether it was the blood or the injury more generally or some remnant of whatever had happened during the fight, he'd gone pale and sweaty. Eli sympathized.

Luria came into the room, winding her way between everyone's ankles as she made her way to the water dish. Laz startled and looked down as she brushed against him; Eli caught the corner of his mouth turning up. The kettle started to boil.

"Laz, could you get that?" Eli asked quietly. To Sam and Ulysses, he said, "Let me go get my supplies." He rewrapped the shirt in an effort to keep the pressure on, then positioned Ulysses so he could help Sam keep his limb elevated. "I'll be right back."

He called Ayala from the upstairs extension. She answered on the first ring, and he wondered if she'd still been awake. She often started rounds at four or five in the morning, which generally led her to an early bedtime. Of course, it was a Saturday night. Perhaps she'd been to the theater.

"Sobel."

"It's me. Sorry to disturb you—"

"El? What's up?" He heard her moving around—carrying the phone out of the bedroom, shutting the door behind her. "Is something wrong?"

"I just need some professional advice. I have a patient who needs his arm sutured—"

"Let someone in the ER handle it," she said automatically.

"I'm afraid that's a bit of a non-starter," he said. "It's me or nothing. So I was just wondering if there are any considerations I'm not thinking of."

"Mm." He heard her inhale, could practically see her arranging her thoughts. "What caused the injury?"

"A knife, I believe."

Ayala hummed. "What happened? Cooking accident?"

"No." He shut his eyes, tried to imagine being in the same house as her. "He was in a fight."

"I see. Is it a stab, or a—"

"A slice to the medial surface of the lower arm."

Ayala hummed. "Lucky bastard if that's all that happened to him. Well, if he was wearing a coat when he got cut, make sure you irrigate it well and check for bits of fiber. If there's no tendon involvement and he hasn't bled to death yet, you should be able to sew it up pretty easily. There's lots of skin on the arm, it's not too difficult." She cleared her throat. "Even a neurologist can manage something halfway decent."

"Thanks," he said dryly, and she chuckled.

"What size sutures do you have?"

"I think I have a four and a five." He sorted through his black bag. He'd added extra sutures after Laz's injury, but it was all very fine stuff, meant for facial injuries.

"A five would work," she said. "Is this that same guy you sewed up a few weeks ago?"

"No." He tried to figure out how to explain Sam, then gave up. "That chap's brother-in-law."

"Danger-prone family."

"You don't know the half of it," he agreed. "Come up sometime and I'll introduce you." They were both quiet for a moment; it had been a long time since he'd thought about introducing her to anyone. Then he shook his head, because he missed her, and this wasn't the moment. "I'd better go before Sam bleeds to death in my kitchen."

"All right," she agreed easily, and they rang off.

When he got back downstairs, carrying several clean towels and a thin blanket, his guests were in the same configuration, save that Luria had taken up residence on Sam's lap. Laz was sitting with his eyes fixed on the table. The air smelled like tea, and someone had poured a cup for Eli with milk and sugar added. Must have been Laz. Eli was—surprised. And touched.

"I apologize for the delay," he said, putting a clean towel on the table. "Had to do a quick consult. Let's get you taken care of." He draped the blanket around Sam's shoulders.

Eli dug through his bag, pulling out a bottle of saline, the sutures, and a package of sterile gloves. "Do you have an objection to morphine?" he asked, finding an ampule.

Sam shook his head. "Should I?"

Eli shrugged. "I've had patients say they didn't want it," he said easily, and saw Laz nod out of the corner of his eye. "It can cause nausea, for example. And not everyone enjoys the effects."

"It sounds fine," Sam said.

"Good," Eli said, "because I may not have anything topical . . ." He rifled through the bag again and sighed. "Sorry. Thought I had the whole kit."

"You weren't expecting us," Sam told him, with a forgivingness that felt rather more appropriate for someone not having enough biscuits when you'd dropped by unannounced. Needs must, he supposed.

He covered the top of the glass vial with a towel and cracked it off. "How much do you weigh?"

Sam looked mildly surprised at the question, though he couldn't have missed Eli drawing the medicine up into a syringe. "Around 155 these days."

"Really?" He ran his eye over the man's bony shoulders and thin arms and decided he might be right. He busied himself putting a tourniquet on Sam's unaffected arm, wiping down the crook of his elbow. All familiar motions, calming in their way. Sam exhaled when the needle went in, like he'd been worried about something. Eli set down the syringe and waited, sipping his tea, until Sam started to slide bonelessly down into the chair's embrace. It didn't take long.

"How are you doing?" Ulysses murmured, coming up behind him and hauling Sam slightly more upright.

"Thy drugs are quick," Sam mumbled, and Ulysses grinned.

"Probably all right to get started," he told Eli, as though quoting Shakespeare were somehow the threshold for being properly anesthetized.

Eli set the mug down. Then he pulled off his dressing gown and set it, neatly folded, on the table as well, to keep the sleeves out of his way. From the corner of his eye, he caught Laz watching him while he scrubbed his hands at the kitchen sink, even though he was definitely not an impressive figure in his T-shirt and pajama bottoms, and felt warmed by the attention. Then Laz shifted and averted his eyes as Eli put on gloves and began to clean out the cut. He looked like he would have appreciated a stiff drink. Instead, he cupped his hands around the tea he'd poured for himself.

"Where were you lads?" Eli asked when the silence started to feel deafening.

"The Union," Ulysses said. He'd stepped away from the table to give Eli more space, but in the absence of Sam to hold on to he had started pacing, which was a bit distracting.

"We gatecrashed a party," Laz said.

"And he was there?" Eli made his first stitch, watching Sam carefully, but the man didn't move. The morphine had been dosed appropriately, or Sam was extremely well controlled.

"We did find him," Laz said, mostly to the table.

Sam mumbled, "A Pyrrhic victory," and Eli snorted.

"Do you think Burnsides's group is related to the Greenfields' death?"

"Yes," Ulysses said darkly.

Laz sat up. "He's using the job to find victims. He's looking for war profiteers, I guess. People who are doing classified research for the military, at any rate."

"So charge in and arrest him, why don't you?" Eli said.

Laz snorted. Ulysses muttered something under his breath to him in Russian. Then in English, Ulysses said, "First of all, I'm not the magic police. I don't have any power here. I don't know why you'd think that."

Eli pursed his lips and didn't respond. Sam's body moved slightly like he was suppressing a giggle.

"Second of all, I don't doubt that he told you"—he looked at Laz—"that he is interested in punishing people he thinks are responsible for the war. But I don't know if I believe him, I don't understand how he did it, and I don't understand the presence of the serpent."

"Understand?" Eli asked. "What's to understand?"

Laz said, "Isn't the serpent a demon? That could have killed them, no question. Maybe the painting was enchanted to call it somehow."

"I don't know." Ulysses cracked his knuckles, one at a time, loud in the small room. "The body we saw sure didn't look like they'd been attacked by demons, and that painting was in their house for a couple of weeks before they died."

"Several people told us that Ryan Greenfield had been acting odd," Laz mused. "And Evie Greenfield told me she'd been having nightmares." He sat up straighter, rubbing his chin. "No, she told me that everything *was* a nightmare."

Ulysses nodded slowly. "What do you think? Some sort of geas?" He paused in his pacing, his eyes straying to Sam, an expression on his face that Eli didn't understand.

"Possession?" Laz suggested. "If something could grab them and drive them around, and then seem to let go for a while, it might leave them questioning reality."

"Could a demon do that?" Sam asked. His eyes were wide, pupils huge as he tried to turn and look at Ulysses. The little ring of green left in them was almost glowing. Eli tugged gently on his arm to keep it in front of him.

"No." Ulysses gently turned Sam's shoulders back toward Eli. "And good luck convincing one to do anything."

Eli frowned, keeping his focus on Sam's arm as he mopped the blood off with clean gauze. The stitches looked rather good, a neat row proceeding along the forearm almost to the elbow. "They're like dybbukim," he said absently.

When he looked up again, everyone was staring at him. "What are dybbukim?" Laz asked.

"They're—I mean, it's Jewish folklore. They're spirits of the dead that possess the living." Eli cleared his throat. "It's a punishment, to be dead but not permitted to go on to heaven. So they have a kind of . . . I don't know what the word is." He picked up the antibiotic cream and put a healthy smear along the stitch line. "They come back to life."

"Reincarnation?" Laz asked, looking interested.

Ulysses suggested, "Metempsychosis?"

"Transmigration, I suppose." Eli picked up the roll of gauze. "I'm sure there's nothing to it. It's just a story I heard, back when I was younger and more observant."

Ulysses leaned against the table. "How do you get rid of them?"

"You get their attention and then you talk to them. Make them feel safe and ask them to leave." He looked up from his work to see Laz and Ulysses exchange a glance. "What were you expecting, holy water? Jews use words."

"We'll keep that in our back pocket for now," Ulysses said. "I'll go to the library and see if I can come up with any ideas." Ulysses ended the sentence with a jaw-cracking yawn, and added, "Tomorrow."

Eli finished bandaging Sam's arm and stripped off his gloves. Sam was still—well, he was kind of blissfully high. Certainly in better spirits now that the suturing was done. While Eli dropped the needle into an old jar and washed his hands again, he stood up, dislodging

Luria from his lap, and turned, displaying his bandages proudly.

"I'm fixed," he announced to Ulysses. "We can go home now."

"It's past midnight," Eli said. "I don't know if the cabs are still running, and I refuse to drive you anywhere until after sunrise. So please, allow me to show you the guest room."

Laz opened his mouth to offer a suggestion and then shut it again when Eli shot him a look. There was a discussion, less protracted than Eli had expected because apparently even Midwesterners could accept an invitation quickly when it was cold outside and they were exhausted.

When Eli returned from escorting Sam and Ulysses upstairs, Laz was washing the empty mugs. Luria was sprawled on the little rug in front of the oven, purring loudly. Eli hesitated in the doorway for a moment, then closed the distance and wrapped his arms around Laz's waist, pressing his forehead against the base of Laz's neck. After a moment, Laz set down the mug he'd been rinsing and turned off the water.

"I didn't know where else to bring him," he muttered. "Sam was so adamant about not wanting to go to the ER, and the blood—I kind of lost my cool."

"It's fine," Eli said. "Come to bed."

"Don't." Laz carefully unwrapped Eli's arms, his fingertips damp and warm. "I'm sorry."

"What are you apologizing for?" He looked at Laz more closely, and the man's continued pallor finally sank in. "All right, what happened?"

"They had us outnumbered and outclassed, and—" He shook his head ruefully. "Ulysses is pretty good in a fight, and I'm not bad, but things were not going our way. They were all trained soldiers, I think. But we got lucky—someone came out of the Union to smoke and started shouting. The gang fled, and when I turned around Sam was on the ground, and I . . ."

He fell silent for so long that Eli said, "You didn't realize he'd been hurt?"

"No." Laz cleared his throat. "I thought—oh, let Ulysses deal with him. I was going to go chase Burnsides. But Ulysses called me back, and Sam was bleeding pretty badly, and I—" He took a ragged breath. "I felt . . . I feel guilty."

Eli shook his head, trying to make the pieces fall into some kind of order. "Because he was trying to hide it from you?"

"I was relieved it wasn't me." Laz's amber eyes were large, his face tense as he waited for Eli's response.

Eli wasn't sure what to say. Relief didn't seem like an abnormal emotion to have when one had survived a knife fight intact. "That's understandable."

"Is it?" Laz's voice was small and choked. "Sam doesn't deserve—I'm the one who—"

"You wouldn't believe how many sorry bastards I see day to day," Eli told him. "I don't think any of them deserve the things that happen to them. Except—you know, a couple of weeks ago, I sewed up some chap's head after he got hit with a beer bottle." He squinted up at Laz to make sure he took the message.

Laz said, "Oy, watch it," in a not entirely awful East End accent. But he was smiling, just around the edges.

Chapter 18

T OO FEW HOURS LATER, Eli woke up to the sounds of people in his kitchen. Laz was still passed out on the far side of the bed, so that left Ulysses and Sam.

He sighed and stumbled downstairs again, pulling on a jumper because he'd forgotten his dressing gown in the kitchen and the house was chilly. As he came through the dining room, he could hear their conversation and paused, just out of sight.

"Where does the coffee go?"

"Oh my god, Ulysses. You have a PhD, can't you figure out a coffee maker?"

A snort. "I've seen alembics that were simpler than this. Anyway, you've got degrees from two ivy leagues and I don't see you coming up with any answers." Eli waited a moment, and Ulysses added, "I think it's missing a piece. There's got to be a candle or something that heats the water."

"A candle?"

"Yeah. The water goes in this side, and then it boils and goes through the tube to this part."

"So the coffee goes in there too?" Sam asked. "Like a Turkish coffee pot?"

"No. The coffee goes in the other part."

There was a considering pause, and then Sam said, "It's light out. We could go home and make coffee in a percolator that doesn't run on black magic."

Ulysses laughed, then coughed and groaned.

"You should've let Eli take a look at you." Sam's tone was concerned, mildly reproachful.

That seemed as good a moment as any to enter, so Eli did. "I still could," he told them, stepping through the kitchen doorway. As he'd suspected, they'd found the antique siphon coffee maker Ayala had given him. Sam was sitting on the kitchen counter wearing the same dirty trousers and undershirt from the night before, barefoot, his long legs dangling, while Ulysses was standing beside him, his posture tense. Eli wondered how badly the ribs hurt. "I have aspirin too, if you want."

"Thanks," Ulysses said, frowning.

Eli stepped past them and got down the French press. "You might prefer this to the siphon," he said, and went to get the aspirin from the hall bathroom.

When he got back, they were bickering happily about something else, but the kettle was on and the French press was set up, so he left them alone and went out to get the paper.

"How's the arm feeling?" he asked when he came back in. Sam was holding Ulysses's hand on the uninjured side, his bandaged limb tucked carefully against his abdomen.

"It's itchy," Sam said.

"Pain tolerable?" Eli glanced at the clock. "The morphine is probably out of your system by now."

"It's fine." He looked down at the arm, as though surprised to find it still wrapped in gauze. Then he looked sideways at Ulysses, expectant but not saying anything.

"Would you like me to take a look at your ribs?" Eli asked finally, crossing his arms in front of his chest.

Ulysses shifted side to side. "Would it help?"

Eli's impulse was to reassure him that it would, but he had the feeling that would be a step in the wrong direction with Ulysses. He tried to think beyond what he'd do if he was running a busy ER. "You're an active chap. Knowing whether they're bruised or broken would probably be useful information, wouldn't it?"

He saw the man readying himself to say no, and then Ulysses and Sam locked eyes and something passed between them. Ulysses didn't sigh, but he looked like he wanted to. "Fine."

Sam kissed his knuckles and hopped down from the counter. "I'll make pancakes," he announced, and began rummaging through the cupboards. "Is Laz coming down at some point?"

Eli shrugged, eyes in his medical bag. "He still has a home to go to." He could feel the two of them exchanging glances above his head. "Take off your shirt, please."

Ulysses did, awkwardly. He was more muscular than his brother, broader across the chest and shoulders, and lightly hairy. No tattoos, nor any jewelry save his wedding ring, but a smattering of thin scars, including five above his collarbone that looked eerily like fingerprints. Ulysses shivered in the cool air. "About Laz," he began, and then was forced to stop when Eli pressed his stethoscope to his chest.

When Eli had contained his annoyance and was satisfied that there was no puncture to Ulysses's lungs, he lowered the instrument. "Laz is an adult," he said stiffly.

"True, but also not the point I am trying to make."

Eli huffed and moved Ulysses's arm so he could examine the bruising on his flank more closely. Against his pale skin, the fight had produced a near-perfect boot print bruise. Eli could practically tell what size it had been. He must have made a noise under his breath, because Ulysses grinned a little.

"I'd say you should see the other guy, but—" Ulysses gestured at Sam, who was cracking eggs into a bowl one-handed. Then he sobered and cleared his throat. "About Laz—"

"Can we just imagine that I'm capable of conducting my affairs with integrity and skip the slightly paternalistic lecture?" Eli pressed down on a spot at the bottom of the bruise. "Breathe. Does it hurt worse with my fingers here?"

Ulysses coughed and made a pained noise. "Yes!"

"How about here?"

His rib cage expanded under Eli's fingers, and then he said, "That's about the same."

"And here?"

The response was more delayed. "That's not awful."

Eli nodded.

"The thing about Laz," Sam said from behind him, and then paused, distracted. The kettle had finally started to boil. Eli heard him pour water into the French press, and then into a mug with a tea bag for Eli. "It's not that he's brittle or anything."

"I'm aware," Eli muttered. He turned Ulysses away from him and looked at how the bruise had spread out on his back, a splash of purple and yellow against the skin where the blood had seeped and pooled, framing the bones hidden beneath. It was almost a painting, livid and grotesque but somehow beautiful as well.

"He's brave, but he's not great with words," Sam said. "You probably know that. He needs a little space sometimes."

Eli did know that. Probably anyone who'd spent ten minutes in Laz's company knew that. "All right," he said, trying for a neutral tone, and pressed his fingers below the rib that had seemed to be the most painful. Ulysses hissed, so he moved his fingers lower.

"He doesn't have the same insulation around his nerves that other people do," Sam said, and that was interesting until Eli realized that it was a metaphor. "Everything is very raw with him. But he doesn't talk about it well."

"I see," Eli said, pressing down.

"Just be good to him," Ulysses managed. "If you're not, I know where you live."

"Yes, I'm quaking in my boots." It would have been unprofessional to cause Ulysses pain on purpose, so he didn't. "Isn't it a bit gauche to threaten someone when you're a guest in their house?"

"That's vampires," Sam said helpfully. "Isn't it?"

"No, vampires need to be invited in so they can kill you. That's just a rule of hospitality," Ulysses said.

"Xenia?"

"I mean, a lot of cultures believe it's bad form to kill your host," Ulysses said, and then twisted away from Eli's fingers. "Or a guest. Watch it, Doc."

"Then pay attention," Eli said mildly. "How does it feel here?"

Ulysses breathed. "That's okay."

"Do I want to ask?" Laz murmured, stepping through the door.

Sam held up the bowl he was working with. "Pancakes!"

Laz nodded, eyes flickering over each of them in turn. His face was carefully blank.

"We had so much fun last night, we decided to do some more doctoring," Eli explained. To Ulysses, he said, "It's not broken, although how you escaped that I cannot fathom. I could strap them for you, but I don't think it would reduce your discomfort as much as a painkiller and an ice pack, and there's some evidence it can lead to additional problems."

Laz peered over Eli's shoulder at his brother's side. Eli glanced back in time to catch his pained expression, but all he said was, "Bummer," in a dry tone. Laz retrieved a mug and poured himself a cup of coffee, then took it and Eli's neglected tea over to the counter where the sugar was. He was wearing the same slightly grimy clothes he'd arrived in, but he'd showered and looked a little more at ease than he had the previous night. Eli opened his mouth to say that he could take the jumper he'd lent Eli to wear home if he wanted, and then realized that he himself was already wearing it.

"It doesn't feel great, that's for sure," Ulysses said. He moved experimentally. "Thanks, I guess. I'll take whatever you've got, painkiller-wise."

Eli considered this, and then gestured at the counter. "Aspirin's there," he said. "Or I might have some hydrocodone, if you want something a little stronger."

"Aspirin is fine." Ulysses struggled back into his T-shirt, and Eli hazarded a glance over at Sam in time to see him raising a skeptical eyebrow. Ulysses must have caught it too, because he said again, "I'm fine."

"Try to take it easy," Eli advised, throwing the stethoscope back into his bag. "Ice is your friend. Heat is also a good option, if you have a hot water bottle or something."

"Will do." Ulysses shook two pills out of the bottle and swallowed them with a sip of his coffee. Eli took his tea back from Laz. He sat down in one of the chairs at the kitchen table, and Laz sat down next to him. Sam was still rattling around with the pancake batter, looking for a pan or a spatula or some such, and for a moment Eli and Laz locked eyes. Laz's mouth turned upward in a tiny smile that made Eli's heart speed up. And he wouldn't have been able to say with certainty that it was magical, but it did feel that way a bit.

L AZ AGREED TO LEAVE with Ulysses and Sam, partly because someone had to drive those yahoos back to the Baskerville so they didn't get waylaid by some misadventure on the way, and partly because he was pretty sure he'd bothered Eli enough for one weekend. Although after the other two had stepped outside, Eli grabbed Laz, shoved him up against the closet door, and kissed him.

It was rough and direct, the type of kiss that was usually a prelude to something else, but Eli let him go and stepped back slightly. "Tomorrow evening?" he asked. "Come by the clinic at six."

"Yes," Laz said, a little dazed.

It was a pleasant enough morning, forty degrees and sunny. The snow was gone, and the pavement was dry as the GTO rolled along it. Sam and Ulysses were speaking quietly to each other, letting Laz stare out the windshield. He stayed lost in his thoughts until they were going along Wilson Street, almost at the Baskerville.

"Can you watch the house?" Ulysses asked abruptly.

Laz ran through a mental list of all the houses Ulysses could possibly mean. "The Fosters'?" he guessed. His brother nodded. "What, like—by myself? No. What would I be watching *for*?"

"Something weird." Laz glared at him, but Ulysses just shrugged. "I don't know, I just have a feeling, no specifics."

"Useful."

"I know." Ulysses inhaled and winced. "You're right, we don't have the manpower to keep a good watch. But I'd like to get eyes on the couple and see if something is going on." When Laz's scowl deepened, he added, "Let's focus on overnights, how about that? If you can take six p.m. to midnight, I can relieve you and do midnight to six."

Laz tried to picture himself sitting out in the cold dark, watching anything for six hours. "That sounds miserable."

"I know." Ulysses's face turned down. "I'm sorry. I'm just concerned about Burnsides and his lot showing up—"

"Fine, fine." He took a deep breath and tried to center himself. "What if they've already been?"

"Last night, you mean?" Ulysses made a huffing noise that probably counted as a laugh with his ribs all fucked up. "They beat us up, and then as an encore they went over and did some dybbuk summoning?"

Laz pulled into a spot along the curb that wasn't directly adjacent to a fire hydrant and set the hand brake. "I think we got the worst of that fight," he said, somewhat unnecessarily. "They probably had plenty of energy left over."

Sam snorted. Ulysses pressed his lips together. "I don't know what it takes to summon and bind dybbukim. I've never encountered them before," he said eventually. "But I wouldn't try it without a clear head."

Laz refrained from pointing out that clearheaded people probably did not summon anything at all. "All right," he said instead. "I'll see you at midnight."

Laz spent the rest of the day puttering around. The Goat needed an oil change, so he did that. He took a nap, or tried to. He fixed a blender, and put in a load of laundry, and resolutely tried and failed not to think about Eli casually wearing his sweater in front of Ulysses. *Again.*

Eventually he went down to find Aunt Cass in the greenhouse.

It was chilly outside, and the structure's interior felt clammy and cold. The humid air had frozen against the glass, giving the last of the day's light a strained quality as it filtered through. Tim was curled up on the workbench with his feet tucked under, a perfect little loaf of a cat. Cass was for once not up to her elbows in dirt or seedlings, just sitting with a large book, adding some notes beneath a detailed sketch of a flower.

"Good afternoon, nephew," she said when he walked in. "To what do I owe the pleasure?"

"Dybbukim."

She motioned to the stool on the far side of her work table. "Your reticence is deeply dignified, my darling, but I'm going to need a bit more than that. What are dybbukim?"

He pulled over the stool and sat. "They're a kind of hard-done-by Jewish ghost, I think."

Cass pursed her lips. "Have you and Ulysses fallen out?"

"No, that—"

"Or your young man," Cass persisted. "He's Jewish, is he not? You haven't had a fight, have you?"

"No!" Laz shut his eyes for a moment. "I'm . . . Ulysses is so far ahead of me on all this stuff. I'm still running my preflight checklist, and he's . . ." He waved a hand at the sky.

She gave him a mildly concerned look. "What is it you wanted to know?"

"I thought," he said slowly, "that you can't just *summon* ghosts."

"Just," she echoed. "No." She re-capped her pen and set it down. "But anything can be summoned."

"What do you mean?" Laz had the uncomfortable feeling that Tim was listening to their conversation, although the cat had his eyes closed.

"A summoning is just opening the door and ringing a bell, metaphorically speaking." Cass cocked her head to one side. "You can make the bell louder through various means—"

"Like a stone circle?"

She gave him a curious look. "That would do it."

Laz had not expected to feel reassured by her words; he was rarely reassured by anything. But it was nice to know he was on the right track. "And if something can be summoned, it can be bound, I'm guessing."

Cass nodded. "Anything can be bound." Neither of them looked at Tim. "It's a rope. The question is how much power you have to put into these things. Stone circles can be used to amplify power, and that along with large sacrifices has gotten a lot of people into a lot of trouble."

Laz looked down at the wooden work table. It was scarred from gardening implements and the passage of years, a patina of dirt and competency rubbed into it. "Thanks."

She nodded. "Take care, Lazarus. You look like you're about to go do something dumb."

"You could probably say that most of the time and be right," he said.

Cass laughed. Laz had other questions, about twenty or thirty of them, but since most of them were variations on 'Why is this my life?' he just got up. He already had his orders, after all. Complaining wasn't going to make any difference.

Chapter 19

L AZ WENT TO THE clinic just before 1700, knowing that he was already getting everything wrong. Not that there was a correct way to go around disappointing people.

The receptionist recognized him, which was a sign either that she was pretty good at her job or that the staff was deeply gossipy about the doctors' private lives. Possibly both. At any rate, it got him the information that Dr. Sobel was in his office.

He knocked, heart already racing. He hadn't slept well, and now everything felt raw around the edges, like his brain was full of too many feelings. He was about ten minutes away from some kind of episode.

Eli said, "Come in," so he went. The doctor grinned at him when he shut the door, then glanced at the old clock on the bookshelf. It was an ornate thing with exposed gears, and they needed to be polished. "You're early," Eli said. "I thought we said six."

"We did." Laz wanted to stay standing, but he wasn't in his CO's office receiving a dressing-down, and civilians tended to get uncomfortable and accuse him of looming, so he sat. "Unfortunately, something has come up, and I can't go out tonight."

He wasn't exactly sure what reaction he'd been expecting. Probably something negative. But instead, Eli kind of stilled and sat back. "What's happened?"

Laz cleared his throat. "We need to keep watch on the Fosters' house in case Burnsides and his goons show up, to say nothing of that snake thing. I'm taking the 1800 to 2400 shift again."

"I take it this is entirely Ulysses's plan?" Eli said levelly, and Laz was instantly on his guard.

"What do you mean?"

There was silence. Eli looked unhappy. "Why are you doing things this way?" he asked eventually.

Laz sat forward in his chair; not that he'd been relaxed before. "We can't just leave them."

"Right," Eli said. "But you're using them as bait."

Laz's stomach turned over. "What are you talking about?"

"Have you warned them?" A sigh at Laz's silence. "Why leave them in danger? You could as easily stake out an empty house."

"Do you think that if we turned up at the door with some crazy story of how their new, extremely expensive painting was cursed, they would take it calmly? They'd say, 'Oh yes, right you are, old chap. Just let us gather our mink coats and we'll decamp to our country estate whilst you keep an eye on things here'?" Laz was vaguely aware that his voice was getting louder, but it was Eli's widening eyes that forced him to rein himself in. "No. They'd have us thrown off their property at best and arrested for trespassing at worst. We don't have any proof. We don't have anything at all. Carla made *that* clear to me when she sold the painting to them."

Eli shook his head. "That's an excuse, Laz. You've not warned them because it'll be easier for Ulysses to figure out what's going on if he can see it in action, and to hell with the poor souls who get caught in the crossfire."

"It's not like that," Laz said. He was grabbing the arms of the chair.

"What is it like, Laz?" Eli asked. His voice was soft but persistent. Laz didn't like it at all. "Because it sounds like Ulysses has made a decision and you're going to follow his orders."

"No—" He felt the accusation like a blow to the stomach. "Is that what you think of me? That I'm just a soldier who does what he's told and doesn't think for himself?"

"I think you feel more comfortable when someone else makes decisions for you." Eli sounded—he sounded sad, goddamn it, which was not fair at all. "That's what soldiering is. That's how they get you to do so many terrible things, by conditioning you—"

"I didn't do terrible things!" Laz was on his feet. "I was search and rescue! Then I flew recon! I can't believe you would think—"

"The war itself is unethical, Laz. Just because you weren't out shooting people doesn't mean you weren't propping up something awful."

And there it was.

Laz thought about the prisoners of war, on both sides. He thought about the children who lived outside Tan Son Nhut and in Udon Thani, how happy they'd been when one of the airmen would sneak them a piece of candy. And he thought about Phra Nok and all the things he'd ever said about compassion. He closed his eyes as everything hit him like a freight train, anger and guilt, residual terror and the horrible, choking feeling of culpability. "South Vietnam is a real place, a country in and of itself," he managed, "and they need our help to defend against the imperialism of—"

"It's a civil war. The US has no business—"

"Because no one else is going to waste their time asking if they should or shouldn't be helping—"

"How many people have died needlessly because the US is unable to admit defeat? Not just Americans, Laz. The South Vietnamese are marching into battle after battle to be slaughtered. Their civilian population is paying the price."

Laz took a shaky breath, but there was no air left in the room. "I already fought in the war," he managed. "I'm not going to re-fight it with you." He turned around blindly, groping for the doorknob.

"Laz, wait—" He heard Eli push back his chair, but it was too late. He rushed down the hall to the staircase and out into the cold, amoral night.

He smoked two cigarettes on the drive over, window down despite the cold, radio blaring something by Stumbling Blindly. It was not exactly a surprise that Eli would say those things about the war. Laz would have guessed that he believed them, had he given it any thought at all; Sam and Ulysses probably believed them too, and Babushka's sympathies were almost certainly with the North. What stung was what Eli believed about Laz himself. The war was not Laz's fault. He had wound up there by accident, and he'd done the best he could.

Absurdly, he thought of a conversation with Mariah when he was seventeen. They'd been sitting in a café in Paris, one of those adorable little spots she favored that always seemed to be on the verge of closing, as though trying to attract customers was too bourgeois. He'd been offered a spot at the Air Force Academy, and Babushka didn't like the idea one bit.

"Of course you can do it, darling," Mariah had said, fitting a cigarette into the end of a long holder. "You are radically free. That means you can make whatever choice you want, so long as you can deal with the consequences."

He hadn't understood. Or perhaps he'd understood all too well. "Babushka will be angry," he'd said.

"She'll get over it. There's worse things that could happen than her grandchildren being Americans."

Radical freedom, as construed by Jean-Paul Sartre, was a trickier beast than Mariah let on. It meant Laz could join the Air Force if he was willing to deal with Babushka's continuing disapproval. Which he was, and he had. But people who refused their orders got court-martialed, sent to prison, stripped of their rank and benefits, and forced to resign.

Eli would probably have gone to prison. He was that type. A Conscientious Objector, emphasis on both pieces. Laz knew people like that, and he envied them the clarity of their convictions, because from where he was standing, nothing was ever as simple as it seemed to be when they were explaining it to him.

These days, Laz was pretty sure 'do what you're told or lose everything you value' wasn't any kind of choice at all, regardless of Sartre's feelings on the topic. That was why everyone—in his flight and every other one—kept making the same choice he had. And of course he couldn't have known where he'd wind up, exactly what he was losing, what he was gaining.

"Look, Ma," he muttered to himself. "I gave up existentialism for Buddhism. How do you like me now?"

He turned into the Highlands and flipped the radio off with an impatient gesture. There was a small side road around the corner from the Fosters' and he turned onto it and parked, getting as many wheels as he could on the grass under a low-hanging tree.

He remembered Phra Nok offering to tattoo him, even though he wasn't a very good Buddhist, didn't really know what he believed, was really maybe looking for a place to hang out and practice his Thai now that his tutor had moved away.

"Why?" Laz had asked at some point. Not right away. Later, after the first one was done.

"If you die tomorrow, you won't get to be a better Buddhist." Phra Nok had grinned at him.

The Fosters were probably objectively terrible people. They were definitely bourgeois, and they were not going to appreciate a warning, were almost certain to kick him out at best and call the cops at worst. But not telling them . . . maybe Eli was right. Maybe that was unconscionable. If Laz got a choice of what to do, they did too. And they needed information to do that.

The Highlands was a dark neighborhood. For some reason that surprised him; the area wasn't especially rural, despite all the big houses and golf-course lawns, but it had no streetlights. A few ambitious individuals had put up Christmas lights already, and they shone like tiny will-o'-the-wisps beyond the road.

Once he and Phra Nok had hiked from the Thai border almost all the way to Sisophon, which was something in the neighborhood of twenty miles, because they could not find a ride for anything. Phra Nok hadn't seemed too fussed about it—but then, he never really did. Laz had spent a lot of the walk meditating on the noble truth of the cessation of suffering.

Unfortunately, that required the cessation of desire, at least as far as he understood. Desire less, suffer less. And Laz was made entirely of desire. Because even now, he wanted Eli to approve of him, and he was going to bring a lot of suffering on himself from all angles to get it.

He got out, exhaling a cloud of smoke, and pulled his coat closer around him. It was a long stomp around the corner and up the driveway, and it was drizzling, which made everything more unpleasant. When he got to the end, he found an evergreen he could hide behind and did so, crushing out his cigarette and kicking old needles over the butt.

Just before 1900, a Lincoln Continental prowled down the driveway and into the garage. Laz watched. He had a moment of foresight—there was an unlocked window at the back of the house where the grade was lower. He was thin enough that he could crawl through, make his way upstairs—

No. He was going to do this the right way, and that required him to knock on the door, like he was going door to door. Excuse me, madam, have you heard the bad news about dybbukim?

He rang the doorbell and waited. After a minute, he heard heels on tile, and a moment later the door swung open. It was Mrs. Nadine Foster, in a pair of yellow slacks and a soft yellow cardigan. She looked at him curiously without speaking, head cocked to one side.

"Hi," he began awkwardly, aware that he looked like he'd been hanging around in the rain for an hour. Also, he was genuinely not sure what the best thing to say was. "I don't know if you remember me. I was here delivering your painting the other day."

She raised both eyebrows inquisitively, and he continued. "I have some bad news about it. May I come in? I'd like to talk to your husband as well."

She nodded and stepped back, then led him through the house along a vaguely familiar path to the wing with the painting. Mr. Fred Foster was there, sitting stiffly in a chair, a book open in his lap.

"Good evening," Laz said. Mr. Foster, who had been a friendly, jocular guy when they'd met, cocked his head to one side wordlessly. Now something was really starting to bother him about the two of them. "I'm here because I have some evidence that a group of criminals is using the S. Rochester paintings to target certain individuals."

Mr. Foster got to his feet, still holding the book, and took a step toward Laz. "What do you mean?"

"The painting is cursed, for lack of a better word, and . . ." Laz cleared his throat. "At least one other couple who bought one wound up possessed by dybbukim, which are a type of ghost, and later they died." He had not thought through the exact mechanism for this before, but now he felt like he was on the verge of putting something together. The stone circle and the paintings. . . . There was something important they'd all been overlooking, and it was why the paintings were cursed but not really cursed. "I realize that I'm a little low on specific details, but the threat is very real. If you'd come with me, my brother can—"

There was a flicker from behind him, and the room filled with a strange blue light. Laz froze.

"Tell me now," Mrs. Foster said. "Tell me about these ghosts."

ELI DIDN'T KNOW WHAT to do with himself after the fight. At seven, he pulled on his coat and left the clinic, walking slowly around the corner to the gallery. He wasn't sure why; Laz had told him where he was going. And of course the place was dark, the door locked.

He stood on State Street, the evening pedestrians swirling around him, and tried not to feel like the world had shifted in a way he didn't understand or care for. He only partially succeeded.

He and Laz had parted on good terms on Sunday. Better than good. Laz laughed at Eli's jokes, stole kisses when they were alone, slept pressed against Eli's side like he was starving for touch. Despite both him and Ulysses being so damn protective of Sam, he'd brought the giant to Eli to patch up. Laz was brave and stubborn and smart, and he cared about people. Eli thought of the sketched blueprint for the prosthetic arm—Laz had left it at Eli's place accidentally.

It was difficult to picture a world where things could turn so radically. Where Laz was unwilling to look at what he was doing. Where someone so intelligent was fine with being blatantly immoral. Where Laz had walked out.

Or was that wishful thinking because Eli had given his heart away too easily? He'd never thought of himself as the type to leap into things unthinking, yet here he was . . .

The next morning, things were even worse. The light of day made his thoughts bleaker; he was left with the sense that this was entirely his fault somehow, that he should have phrased his objections better, should have come up with a different way to approach the subject. Should have, should have. The worst was that he'd set Laz's private landmines off, and he'd sworn to himself he wasn't going to do that again.

He thought at first that he would go around to the gallery at lunch, just to see, but someone had a seizure in the waiting room, and he had a new patient with a tremor to work up, and two migraine patients, and the chap with bradykinesia, and suddenly it was late in the afternoon and he had barely paused to think about lunch, let alone Laz.

It was an old trick, long perfected in response to heartbreaks of the past. And he would have gone on that way, working himself into the ground for a few months, except that at five thirty, after a grueling half hour spent explaining abdominal migraine to a teenage patient's mother, he went back to his office to sit down and found it occupied by Sam and Ulysses.

Sam had burrowed into one of the visitor chairs, legs folded neatly to take up the least amount of space someone that tall could occupy. Ulysses was pacing. More than anything else, that was what set off the little alarm bells in the back of Eli's head.

"What's happened?" he asked, dropping an armload of charts on the desk. He hoped it was just Sam's sutures looking a bit off.

"Where's Laz?" Ulysses asked, his usual charm absent in the face of whatever anxiety was driving his motion.

Eli stared at him. "What?"

"He wasn't at the Fosters' to report when I arrived at midnight. But I knew he'd been irritated with me, and we were a few minutes late. I assumed he'd run off to see you," Ulysses explained, the words delivered rapid-fire. "He wasn't at the house this morning, either, which seemed to confirm my hypothesis that he'd spent the night at your place. But when I went to the gallery to debrief him about last night, it turned out he never showed up to work."

The alarms got louder. Eli shut his eyes, just for a second. "He—he came by here yesterday around five o'clock to tell me he'd be spending the evening out at the Fosters' place. We quarreled. I haven't seen him since."

Ulysses nodded, face tense. "Thanks, Doc."

Sam was on his feet, unfurling like the mainsail of a ship, and Ulysses had a hand on the doorknob before Eli said, "Wait. I'm coming too." He got up and pulled his jacket off the peg, abandoning his white coat in its place. "We can take my car."

The whole drive out, Eli could feel the frustration welling

up within him. He didn't know if he was angry at Ulysses for suggesting the stakeout in the first place, or at Laz for going along with it, or himself, somehow, for general failure.

When they piled out of the car, he got a look at Ulysses's face and guessed he was probably thinking the same things about himself that Eli was. Sam looked sick to his stomach.

They found Laz's car parked around the corner from the house, partially pulled off the road into a thicket. It was covered with rain drops and wet leaves, the detritus of a night and a day outside. Eli didn't think he'd ever felt quite such a sense of dismay over something so normal as a car parked by the roadside.

"What do you reckon?" he asked, as they made their way toward the house.

Sam was wearing that long coat that swirled dramatically around his ankles as he walked. "Those ghosts you mentioned," he said, glancing sidelong at Ulysses. "Dybbukim."

"But they're folklore," Eli protested. "I only meant what happened to the Greenfields had a few similarities."

"Maybe," Ulysses allowed. "But I've been neck-deep in Jewish mysticism for two days, and I think you were on to something."

Eli felt his brows draw together. Ulysses's face looked thin and knackered in the wan light from his electric torch. Perhaps he hadn't been sleeping much, between his research and his teaching and his illegal surveillance activities. "In what way was I on to something?" he asked, trying to keep his voice level.

"I'd never encountered ghosts that possessed people. In fact, the phenomenon doesn't seem to exist in the literature until the Renaissance. Coincidentally when there were a lot of magicians—Johannes Trithemius and John Dee, for example—trying to figure out how to summon and bind various types of demons. The dybbukim aren't that, exactly, but they seem to have the abilities of some kind of lesser deity or spirit . . ."

"A daimon?" Sam suggested.

Eli, who had worked hard to forget what little Greek he'd ever had drummed into him, looked at him blankly. Ulysses considered the word more seriously. "It's as good a term as any."

"Taxonomy aside," Eli said, "your thought is that someone found and loosed something that could possess people?"

"It's not impossible." Ulysses cleared his throat. "There seem to have been a number of stories dating from the same era detailing different types of possession. Some were considered positive and even invited by Jewish mystics, like possession by the dead souls of sages for the purpose of instruction. Others were similar to a living person's soul being overwritten by that of the dead."

"That's what we're assuming happened to the Greenfields?"

Ulysses hesitated, then nodded. "The dybbukim seized both Greenfields and then killed them on departure."

His voice was grim. Eli didn't like it. "You seem to have done a lot of research," he said slowly "Any idea how to get rid of them?"

They stopped under a stand of trees adjacent to the house, and Ulysses lowered his voice. "As you suggested, the texts are rather light on that particular detail."

"Of course."

Sam kicked at the pine needles beneath their feet. "Seems like an important omission."

"Perhaps the—" Ulysses broke off with a noise of surprise and crouched down. "Look," he said, uncovering a cigarette butt.

Sam also peered at it. "Is Laz smoking filters now?"

Eli couldn't remember, and suddenly he had to take a step away from the two of them to breathe. There was something about being in this strange, dark, cold place, with two people he barely knew, that left him feeling helpless and shaken. His heart raced at the thought of what might have happened to Laz; his chest was tight.

Sam put a hand on his shoulder. "We're going to check the house," he murmured. "Are you coming?"

Eli made a concerted attempt to pull himself together. "Yes." He stared at the house, which was dark, as though no one were home. "How do we get inside? Do you think they know? Will they just let us in?"

"If they won't," Ulysses began, one hand in the pocket of his jacket pulling out something that looked rather like a jack knife. Then he seemed to remember that Eli was there and hid it again up his sleeve. "Doc, I'm sorry, but this could get a little illegal."

"Should we call the police?" Eli asked, knowing it was a useless, stupid question, but feeling he had to ask anyway.

Ulysses laughed, but it was a hard, unhappy sound. "No. What are they going to do?"

Eli had to admit that something felt wrong as they approached the house, but he couldn't put a finger on what. There was nothing unusual about a house with no one home. And yet the hairs on the back of his neck were prickling.

They went to the front door and dutifully rang the bell.

No one answered.

"Let's try the back door," Ulysses said, starting around the house.

"Do you think Jimmy Stewart is watching?" Sam muttered, and his husband huffed out a laugh in the dark.

There was a wan, blue light in one of the windows. Initially, Eli assumed it was a television, but there was something wrong about the flicker rate. Ulysses walked over and looked in. "It's the painting," he said, and led them around to the back door.

Eli saw him try the doorknob and get nowhere. "Shall we break the window?"

Ulysses fished something small out of his pocket. "We can be a little more elegant than that." He glanced at Eli, then—skeptically—at Sam. "Try to look like you're not waiting to break in."

There was a silence while they watched him lean one shoulder against the back door and shove a thin piece of metal into the lock. His posture was casual, but the concentration needed to open the lock showed on his face.

Eli shook his head. "When we first met, I thought you two were respectable."

"Really?" Sam sounded excited.

Ulysses didn't look over at them, even though he must have been working by feel in the dim light. "I knew taking this job was a mistake," he grumbled. "People hear you're a professor, that's the first thing they assume." There was a click and the door swung open.

The house was an American attempt to copy the stately homes that dotted the English countryside. High ceilings, elegant molding, solid European furniture. In one room they passed, he thought he glimpsed a pair of Louis XV chairs, doubtlessly replicas, but annoying for what they represented. It was like someone had read *Pride and Prejudice* and decided what they really wanted wasn't a single man possessed of a good fortune but Pemberley.

The Fosters' gallery was lit with an eerie blue-green light that did appear to be emanating from the Rochester.

Sam stepped toward the painting, curious, and then hissed, grabbing for his chest. Eli watched him yank irritably on a chain until he'd fished that little glass nazar from his shirt.

"What?" Ulysses asked without looking over.

"I don't know. Something magic, and not benign." Sam bit his lip. "I guess that's not exactly news."

Ulysses held a hand up to the surface of the painting. "I think it's a portal," he breathed.

"It's a *what*?" Eli asked.

"A door," Ulysses said, "to somewhere else. There's a little world in there."

Eli was trying to look at the actual painting, rather than its glowing surface, because it was different than it had been. Some of the foliage was bent, as though an animal had tracked through the scene, and there was something on the edge of the scene that looked like—"Is that Laz's jacket?"

Ulysses had to take a step backward to see it. "Shit." He glanced over at Sam, frowning. "I wonder why he didn't come back this way."

If he wasn't hurt, if he wasn't captured, if he wasn't—

Sam said, "Do you think there's another entrance?"

Ulysses shrugged. "There might be. That would explain how Burnsides and his gang managed to vanish out of the gallery."

Eli felt a sudden burst of insight. "The stone circle, maybe? When we were attacked and it dragged me into the central part, the summoning circle, it felt like . . ." He faltered, worried that he hadn't felt what he'd thought he'd felt, that he was describing it wrong. "It felt like a jungle," he finished weakly.

Ulysses gave him a long look, then glanced at Sam. "Can you meet us there?"

"Ulysses!" Sam's face was awash with emotions, outrage and fear alongside something deep and wry, as though he'd almost been expecting this. "I'm not going to leave you!"

"We don't need to bet the farm on this," Ulysses said. He looked at Eli. "Keys."

Eli fished them out of his pocket and offered them up. Sam looked affronted, and Ulysses took the key ring and drew Sam away by one elbow.

Then they bickered, and Eli stared at the wall and pretended he couldn't hear everything that was being said. The key points on Ulysses's side were that Sam was already injured and didn't need to risk himself further, and that Ulysses needed someone to stay on the outside who could get help if necessary. Sam, for his part, was unwilling to send Ulysses in with someone who had no experience at watching his back. To this, Ulysses pointed out that Eli was a doctor, and there was a reasonable chance Laz had been injured and would need medical attention.

Eli recognized the concluding tone of voice, the calm way that Ulysses restated his case over Sam's objections, and kissed him, pressing the keys into his hand. Finally, Sam subsided, glowering, and Ulysses came back to stand in front of the painting.

"All set?" Eli asked dryly.

"No sense in waiting," Ulysses murmured. "See you on the other side."

From their perspective, it was as though he took one step and then stood a rather far distance away. Before, it had been difficult to discern the scale of the ziggurat and the plants, but with Ulysses in the painting, Eli could tell that they were large.

Eli looked over at Sam, whose face was still drawn. "I'll—whatever I can."

Sam sighed and waved him off. "I'll see you on the other side," he said. "Take care."

"Thanks," Eli said. Then, turning back to the painting in front of them, he took a single long step.

Chapter 20

For TRAVELING INTO A work of art—another dimension, supplied the part of his brain that had grown up on science fiction serials—the journey was surprisingly short and painless. He stepped, eyes closed, and then suddenly he was standing in a different place, beset by dizziness that brought him to his knees in the soft earth.

He opened his eyes. He was in a jungle. A proper jungle, or at least it felt like one. The air was thick and humid, heavy with the promise of coming rain; it smelled of earth and fresh green sap. The ground was soft beneath his feet. Somewhere in front of him slouched the ziggurat, huge, mossy, rough. His eyes followed the steps of it up to the peak silhouetted against the cloudy sky. He heard Ulysses call, "Over here, Doc!" and made his way toward the voice.

Ulysses had picked up Laz's jacket. A few steps away, crushed into the soft soil, Eli spotted Laz's mala. "Oh dear," he murmured, kneeling. The cord had snapped, but the beads were all still present, and he scooped them up, wrapping them in his handkerchief.

"What's that?" Ulysses crouched next to him. "Those love beads he's always fiddling with?"

"Not love beads," Eli said, feeling unexpectedly annoyed. He pushed the emotion down. "It's a rosary."

"Did he tell you—" Ulysses hesitated, sounding uncertain. "He's not Catholic."

"It's a Buddhist rosary." Eli picked up the last little bead and turned it in his fingers, then dropped the lot into his pocket. "For what it's worth, he didn't explain it to me. He's just not the first Buddhist I've ever met."

Ulysses sighed and got to his feet. "More things on heaven and on earth, Horatio . . ."

"Sorry?" Eli stood as well and looked around, trying to see any signs that might reveal where Laz had gone. It all just looked like jungle. When he turned back in the direction he thought he'd come from, there was more jungle.

"I just mean that it's good, sometimes, to remember how parochial my life has been compared to Laz's." He fell silent for a moment, looking down at the jacket he was holding. There was a spatter of blood on it.

When he looked up again, his gaze met Eli's, sad and worried.

"He'll—" Eli looked again at the blood and exhaled. "I know it looks bad, but it's not that much." That didn't sound very helpful. He thought about Laz's tattoos, the protection he'd said they offered if you were careful what you asked for. "Where do we go now?"

Ulysses looked around, frowning. At last he pointed at a spot in the undergrowth that looked like all the rest of it. "There, that way."

Eli stepped aside. "You'd better lead."

"All right." Ulysses started down the—it wasn't really a path, just a spot where Ulysses seemed to think Laz had gone—and Eli followed. "You're taking this well," Ulysses said after a moment. "One would think you crawled into paintings every day."

"I spent six months working as a locum in the emergency room at Cook County Hospital in Chicago." Eli said. "No one is screaming. No one has been shot. Everyone's blood is still mostly inside them." He shrugged, uneasy but moving forward. "I'll fall apart later."

"I can't figure out how this happened," Ulysses said after they'd been walking for a while. It was slow going, because of the closeness of the undergrowth and Ulysses's lack of confidence in picking out Laz's line of flight. They'd had to backtrack a few times, which didn't help their shared concern. Eli had been on the verge of suggesting they try quartering the brush instead of following the path single file when Ulysses broke the silence.

"What do you mean?" Eli asked. "Surely the dybbukim caught him and dragged him in."

"Surely," Ulysses echoed. "But he was supposed to watch the house, not go inside it. Call for backup if he saw anything. He told me there's a payphone around the corner." He inhaled, considering. "I didn't notice any signs that he broke in. They must have gotten the drop on him somehow. I can't think how they would have known he was there."

Eli's eyes widened. "What if he went up to talk to the couple, the Fosters? Tried to warn them?"

"And it was already too late?" He heard Ulysses crack a couple of his knuckles. "I didn't tell him to do anything like that."

Eli's mouth was abruptly dry, but he forced himself to take a breath and say, "No, I told him . . ."

Ulysses stopped walking. "Eli."

"I told you we quarreled. When he explained the plan to me, I said I thought it was unethical not to warn them." He grimaced against the twisting in his stomach.

There was a long silence, an extended moment of Ulysses staring at him. Eli felt a frustrating, heady rush of anger mixed with a total inability to be of any assistance. Ulysses had been wrong, continued to be wrong, but Eli wasn't in a position to do anything about it. He couldn't do magic, knew nothing about curses, and hadn't been invited to the stakeout. But Eli was right. But it didn't matter anymore.

What Ulysses said though, was, "You two are close."

Eli blinked. "I suppose," he said. "But I don't . . . I mean . . . you've known him for far longer, surely. You're his brother." He spread his hands in some kind of wordless plea.

"Yeah." Ulysses sounded sad. He turned and started moving again, and after a moment Eli followed him.

Eventually they reached a footpath of sorts. Not exactly a clearly broken trail, but something. The humidity was endlessly oppressive, especially in contrast to the Wisconsin cold they'd just left, and Eli was compiling a growing list of anxieties: what if Laz was hurt, what if they'd guessed wrong and there wasn't a way out, what if they couldn't find Laz, what if the dybbukim found them first . . .

The undergrowth was still very close. Even walking hard behind Ulysses, Eli was getting hit by branches. "I blame you for this," he muttered after the third time left him scratched, anger mounting. He felt sticky, not so much sweaty as just covered with humidity that had condensed directly out of the air onto his skin.

Ulysses shrugged. "You decided to come, Doc."

He snorted. "What was I supposed to do?"

"That's usually my line." They took a few more steps. "Look, Laz isn't helpless. Far from it."

"I'm sure he'd be in his element if he were flying," Eli snapped.

That was right about when they found the jumper. It was red, the one Laz had been wearing when he'd come to Eli's office. It had been hung across a branch.

"See," Ulysses said. "He's fine."

"Is that what this proves?"

They stared at each other.

"Did you notice," Eli said, picking the jumper up. "It's so quiet here." He clutched it to his chest. There was something damp on the sleeve; he pressed his fingers to it and felt stricken when they came away bloody. A hole high on the arm corresponded roughly with one in the coat.

Ulysses glanced around. "Now that you mention it."

There were no birds or insects, no small creatures in the undergrowth that hopped away as they approached. Was it because they were actually within a painting? Eli peered at the broad leaves they were passing; they looked like leaves, had the thick, slightly rubbery feel he associated with certain types of plants. Perhaps they were somewhere wholly alien, and plants and monsters were the only things in the environment, but that seemed unlikely, given what he knew about ecosystems.

"This can't be a place," he said finally.

Ulysses looked back at him. "What do you mean?"

"It's created." He reached out and turned a leaf over, tried to decide if the variations in color were genuine striations or brush marks. "It has plants because the painting did, but only the types of plants that we could see from the portal." He shook his head.

Ulysses reached out himself and carefully snapped part of one of the broad leaves off. The edge gleamed wetly, but when Eli ran a finger along it, there was no sap. "I think I'd like to get out of here," Ulysses said at last, and glanced back the way they'd come. "If there's no animals here, we have to worry about what made this path, and when something else might traverse it."

They went on. Eli was sweat-soaked and miserable, legs aching, feet aching. They were, roughly, crossing and recrossing a vast swath of jungle characterized by dense undergrowth punctuated by large ferns and trees. Occasionally, they stumbled over a piece of clothing—Laz's hat and one glove, his bloodied undershirt. Laz hadn't been going in a straight line so much as wandering—perhaps trying to get the lay of the land, leaving the clothes not for someone to follow but as a marker of where he'd been. Hopefully not trying to distract something that was following him.

And then, just when Eli was beginning to think they were going to continue trekking across an unending jungle forever, they tumbled out into a clearing. There were small, scrubby plants in hard dirt for about twenty meters leading up to a natural wall of large rocks. At the far end of this space was Laz, shirtless, sweaty, bloodied, his back to them as he peered around the end of the wall toward whatever was on the other side.

Eli pushed past Ulysses and crashed across the clearing. Laz must have heard his footsteps and whipped around holding a knife, all taut caution and incipient violence, and in a wild moment Eli realized he really should not sneak up on someone who was quite so freshly out of the military. But then recognition crossed Laz's face, and a flurry of other emotions too. For the space of a few breaths, they stared at each other.

"I'm—Laz, I'm so sorry," Eli said. And then, both a surprise and a relief, Laz closed the distance between them and threw his arms around Eli's neck.

❧ ❧

LAZ KNEW THAT HE must be quite a picture: wild-eyed, covered with sweat and blood, stinking of the future. Eli didn't seem to notice, just hugged him, muttering quiet words of apology and regret into his neck. Laz shut his eyes and forgot about everything else, focusing for just a moment on the person in his arms.

Ulysses crossed the open space more cautiously. When Laz felt he could no longer delay, he carefully detached himself from Eli and stepped forward to receive his dressing-down.

Ulysses was carrying some of Laz's things and scowling, which was felt very normal and grounding. "How are you?" he asked.

Laz could only shake his head. "The Fosters had already been possessed, but I didn't realize that until after they'd let me in."

Eli looked aghast. "Oh my god, Laz."

"They dragged me into the painting. We fought and I escaped. But I think they only abandoned the chase because there's no way out of here." He took a deep breath. "How long has it been?"

Ulysses looked perplexed, as though he'd entirely given up on time as a concept, but Eli checked his watch and said, "A bit more than a day. Close to thirty hours now, probably."

"Jesus." Laz frowned, trying to piece things together. "It doesn't feel like that." He took his jacket back from Ulysses. "The light here doesn't change."

Eli looked rough. "We didn't realize you were missing at first. I'm so sorry."

"It's . . ." He trailed off, not sure what he should say. "You're here now," is what he eventually concluded. "Unfortunately."

"Where are the dybbukim?" Ulysses asked.

Laz motioned with his head. "Around there. About an eighth of a mile off."

Ulysses snorted, shoving Laz's coat back into his hands. "An eighth of a mile, eh?" But he went to peer around the corner anyway.

Eli, meanwhile, was ripping the undershirt Laz had abandoned into strips with the help of Laz's knife.

"What's that for?"

"Your arm." He stood up and steered Laz until he was leaning against the rock face. "It's not ideal, but it'll keep you from doing yourself any further damage until we can get it cleaned up."

"Sure."

Eli was silent for a moment, focusing on the injury. "You went to warn them?" he said at last.

"I thought about it and decided you were right. Radical freedom and all that." He tried to grin at Eli, hoping it came out right.

Eli's fingers stilled on Laz's bicep. "It . . . what?"

"Radical freedom? There was this guy, Jean-Paul Sartre, and he said—"

Something complicated was happening with Eli's face. "I know who Sartre is. I just—"

Laz was already leaning toward Eli, and it took just an extra few inches to brush his lips against the doctor's. To his gratified surprise, Eli inhaled sharply and kissed him back, pushing him against the rock face, one hand on Laz's uninjured shoulder. Laz put a hand gently on Eli's hip, steadying him.

A moment later there was a huff from beside them and then Ulysses's voice, exasperated: "There's a time and a place."

"As though he'd know about either," Laz muttered against Eli's lips, before reluctantly releasing him. He turned to his brother to find an embarrassed expression on his face, like he wasn't quite sure where to look. "What did you find out?" Laz asked, just to put him out of his misery.

"The Fosters and the serpent are there." He tapped his fingers against the rock face. "I see a circle of stones that looks very similar to the summoning circle. I assume that's the back door we theorized."

To Laz's consternation, Eli replied, "Do you have what you'd require to open the portal?" As though Ulysses had been talking to him. Which apparently he had.

"I think so." Ulysses rubbed his jaw. "Just need to get them away from it."

Eli nodded. "How long?"

"A few minutes."

Laz was pretty sure he was losing his mind. Eli was nodding and saying, "Can you and Laz circle around behind while I distract them?"

"Hold on there," Laz said. "Do you have a weapon?"

Eli patted his pockets and came up with a penlight, a tuning fork, and a reflex hammer.

Laz sighed. "I'll go with him," he told his brother. "You do the spellcraft. When you're ready, we'll just . . . sprint. All right?"

Ulysses shrugged. He didn't look any happier about the situation than Laz felt, but they didn't have a lot of other options. Laz picked up his knife and spun it. He felt Eli's eyes on him and looked up to see a fond expression on the doctor's face. Impulsively, Laz grabbed his hand, and they went around the corner together.

Chapter 21

ELI WAS TERRIFIED, BUT he decided not to mention it.

Laz's face went mask-like as they approached the creatures, his hand tight on the handle of the knife. "What's your plan?" he muttered.

"I'm going to ask them politely to let us leave."

He could physically feel Laz reevaluating their relationship. "Really?"

"Why not?"

Laz sighed. "It's weirdly British of you to assume that there's some reasonableness lurking within them that can be summoned by being polite."

"We don't lose anything by being polite," Eli said.

"Except valuable time and the element of surprise."

He licked his lips. "Do you want to try to fight all three of them? We've a knife and a reflex hammer between us. And I, for one, am not trained in hand-to-hand combat."

"Why not?"

Eli decided not to dignify that with a response. "How long does Ulysses need to get into position?" he asked instead.

Laz shrugged. "Not too long." The jungle stuck out like an arm wrapped around the clearing, and Ulysses was doubtless making his way through that stretch toward a spot from which he could approach the circle of stones from behind. Eli thought he spotted Ulysses moving through the trees parallel to them, then lost him in the shadows.

"Does this remind you of Asia?" he asked, and then immediately regretted it, but Laz just looked around speculatively.

"The weather is right, but—I don't know if you know this, Doc, they have a lot of cities in both Thailand and Vietnam."

Eli sighed. "I probably deserved that."

"You definitely did." They were getting close to the creatures, and Eli had to fight back a moment of horror. Whether they were or weren't dybbukim seemed like a rather insignificant distinction. Two of the beings were human, or at least they were wearing human bodies and therefore looked . . . well, normal, except that there was something odd and uncomfortable about the way they were standing, as though they had seen others do it but never actually tried it themselves. And then there was the third.

Last time, coming across the serpent in the dark, he'd only really seen it in pieces. He'd tried to tell himself he'd not seen it at all. But there it was, longer than he was tall and holding part of its front end off the ground, as though it was listening to the conversation the others were having. Laz hissed under his breath when he saw this and gripped Eli's hand more tightly.

The serpent's back was dark brown, with irregular black patches that might have looked like rocks or leaves in low light. Its underbelly was a bright, glorious red. And its dark, sclera-less eyes were focused directly on Eli. He straightened his spine and took his hand back from Laz.

"Hello," he said to it, since it somehow seemed to be, if not in charge, then at least there to greet them. "Could I have a word with you?"

The serpent said—something, more a hiss than anything that sounded communicative, but the noise reverberated in Eli's head like microphone feedback. He flinched back, clutching Laz's jumper like a shield. It was the woman who came closer. "What is it you wish, human?"

The way she moved was unnerving—no, it was myopathic. She was dropping her hips as she walked. In humans, this was often caused by a weak pelvic girdle. But the movement was much, much weirder than he'd ever seen. Maybe that was what it was like to move with a snake stuffed inside you. "Ah, hello. I'm Eli, this is Lazarus. Are you still Mrs. Foster in there?"

Mrs. Foster shrugged. "This body is myriad. The name is not important."

Oh dear. Eli swallowed hard. "Very well. We'd like to leave. Laz has been injured, and I'd like to take care of him."

Mrs. Foster looked at Laz, and somewhere hell froze over. "He has intruded in things that are not his business." She turned back to Eli. "We cannot permit you to leave." The snake was slithering toward them now. Eli heard Laz's breathing change, could almost sense the hand tightening on the knife. Eli reached out without looking and put a hand on Laz's arm to steady him.

"Can *you* leave?" Eli asked. "Without being summoned or commanded, I mean. Are you being held here?"

Mrs. Foster didn't respond right away, and when she did, it wasn't really an answer: "We are waiting."

"If you're being held against your will, perhaps we can help," he said. Laz hissed something and pushed, starting him walking again.

Mrs. Foster shook her head. "Even if we believed that, we would not strike a deal with humans."

"Eli," Laz said in a low voice. "This is—"

"You don't believe we can help? Is that it?" Eli asked, turning so he was still facing Foster. The serpent was getting quite close now, and Laz dragged him back a step, then another. "Or you don't want our help? Because I can assure you that while humans have been, well, frankly we have a terrible track record about keeping people in bondage, but we're also quite good at liberation, sometimes. I personally happen to be a big believer in liberation."

"We will not bandy words with you, human," Mrs. Foster said, and twitched the fingers of her right hand.

The serpent lunged before Eli could say anything else. Laz spun the two of them, putting his body between it and Eli, and then Ulysses got the portal open.

Eli had wondered how they'd know when it had happened. The end in the Fosters' house was quiet, and although the flickering light had been noticeable in the dark, he didn't think it would have been especially bright in the daytime. Fortunately, the internal one was like a bomb going off—that, or Ulysses was being flashy with it. Laz hit the dirt and brought Eli with him, shouting. Before the dust had time to settle, Laz was pulling him up, dragging him toward the circle. Eli could hear feet on the ground behind them as they ran, but far more frightening was the noise that he couldn't hear of the serpent moving toward them, fast and implacable.

The circle was much less interesting than he'd imagined, just eight roundish stones the size of footballs in a circle. Ulysses had scribbled on several of them with chalk, and the area within the stones had transformed into a strange, churning opacity. Ulysses was waiting for them at the edge.

"Come on," he shouted as Laz hesitated, looking over one shoulder like he was about to turn and make a stand. Eli shoved him hard and watched him vanish into the circle, then followed him through, Ulysses on his heels.

They tumbled out into the ring of standing stones. Light poured out of the portal behind them, painting everything in the clearing flat and strange. Laz was waiting, half-panicked, as Eli came through, ready to grab him by the arm and urge him to his feet. A moment later, Ulysses did something and the light vanished.

Eli made it all of three steps before his stomach turned over and he had to drop onto the dead, wet, frozen leaves littering the ground. He could feel Laz looking down at him uncertainly as he retched.

He ran out of steam quickly. There wasn't much in his stomach to surrender, and the unpleasant giddiness from the translocation faded almost as soon as it had arrived. Eli sat back on his heels and wiped his face on one sleeve.

It was dark and shockingly cold here after the warmth of the painting. The tops of the trees surrounding them tossed back and forth in the wind. High, thin clouds scudded past a waning moon. And they were out. He was free.

He was free.

Laz crouched down next to him. "You good?"

Eli held up a hand and waggled it side to side. Laz made a noise halfway between a cough and a laugh. "You?" Eli asked.

Laz tilted his head to one side. At some point, he'd put the bomber jacket back on but not the jumper, and his bare chest was exposed to the cold night air. "You know—"

There was a whoop, which made Laz jump, and Eli looked around to see Sam unfolding stork-like from the edge of the woods to embrace Ulysses. Eli looked away. Laz wordlessly wrapped an arm around his waist and pulled Eli into him. Eli looked down at his own hands and found he was shaking. Maybe Laz was trembling too.

Eli could hear Ulysses and Sam talking without really being able to parse what they were saying. His watch said it was just past ten o'clock; they'd been gone for five or six hours. It felt like much, much longer. And lord knew how Laz felt—he'd been in there for more than a day, without food or water. He could practically see the moment Laz realized the same thing, the way the fatigue crashed down over him now that the danger had passed.

Eli took a deep breath. "Want to go home?" he murmured. Laz glanced at him and he shrugged, too tired to feel uncomfortable about the implicit assumption. "I mean—my place. I can make sandwiches or something."

"Yeah," Laz said, with much less hesitation than Eli had expected, considering everything. "That sounds nice."

⟫⟫⟩ ⟨⟨⟨⟨

L AZ WOKE UP TO the sound of voices from the next room. No, one voice, speaking at intervals that suggested a telephone. Something about seizures. He rolled over and looked for the clock. 0430.

Eli, with characteristic efficiency, had watched Laz drink about half a gallon of cold, delicious water, made the two of them grilled cheese sandwiches, and then taken him up to bed, where he'd immediately collapsed.

Eli's bed was very comfortable and warm, and he didn't really want to move. He propped himself up on his elbows. If Eli was leaving, was he supposed to go? Should he get up and find his clothes?

Before he could work up a full head of steam, Eli came back into the room. Laz could see him in the dim light from the clock as he crossed to the far side of the bed and untied the belt of his robe, his slender form shirtless in the dim room for a moment.

"What's up?" Laz managed.

Eli slid back under the covers. "Nothing. Someone had a question. I didn't mean to wake you." He gently pressed on Laz's shoulder until he was lying down again, then threw an arm across his chest and slid closer until the distance between them had collapsed. Eli's skin was slightly cool from having been out of bed, but the places they were pressed together warmed quickly.

"You don't have to go in?" It was a ridiculous, needy question. Laz only let it slip because he was still half-asleep, probably.

"No. I might go round in the morning. It's nothing urgent." One of those slow, calm nighttime silences ticked by, and Laz started to relax. "Feeling better?" Eli asked quietly.

He was. He felt scrubbed off—metaphorically, anyway. Not fixed, but shined up, all his screws tightened. "I—yeah," he managed, running his hand along Eli's arm. "Thanks."

"I didn't do anything," Eli protested. "I just dragged you back here and put you to bed. You're the one who decided to listen to my foolish advice."

It wasn't quite an apology, but Laz recognized what Eli meant. He took a deep breath. "I just wanted everything to have been worth it. All the sacrifices. All the . . ." He broke off, unsure of what he was trying to say, and unwilling to bring all those ghosts into this room by naming them. "But I couldn't save them."

"You tried."

"Tried," Laz said scornfully. "Tried and failed. You're off saving lives every day, and I'm not—I didn't—"

"None of that is your job," Eli said, pushing himself up on his elbows, as though that would give him a better look at Laz's expression in the dim room. "I do what I'm trained to do just as much as you ever did."

"Just shut up and take the compliment, would you?" Over Eli's laughter, he continued, "You're so consistently delightful and clever, and I—man, I am a grade-A mess, and I don't know why you're here." His heart was pounding as he finished, and he was suddenly happy for the darkness, because he couldn't have dealt with being able to see whatever was going on with Eli's face at that.

"Other than I happen to live here?" Eli asked.

"Eli—"

"I know what you mean," Eli said. "I just don't know if I have a good answer for you. You're handsome, sexy, smart, brave, you can fix anything . . . I think you actually have a lot of qualities that recommend you." He hesitated.

"I started out looking at you like you were a puzzle that I could somehow solve. And I found that I couldn't, not really, but by the time I'd figured that out, I was falling in love with you."

Laz inhaled sharply, and Eli shifted. "Sorry, I should have known that would freak you out."

"No, it's—I'm not—"

"I can feel your pulse racing," Eli said, pressing down on Laz's breastbone for emphasis.

"For fuck's sake, Eli," Laz muttered, and with one relatively smooth move rolled them both over so that Eli was pinned beneath him. "You just have to give me a minute to collect myself when you go around saying that kind of thing."

"I didn't mean to cause distress," Eli said, but his tone was a little mischievous now, and he had his hands on Laz's hips, urging him closer. Laz kissed him, kissed the side of his neck just below the ear, his collarbone, grazed a nipple with his thumb, replaced that with his lips and listened to the noises Eli made and the way his breathing sped up. Eli's skin tasted deliciously salty, and Laz licked a stripe down his body, heard Eli's quiet laugh as he squirmed.

Eli tugged at Laz's hair, and Laz moved back up, feeling Eli's breath ghosting over his face for a moment before their lips met.

Eli gasped against his mouth when Laz stroked his hard-on through his briefs, hips pitching up toward his hand, so Laz did it again. Eli's clever hands were on Laz's body, tugging at his waistband, so he pulled back long enough to scramble out of the rest of his clothing. Eli threw a leg over his hips and pulled him closer, friction and warmth building between them faster now that there was nothing but bare skin.

"What," Laz said, and then broke off with a choked noise as Eli rubbed up against him, his erection hot and urgent against Laz's. He tried again: "What do you want?"

He couldn't really see Eli's face in the light from the clock, but he could feel his hands as they stilled for a moment, then stroked Laz's dick again, lazily. "I believe I'd like you to fuck me," he murmured, punctuating his words with a tug that made Laz close his eyes in pleasure.

"Sure," Laz said. He felt flushed from head to toe, slightly frantic at the request. "I can—yes. Do you—?"

Eli twisted half onto his side to search for something in the nightstand, and then pressed a jar of something slippery into his hand along with a murmured invitation.

He was achingly hard by the time he was inside Eli, the other man's fingers digging into his back, body tight beneath him. And the heat, and the—everything. For a few seconds he didn't move, barely dared to breathe, face buried in Eli's neck. Then Eli rolled his hips a little and Laz pulled himself together, burying the strange sacredness of the moment somewhere deep inside of himself. He thrust, and felt Eli respond, and then kept going. And somehow this was something they were doing together, moving in something like synchrony up along a steep parabolic curve.

He tried not to collapse directly on top of Eli afterward, but his limbs were rubbery and hard to control, his heart kicking like mad. Eli laughed and pulled Laz down, hugging him.

Laz felt sticky and sweaty and content. He still didn't know exactly what to say. 'I love you' felt inadequate, and 'you make me want to continue living' felt a little too heavy and dramatic. He had no intuition about this, no ideas about what might be the best answer. Eventually, he said, "I still don't entirely understand why you would, but I'm yours, if you want me. I have been for a while." He shut his eyes when he said it, and hoped Eli understood what he meant.

Eli curled up bonelessly against him, forehead on his shoulder, one leg draped over Laz's hips. "Wow," he said after a moment. "That was hardly self-deprecating at all. We'll make an optimist of you yet."

Laz grinned into the darkness. "Don't get your hopes up."

Chapter 22

L AZ WOKE UP ALONE in the late morning. He vaguely remembered Eli leaving at some point, with a kiss and a whispered reassurance.

He took the time to shower before he wandered downstairs, surprised that Eli was not in the kitchen until he saw the morning paper on the table. It was Wednesday; Eli was at work.

That mystery solved, Laz made himself a cup of coffee and sat down. Luria came in, sniffed one of his feet, and went over to her dish, which was empty. She sniffed it and then looked at him, meowing.

"I don't know where he keeps your food," Laz said. "Also, I'm guessing he already fed you and you're trying to con me."

She meowed again, then lost interest in him. He sipped his coffee and skimmed the paper. The war continued to grind on without him, a fact he had almost come to terms with. An attempt to rescue POWs had failed with the revelation that the captives had been moved. Peace talks were temporarily off in protest over air strikes to Hanoi. Meanwhile in Cambodia, farmers in Battambang province, where he and Phra Nok had been a few years ago, were concerned about the war disrupting the harvest. And GM was raising their prices for the 1971 model year.

He closed the paper and called Carla.

He wasn't exactly sure how to say "Sorry I haven't been at work, I got kidnapped by dybbukim," but she was understanding enough.

"Can you make it in on Friday, do you think?" she asked, her voice surprisingly gentle. He wondered if Ulysses had come looking for him and given her a scare. "We can discuss it then."

He went back upstairs and lay down again but found that he couldn't sleep. Eventually, he got up and disassembled the broken burner on the stove. A quick search of the house revealed four reflex hammers, two tuning forks, six penlights, and no tools at all, so he put on his boots and walked six blocks to the hardware store on Willy Street to buy a handful of implements of destruction.

When he got back, Ulysses's motorcycle was in the driveway, the man himself sitting at the kitchen table.

Laz dropped his bag on a counter and bent over to take off his boots. "Don't you have classes or something?"

"Nah," Ulysses said easily. "Thanksgiving break. Everyone's heading home for the holiday."

"Are we doing anything?"

"Babushka has a dinner planned." He grinned. "I'm sure it's a thinly veiled excuse to get to play with the baby while Obe cooks for her."

Laz caught his brother's humor. "How did he get to be the favorite?"

"Because he has more useful skills than either of us, and he has produced a great grandchild."

"I'm thinking about getting a dog," Laz said. He picked up the percolator from where he'd left it on the stove. "Coffee?"

Ulysses waved a hand. "I'm not staying."

It seemed clear that he was, but Laz remembered he should unplug the stove if he was messing with the burner, so he let it go. Instead, he dug through the bag he'd brought back until he found a stiff wire brush and some sandpaper, then took them over to the kitchen sink. Ulysses stayed at the table, watching him. He didn't seem to have anything else to say, so Laz scrubbed the disconnected coil with soapy water, then used the sandpaper and the brush on the terminals. When the metal was shiny, he dried everything off and bent the ends into a slightly better configuration.

"Is that all it takes?" Ulysses asked, watching him reinstall the burner.

"What do you mean, all?" Laz asked over his shoulder. When he'd gotten the stove plugged back in, he turned the knob to high and watched, arms folded, as the metal slowly started to heat, the last of the water sizzling off it. "Being able to diagnose the problem is more than half the job."

The back door opened, and Eli came in. He cast a worried look from Ulysses to Laz. Laz opened his mouth to say something, because it felt like after everything they'd said last night he should have some words, or a greeting that would—what?

Laz was aware that blind panic was not a helpful response to someone telling you that they loved you, and that, in some way, this was a moment that mattered, probably a lot. And yet his mind felt entirely blank when he looked at Eli, except for the dueling urges to pin him against the ice box and kiss him until he couldn't breathe, and to turn and flee.

Neither was helpful. Neither was even something he could put into practice at the moment. He was too tired and too stubborn to run. His brain was full of static and white noise. Had he ever had a real thought in his life?

Perhaps sensing his turmoil, Eli shot him a crooked smile. "I thought I'd make sure you were doing all right," he said.

Laz rubbed the back of his neck. "I fixed your stove." He turned off the burner.

Eli, for some reason, looked impressed. "Thank you."

Ulysses cleared his throat. "As touching as this is, we should talk about Burnsides and his shtick."

Laz tore his gaze away from Eli. "Shouldn't we wait until Sam is around?"

Ulysses shrugged. "I already discussed this with him. We spent the morning in the library."

"Oh," Laz said, and realized both Ulysses and Eli were staring at him. "It . . . hadn't occurred to me that any of this was the type of problem we could solve with a book."

Ulysses squinted at him. "What is it you think I do?"

Laz folded his arms across his chest. "Other than torture me?"

Ulysses opened his mouth, probably to tell Laz in Russian to go to the devil. Laz would be obligated to say back that he hadn't asked Ulysses to do any of this, that he would have been satisfied—happy, even!—to have left things where they stood after his head had been stitched up. And Ulysses would probably shout back, and they'd have to fight. It would be—undignified.

Instead, Eli cleared his throat. "I trust you are feeling better after your exertions yesterday," he said to Ulysses, leaning back against the counter.

Ulysses looked surprised by the question. "I am, yes. Sleep knits the ragged sleeve of care and—you know."

"That worked out well for Macbeth." Eli pursed his lips. "What about the Fosters?"

"Yes . . ." Ulysses rubbed his jaw absently, like he'd missed a spot shaving. "I didn't speak to them, Doc. What's your impression?"

That seemed to bring Eli up short. "Their bodies were intact," he said after a moment.

Laz remembered the strange tones in Nadine Foster's voice: 'This body is myriad.' He picked up the kettle from beside the sink and filled it. "Can we do an exorcism?"

When he turned around, Ulysses looked troubled. "That's a more complicated question than it seems." He gestured at the other chairs. "Please."

Eli gave Laz a questioning look and then sank into the chair directly opposite Ulysses. Laz found himself hesitating between the two remaining chairs, one next to Eli, one next to Ulysses, like some sort of fucking dog that didn't quite know where its loyalties should lie. To cover over his indecision, he put the kettle on the new burner and turned it on. Then he took the chair next to Eli. Ulysses didn't blink. He also didn't say anything for a moment that stretched uncomfortably.

"Not easy to be the bearer of bad news," Eli said quietly, folding his hands on the table in front of him.

"No," Ulysses said, and for a moment he looked—not old, but there was more than a touch of battle-weariness, the type Laz had seen on the faces of infantry guys on their way back to the States, and he didn't like that at all. "There are two prongs to this problem. One is the exorcism itself. The texts I've seen insist it's possible, but they're very short on details."

"What do they say?" Laz asked when Eli didn't say anything.

"A few of them mention using a shofar . . ." Ulysses looked questioningly at Eli.

The doctor cleared his throat. "It's a hollowed-out ram's horn that can be blown like a trumpet."

Ulysses nodded, once. "Do you have one?"

"No!"

"I'll take that off the list then." He sighed. "The others just say, 'And then I performed an exorcism.' "

"Helpful," Laz concluded. "What's the other problem?"

"The snake," Eli said.

"The snake is also a dybbuk," Ulysses said.

Eli looked deeply surprised by this revelation. "But dybbukim are—"

"The ghosts of people, I know. But ghosts can look however they like." He waved a hand dismissively. "Burnsides is the problem. Him and his gang. Binding ghosts is very difficult magic. Binding *powerful* ghosts is . . ."

The kettle was boiling, so Laz got up and started getting mugs and tea bags out of the cabinet. He deliberated over filling up the teapot, but surely Eli would be heading back to work soon. Might as well do this the easy way.

When he turned around, Eli was watching him with a look Laz couldn't quite put words to. It made him feel warm, slightly embarrassed but in a good way.

Exposed. That was the word he was searching for.

He felt better for having found it.

"How powerful is Burnsides?" Laz asked when he could find his voice again. He wasn't sure how much it mattered in an absolute sense—if the other four guys he was hanging around with were a coven rather than just muscle, he probably had all the power he needed.

"Pretty powerful. And clever." Ulysses glanced at Eli. "Do you know anything about stone circles?"

"The standing stones?" Eli shrugged. "Just what your grandmother told us, which was that they're old magic."

Ulysses looked at Laz sharply when Eli mentioned Babushka. "Don't give me that," Laz said. "You know how she is."

"Mm," Ulysses said, rubbing his hands together. "I admit I know little myself, but they seem to be a key to this. Someone went to a lot of trouble to find them and set them up."

"Why are the stones so important?" Laz asked. "Are they enchanted or something?"

Ulysses nodded. "You're aware of casting circles, which are a traditional method of containing dangerous spells, right?" At what must have been identical blank looks on their faces, he sat forward, the picture of professorial excitement. "Casting circles are a more flexible adaptation of the same idea behind stone circles. In this case, the stones seem to have been set up to both contain the dybbukim and enhance the power of spells cast within the circle."

Laz cleared his throat. "How much enhancement are we talking about?"

"Probably a lot. I don't want to speculate on specific numbers, but it felt . . ." Ulysses shook his head, perhaps realizing that his audience wasn't going to understand whatever unenlightening metaphor he came up with. "I'm fairly sure that in order to send the dybbukim away, we'll need to interrupt his connection to the circle."

Eli looked grim. "You want to face down someone who has no compunction about violently attacking you or ordering a killing, in a place where he has extra power."

"Essentially, yes," Ulysses said. "But I'm going to change the playing field."

"How so?"

Ulysses grinned. "I happen to know an expert in stone circles."

THE GROUP DECIDED TO convene at the student union that evening. While they were waiting for Ulysses and Laz to arrive, Eli made Sam show him his arm.

"Really, it's fine," Sam said. "It looks great. Basically healed."

"It's been four days!"

Sam's green eyes were guileless. "Is that fast?"

"It's about half of what I'd expect." They were in an empty corner by an unlit fireplace. Most students, as Ulysses had promised, were away for Thanksgiving, and the few who were left because of work schedules or late rides seemed anxious to be off. Eli said, "Show me." He hopped up on one of the stout, scarred tables, crossed his arms, and waited. It was a trick one of his attendings had favored over yelling to get med students to do things, and it worked here too. After a few uncomfortable moments, Sam took off his greatcoat and suit jacket and started to unbutton his cuff.

When he rolled back the sleeve, Eli had to pull his penlight out of his breast pocket to confirm what had happened to all his sutures.

He stared for a little too long without speaking, resisting the temptation to run his thumb over the spot where the cut had been. Was still; it would be an exaggeration to say Sam had healed completely in four days, but the gash had been reduced to a thin line, like the tall man had been scraped by a branch while hiking. He could tell Sam was getting a little antsy, but it was bewildering—he counted and recounted the hours since Saturday night.

"You extruded them, I assume?" Eli said finally. Most of the careful stitches were gone. There were two left, at the elbow end of the cut, but they weren't doing much. At a quizzical look, he added, "They grew out?"

Sam nodded. "Is that okay?"

"Fine," Eli said absently. He remembered how deep the cut had been. It had been nasty. "Want me to take those last two out?"

"Can you?" Sam asked. "Here?"

"Sure." He got up and waved at one of the chairs. "Sit."

Sam watched in silence as he pulled the little box he'd stuffed with bandages and other useful items out of his coat pocket. "Do you carry sutures with you?"

"No," Eli said, turning it around to show to him. "You want things to be pretty sterile when you sew someone up. This is just a first aid kit." He selected a pair of small, sharp scissors and cleaned off the blades with an alcohol wipe. "I felt like preparedness might pay off, given the type of trouble you lot seem to get into."

"Us lot?" Sam asked, grinning.

Eli shrugged and gestured to Sam's forearm, which he was positioning on the table. "You could try to tell me it's just the Lenkovs who get into trouble, but I won't believe you anymore." He handed Sam the penlight. "Hold this, please."

"I'm a Lenkov by marriage." Sam pointed the light at the stitches and watched as Eli clipped both.

"Have you always healed this quickly?" Eli asked. Sam gave him an interesting look, and he added, "I'm sorry, you don't have to talk about it."

"No, no," Sam said. "It's not exactly a secret."

"Ulysses and Laz act like it is," Eli said. "And you're my patient as well."

"I suppose I am." Sam watched his arm as Eli carefully pulled the last stitch out. "The answer is no. I was a normal human for the first twenty-four and a half years of my life." He seemed to consider that and then added, "At the time I thought I was normal, anyway. Now I heal a bit faster than I used to."

Eli estimated it was about fifty percent faster, based on how Sam's arm was looking. "How old are you?"

"I'll be twenty-seven at the end of December." He laughed at the expression on Eli's face, and Eli rushed to paste a mask of professionalism over it.

"You act older and look younger," Eli said. "I assumed you were older than Laz."

"We have a complicated relationship." He took his arm back and started to roll down the sleeve. "Thanks."

"You're welcome," Eli said automatically. "I think you scarcely needed me."

"I don't think it would have healed as well if you hadn't sewed it up," Sam said, fingers pausing in the act of refastening his cuff. "Healing quickly doesn't mean my body intrinsically knows how to deal with injuries like that. I'm sure I'd have wound up with some lopsided, ugly scar."

Eli wiped off the scissors again and put them away. "Any other side effects from having been a god?"

Sam pursed his lips. "A few. Animals like me. I can tell where Ulysses is. Sometimes when I panic I can hear everything. Things like that."

Eli shook his head slowly. "That's not really a category I can elaborate on."

"Isn't it?" Sam had an impish smirk on his face. Then, looking past Eli, his expression changed to a real smile. When Eli turned, there were Laz and Ulysses with a small figure walking between them, slow but unassisted.

Ekaterina was wearing a long black cloak of severe style and a round black fur hat that reminded Eli of a shtreimel. Together, they made her seem bigger than she was. She looked at Sam and nodded, her expression friendly but guarded. "Mr. Trouble." Her eyes shifted to Eli. "Dr. Sobel."

Eli returned her nod. "Please, ma'am, call me Eli," he offered. She looked at him and sniffed.

"Gentlemen," Ekaterina said, clasping her hands together. "Let us go, yes? It grows late. I have no wish to be out in the cold all night." Without waiting for a response, she swept away down the hall. Framed by the elaborate marble of the union, for a moment she looked like a figure in a painting herself, proud, powerful, and alone.

Chapter 23

I T WAS COLD BUT not actively raining as they walked down to the lake, which meant the weather was better than the last few times Eli had been down that way. It was one of those evenings that felt too late already. The sort that called for a glass of scotch in front of the fire, not traipsing through the woods on some mad quest.

He fell into step beside Laz for a moment, half-intent on suggesting they decamp and leave Sam and Ulysses to their magic investigations. But Laz's face was carefully blank, the way Eli imagined a soldier's might be when preparing for battle. Not that Laz had ever been that particular type of soldier.

"All right?" he asked quietly, hoping that whatever Ulysses was going on about up at the front of the group would distract the others from their conversation.

Laz looked sidelong at him and shrugged. After another five or six steps, he managed to say aloud, "I've been thinking about what Burnsides's group is trying to do."

"Oh?" Eli hadn't given it much thought, because it didn't seem to matter what name you called it—if the outcome was murder, he wasn't on board.

But Laz was clearly working through the problem from a different perspective. "It's not that I think he's wrong," he admitted. "You only have to look at the sorry bastards who are getting shipped home to see the toll the war takes. But going after one person at a time isn't a way to effect change."

Eli exhaled. "Are you saying he doesn't go far enough?"

"Maybe." Eli must have made a noise, because Laz rolled his eyes. "There's loads of people making an unholy amount of money off the war. I know it sounds a little paranoid to suggest that the reason the peace talks haven't been successful is because the helicopter companies don't want them to be, but—"

Unholy was about right. Eli bit the inside of his cheek. "Not all paranoia is unjustified."

"That's the definition of paranoia," Laz said, and Eli laughed, loudly enough that Sam glanced back at them.

They'd reached the spot where the pavement gave way to the limestone path. Eli looked to his right and saw the cold, black water of the lake standing still under a dark sky. For a moment, he couldn't move, pinned in place by the feeling of absence, the way everything was hidden. Then he recalled that the path had frozen in uneven ridges and dips and hurried forward to offer an arm to Ekaterina.

She ignored him.

They went up the little side trail to the stone circle. The air within the circle felt still, stuffy somehow compared to the cool breeze off the lake, and awareness of the menhirs prickled unpleasantly over his skin. It was still just as odd to see them looming out of the woods. Something deeply rooted told him stone circles needed to exist on plains where they could be seen for miles around. He fought the urge to tuck himself against Laz's side, like a frightened child.

Ekaterina took out an electric torch that could have doubled as a shillelagh and went to work, wandering from stone to stone, muttering in Russian. Ulysses made to follow her until she waved him irritably away, and then he joined the rest of them in the center of the ring.

"How does this work?" Eli asked.

Ulysses didn't immediately answer, and when the silence stretched Sam took a breath. "It's like mushrooms," he said.

Laz snorted, but before he could say anything, Ulysses shot them both a quelling look. "The earth has resonances," Ulysses said. "You can quarry stones in the same area, and shape them in specific ways, and they will resonate with your magic, acting as an amplifier. Like a crystal in an old radio."

From the frustrated noise Laz made, Eli was fairly sure it was also nothing like a crystal radio, but neither of them pressed the subject. Instead Laz, always practical, said, "So what do we do to break the connection?"

"We wait for the expert opinion." Ulysses gestured toward his grandmother, who was on the other side of the circle muttering under her breath. Eli saw brief flashes of something brighter and bluer than static electricity as she stretched her hand toward one of the menhirs. The torch she was holding flickered.

When Eli looked back, Ulysses had crouched down to examine the summoning circle in the middle of the henge, and Sam was watching him like turning rocks over was a spectator sport. Laz was standing at parade rest, his eyes fixed on the woods.

"Do you think they check on this setup often?" Eli asked quietly.

Laz shrugged. "Do you think they see the dybbukim other than to give them orders?"

"Orders," Eli echoed. "That makes it seem like they have a choice."

"You always have a choice." There was something tired and flat in his tone, and it took Eli a moment to realize that Laz was throwing his own ideas back at him. Not like a knife to the ribs, as Eli himself might have done, but as a statement of fact.

He forced himself to stop and consider. "Perhaps I was injudicious when I said that."

To his surprise, Laz shut his eyes for a moment and shook his head. "I'm being an ass." He turned to his brother. "Can you release them?"

"Presumably." Ulysses stood, brushing off the knees of his jeans. "The question is what happens afterward."

Sam looked worried. "You don't trust them?"

"Should I?" Ulysses turned the ring on his finger. "We don't know what they can do, and we don't know what kind of vengeance they might want. Unbinding them may put not just all of us in danger, but the entire city."

Eli cleared his throat. "You don't think they'll just go—where do ghosts go?"

Both Laz and Sam looked at Ulysses, who frowned. "Sometimes they wander. Sometimes they go to the nexus."

"Where is that?"

Eli didn't really expect an answer, but Ulysses said, "Over by the old sanatorium north of the lake" in an offhand way. "Or so I hear."

No one spoke, as though waiting for Eli to come to terms with that, and then Ekaterina cleared her throat and Ulysses whirled to face her. The movement felt like an unusual level of jumpiness for the steady, confident man. Eli was pretty sure this wasn't a performance; there was something genuinely worrying about this place. That was not a comforting thought.

"These stones are not old." She paused, shooting a look at Laz, and added, "Nyet, I know. All stones are old. But these were not quarried long ago." She gestured at one of them. "The cuts are still sharp."

Ulysses nodded slowly. "Where were they brought from?"

"Somewhere in the area." Ekaterina scowled at him. "They are limestone."

Eli found himself trying to calculate the cost of building Stonehenge in 1970. "That must have been tremendously expensive," he said after a moment, which earned him everyone's attention again. "How on earth could they afford it? They're ex-soldiers." He wasn't sure what the average pension was, but Laz didn't jump in to correct him.

Sam coughed, politely. "I may be able to shed some light on that, actually."

Both Ulysses and Laz looked over at him. Ulysses's expression was one of interest and admiration, while Laz had plainly forgotten Sam was standing there.

"What are you talking about?" Ulysses asked.

"Remember how Julie Stricker's group was being investigated for misappropriation of funds?" Sam shoved his hands into the pockets of his coat. "It may be that they gave Burnsides money."

"Like a grant?" Ulysses groaned. "Can you prove that?"

"Not right now," Sam said. "But when I called up the agent in charge of the case, she sounded interested in talking to Burnsides. So I wouldn't be shocked if he's mentioned in the records they've got."

"Who's Julie Stricker?" Eli whispered to Laz.

"Some—" He noticed Ekaterina listening and stopped himself. "Someone who was making life hard for us this fall."

Ekaterina glanced from each of them to each, her face that of a professor amused by her students' antics. Ulysses seemed to understand whatever else was in the air, because he shook his head and said, "Explain later; our time is limited." He looked at his grandmother. "How are they configured?"

"Inefficiently," she said, whatever that meant, and then started explaining the pattern to Ulysses in a way Eli didn't understand. But he also wasn't paying close attention, because he thought he heard a noise from the dark woods around them. It was hard to tell above the wind in the treetops and the rustle of leaves, but it sounded like a branch had snapped.

Beside him, Laz had gone tense. He'd heard it too, then. "What was that?" Eli whispered.

Laz shook his head wordlessly and held up a hand. Eli glanced over at the others; Ekaterina had pulled a grease pencil out of some pocket of her coat and was scrawling a sigil on one of the menhirs. Ulysses was holding the light. Only Sam seemed to be at all unoccupied, and he was watching the Lenkovs work. Eli looked back at Laz, who was creeping to the near edge of the circle in a half crouch. A moment later, he had stepped around the menhir and vanished.

Not knowing what to do, Eli reached out and touched Sam's arm. "There's something—"

That was as far as he got before Sam held up a hand, because this time there were voices on the wind. "—too soon," one was saying. "We don't have anything else lined up yet. Casco said he—"

"Thought we agreed we were going to lie low for the winter," a different voice said, and Sam hissed. Ulysses clicked off the flashlight, and they sank down into the darkness. Eli wondered where Laz was.

The first voice said, "It's not winter yet," and then they were emerging into the clearing. Even with the spots from the flashlight still in front of his eyes, Eli could feel their presence, a change in humidity maybe, or the noise of their breathing and the rustle of their clothes. They were carrying an electric lantern that threw off a surprising amount of light, and Eli really shouldn't have been surprised by the little snort of amusement as the newcomers realized they weren't alone.

"So," said the man holding the lantern. "Lenkov the Bloodhound. I didn't recognize you last time we met, or I would have done a better job on your companion." He grinned, eyes dancing in the poor light from Ulysses's torch. Eli didn't much like the way he said the word 'companion,' and he liked even less the way the man's gaze flitted to Sam. "How's the arm, big guy?"

Something in Sam's face tightened, but he wiggled his fingers and said lightly, "Fine, thanks."

"Happy to take another pass at it, if you like," the man said, and Eli thought this must be Burnsides.

Whatever he'd imagined Burnsides looking like, it wasn't an ordinary man, the type he'd pass on the street without a second glance. Light hair, slightly ruddy features, wearing a black jacket and jeans, hands in leather gloves. He could have been a builder. Eli imagined letting him into his house unwittingly and felt tense at the idea. The four with him had unhappy, belligerent expressions, canvas work jackets and heavy leather boots. They were soldiers still, all of them. As Eli inspected them, he thought he saw Laz, bent low in his dark clothes, ghosting between the stones.

"Where's your other friend?" This from a woman with a suspicious expression. "The officer."

"Maybe he came to his senses," said one of the guys standing behind the two talkers. He had an accent that suggested he was from the East Coast, although Eli couldn't say exactly where. "Some replacement they managed to find. At least that guy knew which end of a knife to hold."

Eli drew himself up to his full height of five and a half feet. "I can assure you, I know how to cut people." Sam made a choked-off noise, and Eli glanced over his shoulder at him and Ulysses. Ekaterina was no longer visible. Thank god for small favors. "Look, we'd like to find a peaceful resolution," he said, because no one else was speaking and he felt like someone probably should.

"What does that mean?" Burnsides asked, narrowing his eyes like he'd realized Eli was someone he needed to deal with and he wasn't happy about it.

Eli said, "You have to release the Fosters." He could feel Sam's hand resting almost casually between his shoulder blades, strong fingers twisting into the back of his coat. He didn't turn his head to see what Ulysses was up to. "Once you've let them go and they're safe, we can talk about everything else."

"Everything else," Burnsides said. "Right." He gestured to his gang without taking his eyes off Eli. The light danced as the lantern swayed at the movement. "I think you might be a little ambitious there."

Burnsides was standing a little closer than Eli was comfortable with, more than halfway across the circle, and Eli didn't want to retreat but he also didn't want to be anywhere near a man who was so comfortable with violence. A man who was raising a hand, almost casually, but whose face was cold and intent. He moved like the serpent, but he was worse, because at least Eli had half an idea what the serpent would do if it got too near.

Sparks crackled to life, and something kicked up dirt where Eli had been standing a moment before. Eli stumbled back and tripped over Sam, who had jerked him out of the way, and wound up on his knees among the wet leaves and earth.

Eli had seen Ulysses do magic, but it had been a slow process. How had Burnsides just—where had that come from? Was it because of the circle? Was that what Ulysses meant by power amplification? It was—

Eli looked up in time to see Burnsides step toward him, hand outstretched. Ulysses was saying something, but Eli couldn't hear it over the rising wind and the ringing in his ears. And then he saw Laz melt out of the shadows behind Burnsides and wrap an arm around his throat.

For a terrible moment, he thought Laz was going to snap the man's neck. Eli met Laz's gaze, knowing his own eyes were wide and terrified, and then something in Laz's grip shifted, and he was holding his knife against the guy's cheekbone, Burnsides's thyroid cartilage nestling into the crook of his elbow.

Eli let himself exhale.

Burnsides started to twist, only to be brought up short by the knife. "Crafty." His voice was nonchalant, but he was gripping Laz's knife arm. "Barry?"

"Never trust an officer," the woman muttered darkly. Barry, presumably, was circling around to the left, a knife in his hand. Sam cleared his throat meaningfully and Laz twisted in that direction, keeping Burnsides between him and the would-be assailant. Laz didn't quite look panicked, but he was wide awake.

"I dig it," Burnsides said. "Points for panache. Still . . ." And he made a little stirring motion in the direction of the summoning circle with the hand that wasn't gripping Laz's arm.

Eli didn't pretend to understand how the passage between the world he lived in and the world of the painting worked. The portal had seemed complicated to open from inside the painting when Ulysses was doing it, but now it irised wide with a bright flash.

Eli flinched at the sudden light. He swiped an arm across his stinging eyes and refocused in time to see Laz take an elbow to the ribs and stumble backward. Then Barry fell on him.

Laz moved fast and fought efficiently. It was almost like watching someone dance. Barry came in and Laz stepped to the side. The knife flicked out and Laz ducked, came up behind him, and pulled him backward. The man stumbled, face going blank, and Laz flipped his own knife around and caught him in the temple with the butt of it. Barry went over—unconscious, Eli hoped.

Laz barely had time to look around before the woman was flying at him, a knife of her own clenched in her left fist. Eli must have made a noise or something, because Sam's hand was on his shoulder, tight fingers digging into his trapezius with a strength Eli wouldn't have expected, keeping him pinned in place.

The woman was a better fighter than Barry, that was clear. She had the same ruthless proficiency of movement as Laz, and she didn't let him draw her into making mistakes. Eli wanted to close his eyes, but forced himself to watch, heart beating wildly, because if something happened someone had to help Laz. He had to.

He had to.

The woman feinted forward and Laz shifted his weight onto his back foot. But then he sprang after her as she retreated, and while he was preoccupied with dodging her follow-up slash, the biggest guy in the bunch moved suddenly toward them. Laz twitched away, then had to raise his knife arm in a blocking gesture as the woman swung her fist at his head.

That was where things went wrong. Laz miscalculated, and the big guy reached out and grabbed his arm in one rapid, fluid motion, wrenching it down and twisting it behind his back. Eli heard him shout with pain, and a dull noise as the knife hit the ground. Laz's shoulder didn't make a sound when it came apart, but Eli felt the wrench of it in his back teeth anyway, saw the look of horror and agony on his face as the joint dislocated.

Sam wouldn't let him go, hissing caution in his ear as he tried to scramble across the circle to Laz. "They will kill you. Wait." And maybe he was right, but Eli couldn't just—

"Put down the knife, Dr. Lenkov," Burnsides said, holding up a hand. Eli twisted enough to see that Ulysses, who'd apparently been occupied all this time chalking an increasingly complicated series of sigils on the nearest menhir, was holding a knife—a small one, silver blade with a black handle. And then he dropped it.

Burnsides turned, his eyes sweeping over the rest of his crew. The man Laz had knocked out was starting to come round, one of his comrades bending over him. The third man was holding Laz in place—by his other arm now, thank goodness. Laz, on his knees, was silent, but the sheen of sweat on his forehead and the awful oatmeal color of his skin said too much.

Burnsides didn't seem to care. "How's Barry?" he asked one of the other members of his crew.

"He'll live." The man examining him didn't look up. "Nothing seems to be broken."

"We should teach the captain here a lesson." Burnsides retrieved the knife Ulysses had just dropped. "Jimmie? Lefty? Either of you care to do the honors?" He looked at the woman, and at the man holding Laz down.

"Ah, just give him to the snake," the last guy said. He had his arms folded and he didn't look happy. "I don't want his blood on my hands, and neither do they."

"Fine." Burnsides turned and watched as the serpent slithered into the summoning circle, followed by the Fosters. Their faces were blank; Eli wasn't sure if it was apprehension or boredom. When Burnsides looked back at Laz, he was grinning. "On your feet, Captain," he said mockingly, and the tall man started to haul him up.

Laz shouted when his arm was jostled. It was too much; Eli jerked out of Sam's grasp. It took him five quick steps to close the distance and shove the tall man away from Laz. "You're going to damage the joint capsule," he snapped, and the man was so surprised he actually stepped backward.

"Your timing is something else, Doc," Laz said through his teeth, and Eli looked around to see a couple of knives being pointed in his direction.

Laz was still kneeling, his injured arm clutched to his body. Eli stepped over, tucking himself against Laz's good side. "Lean on me," he said quietly, and let Laz haul himself up.

"Go on," Burnsides said, and gestured toward the summoning circle. "Our friends would love to meet you."

Chapter 24

E LI LOOKED AT LAZ, and he looked wretched. It was unsettling to see him still and pained, gazing at the serpent with a defeated expression. After a silence that went on for probably twice as long as was reasonable, he inclined his head fractionally toward Eli and said, "Got any ideas?"

"I'm still not trained in unarmed combat," Eli said quietly, and Laz grinned, despairing and beautiful.

"Words it is."

Somehow, as though moving with someone else's legs, they stumbled the few steps to the summoning circle. Eli's vision flickered like a poorly tuned television for a moment as he stepped in, and his stomach twisted, but he'd been nauseated from the get-go and so hardly noticed the transition. Outside of the circle, Ulysses was saying something to Burnsides—shouting, maybe—but it felt muffled and distant. The wind was rising, but within the circle everything was still and quiet, or else he couldn't hear anything above his own pulse thudding in his ears.

They'd stepped into a space that felt like a closet, or a phone booth. It was small and too warm. It was dark. The air was close. And when he opened his eyes, the serpent was leering at him, all its fangs on display.

Eli forced himself to acknowledge Mrs. Foster instead. She'd seemed to be in charge the last time they'd met, if that idea meant anything in this context. She was probably the one to attempt a parlay with now. He steadied himself, tightening the arm he still had slung around Laz's waist, even though Laz didn't need it to stand. Maybe Eli did. He said, "Greetings."

Mrs. Foster's eyes were immediately on him, and he regretted having spoken. "Human. We meet again."

"I offered you liberation, when last we spoke." There was not a twitch of recognition on her face, though it couldn't have been more than twenty-four hours ago. "I'd like to discuss terms."

"We will not bargain with humans. You have no honor."

Eli shrugged. "Won't you reconsider? I would give you freedom. Isn't that worth anything to you? Would you prefer a life of service and bondage?"

Mrs. Foster tilted her head to one side, almost like a bird. "Our freedom is our right, not yours to give or take as you please. We will not trade one master for another."

Outside of the circle, as though to punctuate her point, the menhirs suddenly lit up, bathing the entire area in an eerie yellow-white glow. Laz jumped when it happened, and Eli felt the fingers of Laz's good hand clutching at his coat. Who the hell had done *that*? He darted a glance at Ulysses, and found him struggling with Burnsides and the woman. Not him, then. Not Burnsides either. Sam was being held on the opposite side of the clearing by the man who had dislocated Laz's shoulder. Could Ekaterina have managed such a display?

"We would not ask you to trade," Eli told Mrs. Foster. He forced himself to release Laz, to stand up straight and put his hands in his pockets. "I want to discuss the terms of your leaving our realm."

Mrs. Foster looked at Eli for what felt like a long time. Mr. Foster and the serpent both turned to look at Eli as well. After a while, the serpent said something in that wince-inducing language and Fred Foster nodded.

"If you wish to treat with us, you will allow Nakhash to join with you," he pronounced. "Demonstrate your trust."

Eli looked at the serpent and shivered. "Join with me," he repeated. The fight seemed to be going on forever outside. Was Ulysses trying to reach the knife he'd discarded? Sam? He couldn't think about that now. Just being this close to the serpent was making him sweat, his heart racing unpleasantly. "And you'll—"

"No conditions," Mrs. Foster said. "You will join. And then we will judge the merit of your request."

"Eli," Laz said, his voice hoarse, loud in the small space of the circle, "this is a bad idea. Do I need to say that it could kill you?"

Outside, Ulysses said something inaudible, followed by a bright flash and a weird sensation of pressure and release, like Eli's ears had just popped. Laz flinched. Eli didn't think they were winning, somehow.

"I'm sorry," he said to Laz. And to Nakhash: "Do it."

He'd envisioned the snake squirming down his throat. The idea of the unwanted intrusion was terrible, but the smooth coldness of Nakhash as it wrapped itself around his legs was worse, somehow. But then the serpent dissolved into mist—and it was there, in his mind.

Nakhash was not her real name. She wouldn't reveal that to him, but she was surprisingly gentle as she arrived. His body revolted at her presence, but she gripped him tightly and wouldn't be thrown, like he was a panicky animal. And then they were somewhere else.

When he stopped retching and looked up, he was on the dais in a lecture hall that seemed vaguely familiar. Some room at Oxford she'd fished out of his memories, no doubt, although he couldn't quite place it. Mrs. Greenfield had said it was like being in a nightmare to be possessed by the dybbukim, or so Laz had reported. Eli understood that now. It was dreamlike, the reappearance of a place without the exam he'd written or lecture he'd attended. But it lacked the immediate terror of a nightmare, the lurking sense of something wrong. Perhaps because he knew what was going on. He got to his feet and looked out at the audience.

A woman sat in the middle of the block of seats he was facing. She was dressed in dark clothing, and a veil obscured her face and hair.

"What shall I call you?" he asked when she made no move to speak.

"Nakhash will do," she said. It was the Hebrew word for snake; he knew that in the way one knew things in dreams, or else the connection between them was somehow shared and she knew it. Different kinds of possession, Ulysses had said. Nakhash said, "Make your case."

"To you alone?"

"Yes."

He cleared his throat, although in the absence of a physical body it was the most useless of tics. "You want to leave here, I imagine." He was glad in a way that they were alone; her hostile silence was already oppressive. A greater audience would not have helped. "You were imprisoned unfairly. I don't—I'm not familiar with what you might need to be able to go. But I'd like to help."

He wasn't sure if that was what she'd been expecting or not. There was a long silence. "A negotiation implies a give and take. What do you wish in return?"

"That you depart, leaving the minds and bodies of the Fosters intact," he said promptly. "And mine as well. And that you will not do this again."

"We did not choose to do it the first time." She sounded bland, but he felt something tighten within his chest. Her power, perhaps. She had some grip on him, on his physical body.

"I don't mean to imply that you did." She could kill him. And he hadn't even kissed Laz goodbye.

Laz would have been furious if he had.

Nakhash vanished from where she'd been sitting and reappeared closer up, startling him with the suddenness of the movement. "What do you imply?"

"That when Ulysses frees you, you choose to depart." He hesitated, and added, "Forgoing vengeance."

She could at least tell he was in earnest; sincerity was nearly all he had to offer. "Why?"

"Because it doesn't help anything?" Eli tried to marshal his thoughts. "Would killing Burnsides and his gang make your . . . your existence, such as it is, better?" She didn't answer. "Or killing us, for that matter?"

"Perhaps it would." She vanished again and reappeared nearly beside him on the rostrum. "Why did you come here?"

"I thought I could help."

"And you trusted us not to hurt you."

"I did." Her eyes were hard on his face, burning through the veil. "Was I wrong to?"

She walked around behind him like a tiger, sizing him up. "You place a lot of value on choice. Even when it could lead to your death."

It was true, and he didn't really know what to say. He pictured Laz for a moment, making tea in the kitchen. "I suppose I do." He straightened his shoulders and put his hands in his pockets. "I think Burnsides taking the choice away from you was beastly. I don't know if you would have joined forces with him on your own or not, but you should have been given an opportunity to choose."

Nakhash stopped in front of him, standing still in a way only ghosts and very deep-sea creatures could manage. She didn't breathe. Was he breathing? Was he only breathing out of habit? "If I choose Burnsides, what then?"

"Then I'm dead anyway," Eli said slowly. "But I was asked to join with you to demonstrate my trust. So I'm going to trust that you won't do that."

He felt his heart start to slow from its racing and knew, somehow, that Nakhash was doing it. It passed from tachycardia to merely a bit above normal and then continued to sink. He started to feel dizzy and nauseated again. Black spots bloomed in front of his eyes.

"That is your choice? That I can kill you where you stand—if I have chosen?"

He couldn't decide if her flat voice was mocking. It was hard to get his breath now, habit or not. He managed to say, "Yes."

And she let go. His heart rate kicked back up. For a moment he had a rush of lightheadedness and nearly passed out anyway. He gripped the lectern.

Nakhash said, "Very well." Before he could say anything else, she reached out and pressed a hand to his forehead, and he was falling . . .

L AZ WATCHED ELI CRUMPLE with a sense of impending doom. He managed to catch his limp body one-armed and lower him to the ground in a semi-controlled way, kneeling uselessly beside him. The other dybbukim stared at him through the eyes of the Fosters. He couldn't operate his left arm, could barely focus past the pain, and he didn't know what to do. Eli seemed to be breathing without issues, if a bit quickly, his pulse fast but strong. Laz looked up helplessly.

"Please," he said. He wasn't sure what he was supposed to say. "Leave him alone."

Nadine Foster looked at him curiously. "He agreed."

"What kind of a choice did he have?" With his good arm, Laz tried to pull Eli's body closer to him.

"As much as we did."

Laz didn't have anything to say to that, so he didn't speak. Time might have been passing around him, or it might have been stopped for all he could tell. Eli was pale. His breathing was slowing. Laz didn't know if that was a positive or not. The slightly bluish color of Eli's lips suggested it was not. "Help him," he demanded, unsure if he was talking to the Fosters or to himself.

Nadine Foster looked pitying. "Only he can save himself now."

And then at some moment that seemed no different from the last, Nadine Foster made a low noise and looked over at Fred. For a long stretch of seconds, neither moved nor spoke. Then she nodded. "It is concluded."

The bubble around the summoning circle burst noiselessly, cold air hitting Laz's face again. The sounds reached him again, too. He'd lost track of the fight. When he looked up, it was to see one of the goons throw Sam to the ground, hard enough that he skidded across the mulch, just within reach of Laz's discarded jackknife. Laz felt his eyes go wide as he realized what Sam intended.

Sam's outstretched palm closed around the handle and he rolled to his feet, just in time for the goon he'd been tussling with to tackle him at waist height. The knife went flying again, and fetched up at the edge of the summoning circle.

Laz scooped it up with his right hand and tossed it to Ulysses. It was an easy, graceful gesture, ruined only by the fact that the movement sent the other shoulder into torrents of agony. But Ulysses caught it.

It felt like slow motion. Laz had a flash of premonition that raced ahead of Ulysses's movements as he flipped the knife open and sliced his palm.

The white chalk sigils Ulysses had drawn gleamed like circuits for just a second, and then he slammed his bloody hand against the menhir. Laz curled forward, shielding Eli's body just before something exploded. His shoulder screamed in agony as he tried to cover his head and Eli's. And then, when it was done, he opened his eyes just in time to see the Fosters stepping out of the summoning circle.

Laz had been in brawls before, mostly with Ulysses at his side, and he knew he needed to get up. Ulysses was standing next to the menhir, drained but triumphant. Burnsides looked angry—no, furious. And he still had fists and a penchant for violence, and several friends who felt the same. Laz needed to get up. Sam was still on the wrong side of the circle, doing a reasonable job of staying out of the range of Jimmie's knife, but that also meant he couldn't help Ulysses. Laz needed to move—

He couldn't.

The fear wrapped around his windpipe like a gloved hand. Something closed up in his chest and he couldn't breathe, couldn't move. Ulysses needed him, but the klaxons and smoke were drowning out his ability to get his limbs to move.

He made it to his knees, then one foot, pushing against a headwind. He was standing. Ulysses started to turn toward him, and—Nadine Foster touched Burnsides's shoulder. He froze. Laz froze.

For a long moment, it felt as though all the shouting had died away. Laz heard the wind rushing in his ears, or maybe that was his own breath. And then Burnsides fell down.

Fred Foster was at Jimmie's side, and as she went down Lefty turned and ran into the woods. Laz heard a scream from not very far away, and then silence.

He looked over at Ulysses. Sam, apparently uninjured, had scrambled over to his husband's side and slid an arm around his waist. When Laz looked back, the other two members of the gang had also fled. Good riddance.

"Is Burnsides alive?" he asked, not caring too much about the answer.

Ulysses looked but didn't move. "Think so." He coughed a little, leaning on Sam. "How's Eli?"

Eli was still unconscious. Laz knelt beside him again and checked his pulse. He forced himself to say, "He's breathing. But that doesn't mean anything." He wanted to look away. Eli's face was slack but perfect, without any sort of injury. He should have been fine. Laz hugged his own bad arm closer to his body. "I don't even know if that serpent—the dybbuk—is still inside him."

Babushka came into the circle. Her hair was slightly mussed, but otherwise she looked untouched by the fight they'd just endured and unscathed by whatever she'd done to the menhirs to get them to glow like that. She glanced at Ulysses, nodded brusquely, and made her way to where Eli lay sprawled in the leaves.

Distantly, Laz heard a tenor voice say, "Nadine?" in a quavering, startled tone that was exactly the same as Fred Foster's had been and yet entirely different.

Babushka knelt down on Eli's other side, grumbling, and reached out to touch his face. For a long, stomach-turning moment, there was silence. Then she said, "It is gone." But Laz hardly heard her, because at that moment, Eli opened his eyes.

Laz was pretty sure he wasn't keeping the emotion off his face very well, but Eli didn't seem to mind. He looked at Laz, then at Babushka, and shook his head. "Sorry . . . can you say something I wouldn't expect you to say?" he murmured. His voice sounded hoarse.

"You're lucky they don't give the bronze star to civilians," Laz said. "Or I'd make you sit through all that ceremonial bullshit." He darted a quick glance at

Babushka, but her expression was indulgent. Eli didn't say anything, and Laz managed to add, "All's well, Doc." Eli glanced pointedly at his shoulder, and Laz suddenly couldn't stop himself from laughing. "For some value of well."

Eli sat up and wrapped his arms around Laz in one slow, gentle, decisive gesture, there in front of Babushka and god and everyone, and after that if Laz was laughing or crying, who could really have said.

Chapter 25

L AZ CAME DOWN THE hill into James Madison Park walking carefully, because it was slippery and the last thing he needed was to fall on his ass when he was already wearing a sling. The dog trotted along at his heels, unconcerned, because he had four legs for traction and a shorter distance to fall, lucky son of a bitch that he was.

Eli was sitting on a bench a ways along the lakefront. At first, he seemed to be deep in meditation, staring out at the icy lake and the sun sinking down toward the horizon, huddled down into his coat against the December wind off the lake. Then something alerted him to Laz's presence and he looked over, his face lighting up.

It lasted until he noticed the dog.

"What are you doing with a dingo?" he asked when Laz was close enough to hear him.

"He's just a mutt. A friend of my sister had to move their elderly mother into their house. Turns out she's allergic to dogs. I said I'd take him, at least until they can find somewhere better."

He sat down next to Eli on the bench. The dog settled on the ground between them with as much dignity as he could manage, resting his muzzle on Laz's leg.

"What's his name?" Eli asked.

"Oliver."

Eli snorted. "That's an absurd name for a dog."

"It's no worse than Luria," Laz contended. "I had to go to the library to look him up."

Eli made an indignant little noise that left Laz fighting a grin. "He's a giant in the field."

"Mm. Well, for the record, I didn't name him Oliver." Laz scratched him behind the ears, because hearing his name repeatedly made him nervous. "It seemed rude to change the name he's become accustomed to."

Eli stretched out a hand and allowed Oliver to sniff. "He seems nice. For a dingo."

Oliver licked Eli's fingers solemnly. When no pats were forthcoming, he moved over to Eli, poking his nose directly into the doctor's thigh.

"He likes you."

Eli sighed. "He can't sleep on the bed."

"No, of course not. He has his own bed to sleep in." It had been three nights, and Oliver had slept in his own bed for two-thirds of them, so Laz figured his statement was probably true.

And yet Eli still looked skeptical. "Is this a one-time thing, or are you going to adopt a dog every time I go to a conference?"

"Why, do you want one too?" Laz grinned, and then Eli grinned and scratched Oliver behind the ears. "How was your trip? You look tired."

Eli shook his head. "My flight back was delayed, and when we finally landed, the roads between here and Chicago were a bloody mess, so I stayed at Ayala's overnight. Then when I got up this morning, my battery had died."

"You could have called."

Eli waved a hand. "I didn't want to trap both of us in that hellhole. Anyway, Ayala jumped it for me, so I just had a somewhat harrowing drive back."

Laz considered all this. "I'm getting you snow tires for Hanukkah."

"I don't need snow tires."

Laz ignored him. "When is it?"

"Hanukkah? I don't know," Eli said. "Sometime this month."

"You don't know?" Laz prodded.

Eli made a face. "I'm a childless adult and my nearest family lives two hundred miles away. Why would I know?"

"Let's have a party," Laz said. "You haven't met Celeste yet. We could do it this weekend, before Sam and Ulysses leave."

"Where are they off to?"

Laz made a dismissive gesture. "Honeymoon."

Eli shot him a look, as though inquiring whether Laz wanted to discuss that topic, and Laz turned his eyes toward the vast expanse of the half-frozen lake. Eli angled his body toward Laz's, leaning closer. "Did you talk to him?"

No need to ask about what. "Ulysses talked."

There was a short silence that strongly implied, 'and . . .?'

Laz huffed. "There's nothing in the literature about whatever the serpent did to you." Laz looked down at Oliver, who was trying to crowd into the space between their legs, and shifted closer to Eli, closing the gap. No need to let the dog up on the bench immediately and let Eli believe he had no manners at all. "He thinks if it was harmful, we'd know by now. But you could try doing an EEG and see if anything weird shows up." He wasn't sure what to say about his brother's newfound faith in the EEG.

Eli nodded, reluctantly, and Laz thought he probably understood. He said, "That would work better if I had a baseline on myself, but . . . I'll think about it." He scratched Oliver under the chin.

"You feel normal?" Laz wasn't sure why he'd made it a question, and Eli's quirked eyebrow suggested the same. "I mean . . . no bad dreams, no flashbacks, or—"

Oliver huffed and folded himself up until he was lying across Laz's boots. Eli looked down at him, then up at Laz's face, and shook his head. "Nothing like that." He looked out at the lake again. "I've been taking the memory out and looking at it sometimes. It wasn't pleasant. But things are fine now."

"There's something to that attitude." Laz looked at the edge of the sidewalk, where water from the lake had been blown up onto the cement and frozen into sheets and rivulets. "The Fosters are doing all right, I guess."

"Really?"

"I'm not their shrink, man. I don't know." He tried to shrug and regretted it when his shoulder complained. "Far as I know, they're up and about."

Eli accepted this. "And Burnsides?"

"Jail." Laz tried not to say it in any particular way, because he still wasn't sure what he thought about it. It was justice, after a fashion, and yet. "I don't know all the details. I'll probably have to testify if it goes to trial." He shook his head, dismissing the idea. "How was the conference?"

"There was one panel all weekend that touched on magic, and only a handful of us attended. It's an under-researched area, which is a pity. Since your grandmother came to the clinic, I've realized that a lot of my new patients are bloodline magic people, and more are common magic users. I don't know if she's sending them my way or if I was just daft before and didn't notice. But almost no one is thinking about this." He sighed. "Of course, most of them are taking a lot of herbs, and I don't know what they're supposed to accomplish or how they interact with what I prescribe."

"You should talk to Aunt Cass. She's the herbalist."

Eli nodded. "Maybe I can have her come down to the clinic and give me a crash course." There was another pause as Eli collected his thoughts. "I talked to one of the presenters who was doing work on magic and aphasia—the thing Virgil has. She's going to send me some of her research." He finally seemed to give up and leaned into Laz, resting his head on Laz's good shoulder for a moment. "It annoys me that there apparently isn't any research. That science has just abandoned us."

Laz could have told him that, and yet Eli's frustration was oddly touching. "I've lived most of my life out here," he said eventually. "You get used to it." He reached down and grabbed Eli's hand, lacing their fingers together. "Want to get takeout? I can take a look at your alternator, make sure there's nothing wrong with it."

"The alternator is fine. It was the battery." Eli got up and tugged Laz to his feet. Oliver surged to his feet as well, excited by the prospect of going somewhere. "Did you know they're planning on moving a synagogue to this park? The first one built in Madison."

"I think I saw an article about that." He looked sidelong at Eli. "You're not going to get all metaphoric about it, are you?"

"No, not at all." Eli scowled and looked away. "Tell me about this Hanukkah party you're planning."

"Drinks? Cheese and crackers?" Laz shook his head. "What do normal people do?"

"Why do you care?" Eli let go of his hand and fussed about, untwisting the sling where it went behind his neck. "As long as you're not going to lean on me to make latkes or something."

Laz tilted his head to the side. "You'd do it if I asked, though, wouldn't you?"

"Probably." Eli considered the situation, smiling faintly. "I suppose I would."

Oliver, apparently growing bored, started back up the path out of the park, and Eli followed him.

Laz watched them go, feeling a strange, light emotion unfold in his chest. Not hope, which was a bunch of bullshit as emotions went, but something he tentatively identified as happiness. Still not an emotion worth putting a lot of weight on, but he wanted to enjoy it while it lasted.

Eli turned around to look at him and saw that he wasn't walking. "Your dingo is going to get away," he drawled. "And he doesn't really look like the type of beast with a lot of street smarts."

"He'll come back," Laz said, and whistled. Oliver glanced over his shoulder and then turned, padding back toward them. Laz jogged a few steps to catch up with Eli, who was looking at him quizzically. "What?"

Eli shrugged. "You just had an odd expression on your face."

Laz pressed the back of his hand to his mouth, as though that would tell him anything. "I was just thinking I was lucky to meet you."

"Careful," Eli said. "People will think you like me."

"Wouldn't want that," Laz agreed, and then leaned down and kissed him. It was just a quick brush of his lips across Eli's; his face was cold, and so was Eli's, and Eli was grinning at him a little dopily, and, for a moment, he feared he was going to explode. He took a breath. "Come on, I'm freezing," he said, taking Eli's arm to turn him back up the hill. "My car is back at the house. Want to get a pizza? I can drive us back to your place."

"Yeah, all right," Eli said. "But why don't I drive, since you're down an arm."

Laz grumbled. They walked up the hill together, Oliver prancing along at their heels, and for a moment Laz let himself consider his path as bent by an object with a greater gravitational pull than the Earth. And he smiled.

Acknowledgments

Many years ago, I somewhat impulsively moved to Ho Chi Minh City, Vietnam after graduating from college. Although it was not always an easy place to live, this sparked a lifelong love of Southeast Asia. I don't think it would be correct to say that experience led directly to this book, or even to my interest in the 1960s, but there's definitely a thin, wobbly line connecting the two.

I am immensely grateful to the Vietnamese department at the Southeast Asian Summer Studies Institute (SEASSI), led by Thay Bac Hoai Tran, who had the unenviable task of dragging me through both elementary and advanced Vietnamese, and to the wonderful instructors in the Thai departments at both SEASSI and UW–Madison, who as a group took my Thai from zero up to adequate. (Please don't blame them for the Thai Laz speaks in this novel.) I also had a lot of friends and teachers in Vietnam who showed me around, corrected my grammar, and otherwise coddled me during my HCMC era—too many to list here, but I'm still so very grateful for the affection and assistance. I also appreciate all the Vietnamese people who have talked to me over the years about the war and their experiences, as well as the veterans (of the Vietnam War and others) I know.

Vietnamese is written in a Roman alphabet, but with many diacritic marks indicating vowel differences and tones, all of which I have omitted. I have also used Anglicized spellings of some Vietnamese words. Thai has a larger alphabet than English—forty-four consonants, and additional letters for the vowels. It also has five tones. This means that any system of romanization is going to be flawed—Thai is being squished into too-small a container. I've romanized the Thai (including place names) using the Royal Thai General System of Transcription, or RTGS, which is the official system of the Royal Institute of Thailand. The biggest difference from English orthography is that it uses an "h" following certain letters to indicate an aspirated sound, meaning you make a puff of air after the initial consonant, so "phra," a title for a monk, is pronounced like "pra," rather than like the Italian "fra."

I owe a debt of gratitude and honor to Dr. Patrick Kerns, who not only checked most of my neurology stuff but told me about several exciting techniques that I was unaware of. He's also been a good friend for the better part of two decades and a supporter of the series.

This book was alpha read by Bryan Metrish and beta read by Blaine Maisey, Katy Williams Pruitt, Barbara Njus, and by the Middle Lions (Monique, Alice, Justin, and Wendy). Rowan McMullin was my book doula, and as usual helped with a million tiny tasks and decisions, and also read at least three different versions of this manuscript. The inimitable Eliot West edited it. Beneli Andert proofread it. Dr. Jesse provided research assistance. Remaining mistakes are on me.

Looking forward, I hope that book 5, tentatively titled *Renaissance*, will be out at the end of 2025 or early 2026. It will offer a conclusion to Sam and Ulysses's arc. Laz and Eli will appear in it, and then they'll be back as the main characters in book 6.

Finally, while in the midst of revising this book, I happened to go to a reptile expo where I met a Burmese python named Toast. Toast was thirteen feet long and two of my hands in circumference at its widest bit. It was lying on the thin carpet of the expo center, coiled into a spiral with its head in the middle, not really asleep but not doing anything much while people stopped to pet it. After watching for a while, I realized it was carefully lifting the bit of coil the person petting it was touching, just a little bit, like an affectionate cat. I'd just like to say that I hope no one equates the fictional serpent Nakhash with real snakes like Toast, who are delightful creatures (if you are not a mouse or rabbit).

I can be found on social media as @pretense_soup (Instagram, Threads) or @pretensesoup (Mastodon, Bluesky). My website is ehlupton.com. There are a few free extras there, as well as my blog and a spot to sign up for my newsletter. If you enjoyed the book, I hope you will look me up, or even tell a friend.

About the Author

E. H. Lupton (she/they) lives in Madison, WI with her husband and children. Her debut novel, *Dionysus in Wisconsin*, was shortlisted for both the Lambda Literary Award and the Midwest Book Award. She is also the author of the novels *Old Time Religion* and *Troth* (Winnowing Fan Press, 2024), and novella *The Joy of Fishes* (Vagabondage, 2013). Her poems have been published in a number of journals, including *Utopia Science Fiction*, *Paranoid Tree*, and *House of Zolo's Journal of Speculative Literature*. She is one half of the duo behind the hit podcast *Ask a Medievalist*. In her free time, she enjoys running long distances and painting.

More From E. H. Lupton

The Joy of Fishes (Vagabondage Press, 2013)

Wisconsin Gothic series (Winnowing Fan Press):
Book 1: *Dionysus in Wisconsin* (2023)
Book 2: *Old Time Religion* (2024)
Book 3: *Troth* (2024)
Book 4: *Lazarus, Home from the War* (2025)
Book 5: *Renaissance* (TBD)